Cry of a Cactus Wren

Cry of a Cactus Wren

Requiem for a Gunfighter

Donna M. Vesely

FIVE STAR
A part of Gale, a Cengage Company

GALE
A Cengage Company

Farmington Hills, Mich • San Francisco • New York • Waterville, Maine
Meriden, Conn • Mason, Ohio • Chicago

GALE
A Cengage Company

Five Star Publishing, a part of Gale, a Cengage Company

LIBRARY OF CONGRESS CATALOGING-IN-PUBLICATION DATA

Names: Vesely, Donna M., author.
Title: Cry of a cactus wren : requiem for a gunfighter / Donna M. Vesely.
Description: First edition. | Farmington Hills, Mich. : Five Star, a part of Gale, Cengage Learning, 2019.
Identifiers: LCCN 2018044046 (print) | LCCN 2018052046 (ebook) | ISBN 9781432852238 (ebook) | ISBN 9781432852221 (ebook) | ISBN 9781432852214 (hardcover)
Subjects: | GSAFD: Western stories. | Suspense fiction.
Classification: LCC PS3622.E86 (ebook) | LCC PS3622.E86 C79 2019 (print) | DDC 813/.6—dc23
LC record available at https://lccn.loc.gov/2018044046

First Edition. First Printing: July 2019
Find us on Facebook—https://www.facebook.com/FiveStarCengage
Visit our website—http://www.gale.cengage.com/fivestar/
Contact Five Star Publishing at FiveStar@cengage.com

Printed in Mexico
1 2 3 4 5 6 7 23 22 21 20 19

PREFACE

I live in a region full of legendary frontier ghosts, but *the ghost in the legend* or *the legend* in this story have no referential basis whatsoever. So far as I know, the Mescalero Apaches never had a sacred valley haunted by a horseback-riding skeleton with a Spanish blade in its back.

There is a real La Luz Canyon in the Sacramento Mountains of southern New Mexico, where Hispanic settlers had ranches in the 1850s, but there is no side canyon off the La Luz called Puma Canyon so far as I was able to find among the multitude of canyons in the range.

This being an English language work located in a place where Spanish has been and is a principal language, a few words about the Spanish used: some of it is still used today on the border where I lived and can have different connotations elsewhere, say in California, even in Mexico. Some terms or phrases may no longer exist in modern Spanish or may have outdated meanings from the nineteenth century, for example, *jumadera*—old meaning, "cloud of smoke"; modern meaning, "drunken, drunkenness." I have tried to stay true to the Spanish vernacular of the locale and the historical time period of the novel, using referential material not exclusively but including library-archived civilian and military autobiographies, journals, diaries, newspaper articles, etc, and, especially kept close at hand, *A Dictionary of New Mexico and Southern Colorado Spanish* by Ruben Cobos, copyright 2003, published by the Museum of

New Mexico Press, Santa Fe.

Actual living historical figures of territorial New Mexico realistically flesh out the characters in this book. However, all characters are totally fictional and are figments of the author's imagination. Historical events and places alluded to have been researched for accuracy, but an author can only be as accurate as the historians' work relied upon. There are a lot of discrepancies and inaccuracies written in historical works, so please forgive any disparities that might be found.

Having lived in western Texas and in southern New Mexico for many years, and having worked on the White Sands Missile Range in the Tularosa Basin as well as having been a hiker, mountain climber, and horseperson, I have personally been to the places I write about, some of which are closed to the public. For instance, a spring-fed lake hidden at the top of a mountain in the Cornudas Mountain range on a private ranch (not open to the public then or today) inspired the lake-in-the-sky village on the mesilla mentioned early in the story.

All in all, this story is meant not so much to enlighten as to entertain and take the reader out of his/herself for a little armchair getaway.

—Donna M. Vesely, Canutillo, New Mexico, 2017

Prologue

The Legend . . .

. . . tells of a skeleton of a man, with a Spanish blade in its back, slumped on a pale ghost horse, with sooty eye sockets and sooty nostrils and sooty mane and tail, which eerily screams as it gallops up and down Squawman's Valley. The Apaches regard the valley as sacred. It has become a part of the lore of the land that the forbidden valley is a place no man ventures without meeting up with himself. A valley of no return.

Chapter One

The cry of a cactus wren repetitively rasped in the heat-shimmering silence. From its bristly perch of a cholla, its beady eyes mirrored the watery, dark silhouette of a man on a horse emerging larger and clearer from white gypsum dunes.

He came out of a baked, bleached, and broiled country, where hawks lazily glided on air currents at the heights of a great upthrust of bisque-colored rock. The rock loomed like a riven prow of a petrified ship over vast salt flats of a dried-up ancient sea. The flat-topped ridge of the plateau mountain range possessed a mystical aura of forbidding isolation.

The lone rider appeared carved out of the ancient cliff-sides. The horse was a smoky beige dun, ears, eyes, and nostrils shaded the same as its dark mane, tail and legs the color of the sooty shadows in the recesses of the cliffs. Horse and rider blended in with the desert environment.

Eyes gleamed like silvery slivers of ice in the shadow of the dust-coated, sun-bleached, wide-brimmed hat. The eyes conveyed a cold indifference to life and even to death and gave the cleanly chiseled face a visage of fierce fearlessness. A long-barreled forty-four strapped low on his thigh invested the fearlessness with a deadliness that even the most foolhardy of his kind would think twice about before daring to defy.

He rode easily and unhurriedly. His gaze was fixed straight ahead, but there was an intensity beneath the surface of his casual bearing that gave the impression not a creature stirred for a mile around without his awareness. He knew he was being watched.

There were no people. No naked brown children playing in the powdery dirt. No barking dogs. Mesquite-pole pens went empty. No wood smoke came from the ramadas of outside kitchens. No *chile ristras* drying red in the sun. Fields of cornstalks and pumpkin vines lay to waste, sun-scorched and withering but for some moist green patches—a sign of life. Dust devils whirled around corners of deserted adobes. A wooden shutter repeatedly banged somewhere, as if by a pissed ghost. In his all-encompassing observation, over the harshly serene abandonment, like a forsaken gesture begging divine pardon from the savagery of a hostile land, stood the heavy wooden cross of a church.

He sensed the stealthy observation of his passage from the belfry. It faintly rang a ghostly peal. The slow *clip-clop* of the horse's hooves on the hard, dusty ground echoed in the haunted quiet, distantly punctuated by the pissed ghost's banging. The corner of the lone rider's mouth twitched the suggestion of a humorless grin.

Waxed with the sky's dusky light, a pair of haunted green eyes gazed from the belfry at the wagon road's slate-gray scar on the purple-mottled face of the late evening desert. The road dipped and rose and disappeared until it was seen again, a straight ribbon that reeled out in the lower distance toward the tiny lights of the town.

Behind the vacant green gaze were fiery flashes of a violence so awful that for the past seven years the mind within had locked the memory in a deep chamber of oblivion. But then this evening the devil out of the desert foothills had unbolted the heavy door, and it fell open, freeing through the slender crack the horrors that clamored insanely to get out.

The ghostly hamlet left behind on the mesa, the rider rode along the featureless, flat desert floor, monotonously bristled with widely spaced scrub brush so uniform in growth it appeared as if a giant hand with giant scissors had clipped it all flat-topped for miles around. He came to a cluster of squat adobes haphazardly arranged like so many pebbles strewn by the whimsical hand of fate in the middle of the windswept plain. Up close, the settlement assumed a more orderly appearance with a water well centrally anchoring the adobe structures to impart overall the semblance of a small town.

Chickens squawked their complaints and flapped their wings in elusion of the pale dun's high-stepping sooty legs. Midge-clouds hovered in bronze sun-shafts like desert heat waves in the cooling-down part of the day. Saddle horses, the few that there were, ear-twitched and tail-switched, listlessly chasing off pesky gnats. Through the general stench of sun-baked animal and human waste matter wove wafts redolent of roasting corn and a telltale aroma of tortillas cooking on comales, blue-hot sheets of tin fixed over red-hot mesquite-wood coals.

Barefoot children playing in the open quickly disappeared from sight. He rode past a long building, pockmarked with bullet holes and cankered with exposed patches of the straw-reinforced mud bricks where white gypsum plaster had fallen away. Doorless black holes to windowless sleeping rooms were fitted with Mexican blankets for privacy, some of which for ventilation had been flipped over viga studs aside each crib opening.

Two loafers idly leaned against wall space of the long adobe. They wore embroidered sombreros with huge brims and buckskin strings, and silver conchas adorned their leather dress.

Each one's hips carelessly boasted a low-slung holster. The dirt-ingrained hands of one, tall and lanky, fondled a coiled rope of braided rawhide in the absent manner of a snake charmer. The other, short and rotund, observantly lifted a cornhusk cigarito to his mouth between pendant gray moustaches that hung from his doughy face like Spanish moss.

Their watery, bloodshot eyes weighed the heavy sacks slung over the saddle of the slow-prancing zebra dun. They watched the rider pause long enough to let the horse have its fill at the wooden trough next to the well. Anyone could see the heavy sacks were not grain for the horse. The two loafers contemplated the sacks but not without heeding the looks of the gringo as his shadow obliquely broke over their well-weathered, leather-clad forms.

A lady with frizzy hair the color and seemingly the texture of grama grass, cheekbones and lips berry-stained, swung hips caged in whalebone in time with the high-stepping fores of the horse. "Hello, mister," she purred in a whisky voice. "You look like a real man who would like some obligin' company."

Her sashaying promenade, in fancy but faded and soiled taffeta skirts that had lost their froufrou and inevitably seen better days in better towns, came to an end with one chicken-claw hand on a thrust-out false hip as she stared after the horse and its rider, neither of which had shown her so much as a flicker of acknowledgment. A sneer pushed the smirk off her disease-emaciated, painted face.

An untimely bray of laughter burst out of the doorless doorway behind her. The spurned lady made a jeering face at the sounds of revelry, then briefly searched the ground for a rock of dimensions suitable for her intentions. She snatched it up, pitched it full force, and hitched up her pathetically humbled dance-hall skirts and ran faster than the speed of sound—specifically that of chairs crashing over and roaring oaths of outraged surprise.

She peeked out from the darkness of a tiny jacal crouched between two mesquite trees and with a sotol stalk in the front yard, sticking up like a flagpole of a desolate dominion.

The likes of a snarling wolf came stumbling out of the saloon with such vigor, he nearly fell on his hairy face. Lurching to a halt, he brandished two double-action pistols. His murderous glower leered up and down, left and right, and landed on the back of the lone rider on the smoky beige horse.

"Hey! You!" he yelled. "Hey, yellabelly rock-throwin' bastid! Turn around! I'm talkin' ta ya!"

Where the two loafers had been was only bullet-pocked wall space. The lady squeezed her eyes shut tight, listening to the wolfman's accusations and insults.

"Who the hell ya think yar? Throwin' rocks like a idjit! Turn around, damn it! I'll plug ya right in the back, goddamn chicken-shit coward! You deaf? I warned ya!"

At the sound of the pistol shots, the frizzy-haired lady opened her eyes and peeked from the dark doorway. Other eyes peeked from other dark doorways.

The rider pivoted the bit-chomping dun around.

The wolfman growled an oath at his astonishingly bad luck. It was plainly incredible to him that all four shots had missed their mark. Even if he had been blind drunk, which he was not, the proximity should have made the stranger's back as sure a target as the broad side of a barn. Only God or the Devil could have diverted the course of the bullets for them to have missed their mark at such close range.

He saw it was more likely the latter, the Devil not ready to make claim on the soul He already possessed. If the reptile-cold stare was not enough to sober the wolfman, it succeeded in penetrating his alcoholic fog and unnerving him. His bow legs visibly trembled. But even drunk, he knew something had been started that could not be reversed. He met the icy stare from Hell with forced bravado.

The devil horse walked toward him. The wolfman emptied both barrels out of sheer panic. The icy-eyed stranger kept coming. Unbelievingly, the wolfman staggered backwards.

The frizzy-haired lady and every furtive spectator thought the stranger was going to walk the horse right over the wolfman. Instead, his right foot left its stirrup with such swift action that all anyone clearly saw was the struck victim's arms fling up and outward as if in surprised surrender before he went sprawling flat on his back.

The wolfman's six-shooters went spinning in the dirt. Clutching his throat with one hand, the wolfman rolled on a hip and reached for one of the lost weapons. The pistol danced away from his outstretched fingers to the dust-spurting tune of a lightning-quick, palm-fanned, single-action, converted, old army Remington.

Bloodily foaming at the mouth, the wolfman's rabid glare shot out pain-twisted hate. It was a glare that established a lifetime vendetta.

Two men came skidding out of the saloon on spurs, hands high and wide of their gun belts.

"Don't shoot, mister! We jes wanna git the hell outta town!"

"Then git," came a soft growl.

"It all right we take him?" one of them politely asked.

The answer came—a hastening jerk of the forty-four's long, octagonal barrel.

As they lifted their felled comrade, they jammed his retrieved revolvers into his holsters and hauled him, boots dragging, to his horse. In less than a minute all three were making dust out of town.

The frizzy-haired lady's carbon-rimmed, jaundiced eyes were wide upon the stranger. She watched him loosely rein the horse around and continue in his previous direction, but not before she felt branded by the searing cold glints of his eyes, which seemed to crinkle a secret smile directly at her. She felt *accused* and *condemned.*

She backed away from the doorway, deeper into the darkness of her mean shelter. She whimpered. Chills crawled up her spine as if she were touched by the cold draft of a tomb. She lay down on her filthy, flea-infested pallet and stared up into the dark at the low ceiling. She was found that way a few hours later by one of her regular customers, who got the surprise of his life when he crawled in next to her. The consumption had at last consumed her.

Chapter Two

The sudden lull in laughter and conversation alerted him. He had his elbows down on the bar, the sacks of gold at his feet. There were no reflective surfaces, no glass or mirror, to see behind him. He sensed someone close.

He was still.

Everyone was still.

Time seemed to stand still.

In the next split fraction of a second, he was crouched, with gun drawn and palm poised over the cocked hammer.

The people who witnessed the scene later testified among themselves that it had been only by the miracle of the saints who watched over her that he had not pulled the trigger. The mind of even a gunman as swift as the pistolero americano could not function as fast as his self-trained reflexes. Each singular act from the draw to the squeeze was done in one unbroken motion performed without thought and as mechanically as if the weapon functioned with hair-trigger precision itself. Conceivably, he had expected El Lobo, whom he had earlier disgraced and humiliated, or any one of a number of reputation-seekers that haunted his kind's every wakeful and sleeping moment.

While his gun was still trained on her, he drew himself up to his full height. She pressed so close that the mouth of the long barrel got lost in a deep fold of the dark rebozo that cloaked her from head to hips. Her face was darkly shadowed in the hood as his was beneath the low-set hat brim. From their respective shadows, soulless blue eyes and haunted green eyes locked in an emotionless embrace. Then, as suddenly as she had appeared, she turned and made her way back out of the cantina into the street.

He struck a sulfur match with a thumbnail and motioned to the *cantinero.* The cantinero poured more *pulque* into the glass and took the opportunity to make a furtive study of the clean-shaven face behind the match flame. A cloud of cigar smoke broke over the lowered hat brim, which abruptly came up. Dark-gold lashes revealed eyes colder than death itself. *Desalmado.* Without soul. The soulless eyes of such a man, the cantinero thought, would make the Devil himself shudder. Or laugh with delight.

The suspense anticlimactically broken, finger snapping, foot tapping, and hand clapping to the fevered tempo of a guitar pervaded the smoky atmosphere. Everything was back to normal at an accelerated pace that might have come from relief or disappointment. A few loudly and dramatically strummed chords commanded everyone's attention.

"*¡Oiga! Candelario canta,*" the cantinero said.

After a while, the gunman glanced over his shoulder. The guitarist gave him a wide, toothy grin and sang with animated fervor, nodding a sleek, black head. The gunman slid his gaze over the faces in the murky tallow light. Floppy brims of sombreros bobbed up and down over wide, mustachioed grins. All eyes were upon him.

Generally, no songs glorified his kind. No dime novels immortalized his kind. Like those of his kind, he eschewed notoriety. Anonymity was his trademark. The nature of his work straddled the fine line between lawfulness and lawlessness. His employers could be an individual or a collective body of individuals and who invariably regarded himself or themselves as God-fearing, law-abiding citizens who hated violence but were forced to employ violence to stamp out violence, or were forced to seek a personal justice that bureaucratic blindness, bigotry, or bribery, or all three, denied them. Rarely did his employers respect him for his profession—*fear* was not respect—and they respected less their own association with him. They were glad and relieved when the association came to an end, whereupon he, the persona non grata, collected his pay, expected no thanks, and rode off to disappear into the sunset—nameless, faceless, without trace as if he had never been there.

The corrido was about him. It drew attention to him he did not want or like. The hero kept his back turned to his adulators and his face to the dark bottles and glasses on the rough shelves behind the jerry-built plank bar. The guitarist put to music lyrics that romanticized his swift deadliness with the foot and the gun, how he had turned the much feared and hated killer El Lobo from a growling wolf into a bleating sheep. No romantic ballad was complete without its amorous implications. And leave it to a Mexican guitar player to make two wordless stares sound like a love affair.

"Señor, eet ees their way to show for you their respect," the cantinero said. "El Lobo . . . mucho mal hombre."

"Mucho borracho," the gunman drily corrected.

"Drunk or no," the cantinero snorted, "veeshus keeler!" His shiny anthracite eyes flashed, and the fat caterpillar of black hair riding his upper lip curled with contempt. "They say he work for beeg men een El Paso, do their dirty work een salt war. You know about that, eh?"

The gunman nodded. The "war" over the control of the salt lakes, between Mexican peons, who for generations had freely mined the salt on the American side of the Rio Grande, and greedy U.S. legislators and politicians who wanted the potential profits from claiming the salt lakes and charging for the salt, had been going on for decades. In Uvalde he had read the outdated news in an old copy of *The San Antonio Express* that, the past December, white American ringleaders were shot in a small Mexican town on the American side of the river by a Mexican firing squad from the other side of the river. The Texas Rangers were called in, and the mob held them prisoners, then allowed them to leave without their weapons, after which the Mexican mob looted the little Mexican town.

It appeared by the cantinero's remarks that nothing had been resolved over the past eight months since the Mexican mob incident. The "salt war" seemed to be becoming another military affair, like the Lincoln County War, which he had read about in a more current copy of the *Express* while in Uvalde getting a haircut and a shave in the barber shop after a hot bath. The barber had a special going, three for the price of two, and he had been able to get caught up on the news. When the Lincoln County sheriff's own deputized posse made themselves "the Regulators" and shot him and his official deputy, that long ongoing feud had been settled by soldiers from Fort Stanton, who marched into the town of Lincoln with a Gatling and a howitzer. The army ended that civilian war only a month ago. The famed Billy the Kid had been involved. Seemed there was no newspaper he could pick up and read on the frontier anywhere in which the kid outlaw wasn't mentioned. No doubt, the gunman wrily thought, the Kid enjoyed the publicity, and the publishers enjoyed the newspapers he sold without their having to pay him a hawker's dime.

The cantinero got all riled up. The subject matter touched a sore spot in every patron of the establishment. The cantinero raised a fist. He was no longer speaking English, since he was no longer addressing the pistolero americano but the whole room of patrons. "The gringos hire that pack of coyotes to work over the people!" A roar of heated affirmation rose up in the suddenly close room. Glasses clinked. Liquor poured.

The pistolero americano was forgotten in the political fervor. He shifted his weight over the sacks of gold at his feet, hoping they would remember he was their hero.

This was Comanchero country. Every peón from here to the Staked Plains was a likely candidate, if not an active member of the covert community, then a collaborator in one form or another. Sheepherder, farmer, shopkeeper, cantinero, vaquero, even *padre* by apparent occupation, Comanchero by clandestine profession or association. Even if one did not him- or herself rob from the Anglos and Spanish *ricos* and trade the booty with the hostile Indians, he or she inevitably had a relative, friend, acquaintance, or lover who did. Secret loyalties to the underground brotherhood were strong, however strange, bound by flesh, fraternization, or fear, most of the time all three. In spite of these people's celebration of him as a hero, he wouldn't trust any one of them not to castrate him for a copper tostón should their hated enemy, El Lobo, put the bounty on the hairy skin of his balls. Of all Comanchero contraband, human life was the cheapest, and a gringo's life even cheaper.

He lifted his gaze to see the cantinero demanding, practically in his face, "Hear sheep burn alive? Terrible, my friend. Sound human. Like *bebés,* they cry. The cries of those poor sheep burning alive don't let a man sleep all night. Puts a pain in his chest and brings tears to his eyes. You want to shoot them until they are all dead, and you don't hear no cries of their pain no more."

The gunman said nothing. His eyes were slits of frigid dispassion seeing back in time as he indifferently mused upon the madness of men. He sipped at the bad pulque, which left an unsavory taste in his mouth. A vestigial soreness in his gut reminded him of another unsavory taste—slop of a worst sort, mucous slime forced down a throat that kept locking up to try to block its passage into a gut that kept sending it back up . . .

dank, underground darkness . . . lice-and roach-infested . . . where he might have rotted to hell if not for one daring and devious señorita. Raquel. Held against her will by one General Hinostroza.

Raquel had seen her chance for escape in helping the gringo prisoner to escape. Only the gringo prisoner was one step ahead of clever Raquel, seeing through her ploy to use him as a decoy to lure the guards in one direction, while she made her getaway in another. With a few little last-minute changes in Raquel's well-thought out plan, together they had made their escape, not to mention with the good general's gold. The good general without a doubt had obtained it no less virtuously, considering it was American gold, and he was in the side business of rustling Texas longhorns across the border and selling the stolen American stock back to Americans in Arizona and California.

Though the bruises and lacerations from the general's polished, black military boot and the rifle butts of his bandoliered *guardia* had faded from visible evidence on his muscularly lean body, the crude imprints were still deeply rammed in his memory, and the reassuring touch of his moccasined toe against the two twenty-five-pound sacks that lay on the dirt floor at his feet helped ease the vestigial soreness in both body and mind.

As for Raquel . . . last seen in the Sierra Madre wilderness with her fugitive lover and his band of *bandidos,* drunkenly celebrating their new wealth in Raquel's share of the glittering yellow Liberty heads and heraldic eagles, which would make them as strong as an army and enable them to buy American weapons and ammunition for their guerrilla warfare in the land of revolutions.

Chapter Three

The physical closeness of their faces over the bar seemed to remove former social restraints, and they were friends.

"Amigo, a drink on the house!" The cantinero brought a glazed clay jug out from under the bar and poured two glasses. He raised his glass before gulping down the liquid. *"¡Salud!"*

The gunman tentatively tasted the clear liquid in the clean glass, discovered not just a little better grade mescal than the piss-colored pulque, but an agave liquor meriting the name tequila. He gulped the liquor all at once and savored the smooth burn down his alimentary canal to his stomach, where it mushroomed into velvet heat that radiated throughout him and caused an almost instantaneous rush of sublime lightheadedness. He soundlessly sucked his lips against his teeth.

"Muy fino."

Pleased by the compliment, the cantinero poured two more shot glasses and asked, "Mind you me ask, amigo, what were that theeng weeth you and the señorita?"

The gunman lifted his icy gaze to the cantinero's face. "I was hoping you could tell me."

The cantinero shrugged. "What I know about her ees only what I hear, *¿sabé?* They say she, you know"—drawing circles with a finger aside his temple—"not all there. *Loca.* She leeve up there een the empty village weeth only the ghost of a padre."

"How did the padre become a ghost?" the gunman asked, tongue in cheek. Mexicans loved their ghost legends. His own favorite was the legend of La Llorona, the Weeping Woman. Mexican mothers threatened their children La Llorona would come and get them if they didn't behave. La Llorona's restless spirit haunted riverbanks, or any water way, dry wash if there was no local wet stream, wailing banshee cries, remorsefully lamenting the loss of her children drowned by her own hand. Someone had told him it was a legend handed down from the Aztecs, but the Aztec mother had used a dagger to slay her baby. The tale varied region by region, but always the distraught mother had killed her baby or children to spite a lover or husband for his infidelity. The gunman wondered if the cantinero's ghost story might be as good.

"The Lobo gang, they ride their horses over the people's crops. Shoot at any man, woman, even *niño* show hees face. The padre try talk weeth them. They shoot heem. Dead!" The cantinero snapped his fingers. "Like that! A man of God they shoot like a snake! Now you know why you hero to these peoples. El Lobo *mucho mal hombre.* Heem and hees gang."

"What happened to the people?"

"The peoples, they farmers, *pastores, artesanos* work weeth the leather and wood. They raise a few cattle for their own use. The Lobo gang stole them. The peoples they no fighters. After El Lobo burn the sheep and use the goats, chickens, pigs for target practice, the peoples go. They can't win against hombres like that. They say before El Lobo gang come to work for the salt ring een El Paso, they do dirty work for beeg ranchers een the range wars over there een Texas."

"This is Texas," the gunman said. Although it was true, there was no law in the county other than a small unit of the Texas Rangers based at the little settlement of Ysleta near El Paso. By the time the Rangers got wind of any criminal doings in this most remote part of the county, it might as well have been on the moon. The gunman understood why the Lobo gang could get away with criminal behavior when any posturing of the law was a hundred miles away. That was his job, to do when there was no law, or the law was ineffective or too far-flung, hired by private parties who had the money to afford him to administer justice according to their regulations, since he was their employee, not the employee of any county, state, or federal government.

"*Sí. Yo sé, pero,* I mean *over there* een Texas faraway from here many days east. I never been there. I think Texas she ees beeg like Mexico she ees beeg."

The gunman wordlessly agreed with a nod of his head. He had been coming through Texas for over a week from the *brazada.* By now he had aimed to be in central New Mexico Territory, and he was still in Texas.

"Eet ees believe El Lobo wants the grass een these parts for heemself. To bring een cattle before the beeg cattlemen come and claim eet. That's why he want the peoples out. That's what I hear. He don't want to work for the beeg men no more. He wants to be the beeg man." The cantinero shrugged. "*¿Quién sabe?* Who knows? Weeth a man like that, eh?"

The gunman made no reply. The cantinero turned his conversation back to the girl. "Strange how Dominica come een here like that, eh?"

"Dominica?"

"That ees what she ees called. She never come to town before."

"You never saw her before, but you know who she is?"

"Who else could she be, amigo, eh? Where else could she come from but up there een the village on the mesilla?"

The cantinero called out to a group at a table close to the bar and asked if any of them knew the girl. Rapid Spanish assailed the gunman's ears from all mouths at the table at once.

"Sí, amigo. Eet were her," the cantinero said. "I used to keep the padre's wine een my stock. I regret that loss. Carlos Valenzuela used to breeng eet. Diego over there, he knew Carlos. The padre, he used to come when he were sent for to geeve the last rites to somebody, *¿sabe?* More than a few times he geeve the last rites to customers right there on the floor." The cantinero jutted his chin indicatively. He made a pass over the bar with a smelly, damp cloth.

"The way he tolded eet to me, her peoples was *emigrantes.* Could be seven, maybe eight years ago now, they was camp-ed een the mountain pass up there." The cantinero jerked his head in a general direction toward the plateau mountain that rose out of the desert like a great barrier wall to the east. "There ees a old stagecoach station up there I am tolded. Eet ees a favoreet place to stop for to rest and get water by travelers of the El Paso-San Antonio road."

The gunman was well acquainted with the old Pinery. The abandoned way station on the old Butterfield Overland Mail road was more than a favorite stopping place for emigrants, freighters, soldiers, outlaws, and drovers driving cattle from Texas to Arizona and California; it was the *only* place between long stretches of waterless desert. The long-deserted Butterfield station where fresh stagecoach horses had been kept, with sweet spring water and grass for livestock, was an oasis for travelers of the bygone Butterfield route. And it was a favorite place of Apaches for ambushing the travelers.

"Thees place right here," the cantinero said, emphatically thumping a burly arm on the rough-hewn pine bar, practically making it jump, "were stagecoach way station once."

"What about the girl?" the gunman prodded.

"Like I said, I only know what I hear. Her whole family were supposed to be massacred up there een the pass by the old station. How the girl escaped nobody know. The religious say the saints preserved her life and took away her memory of the horrors she must have seen. Some call her *la loca santa.* The holy crazy one. She come een here like that and up so close to you and look at you like that. *Escalofriante.* Give me the chills. I am not the only one to cross myself, señor."

That was true. In his peripheral vision, the gunman had seen a lot of hands making the sign of the cross from foreheads to chests and shoulders as the girl made her exiting passage.

"She ees call Dominica. For the day the Indian *mujer* bring her to the church. *Domingo.* The padre learned about her people, their massacre, from the Indian mujer who finded her."

"Indian woman."

The cantinero, putting the cork back on his private jug, started slightly. The sand-dry croak of a whisper that had come from the parched lips in the hatbrim-shadowed face sounded like the voice of the dead risen from the grave. He almost crossed himself. But the gold coin pushed across the bar at him warmed his sepulchral chill. He shrugged.

"Sí, amigo. It ees said one side of her face all scar. Very bad. Like burned. Or something. When she bring the girl to the church and tolded the padre about the girl's peoples, she went back een the mountains from where she came-ed. The padre deedin learned nothing about her but for her scar face. It ees her face they say make her once seen, always remembered. Somebody say she were seen een the mountains north, een New Mexico, squaw of a squawman." Again he perfunctorily jutted his chin in the general direction of the mountain ranges to the east. Counting out some coins in change, he glanced up, because he had the feeling he was talking to himself. He was.

The cantinero pocketed the quarter eagle and put the silver peso and two-bit pieces into the money box. He watched the figure recede through the murky haze of tobacco smoke toward the open doorway. The pistolero americano walked lightly and quietly, no spurs jangling on the hard-packed dirt floor. The brown *jerga* fell to a ragged hem around high moccasins. Even burdened by two heavy sacks slung over a shoulder, which the cantinero figured held gold coins as a sure bet—supported by the quarter eagle in his pocket—the pistolero americano moved less like a horseman and more like a ground animal. Catlike and deadly.

Chapter Four

Reflected in the tiny twin mirrors of the cactus wren's eyes, the crest of the sun glimmered like a glowworm crawling along the flat rim of the great plateau. A breeze picked up and feathered seed-plumed tips of bunch grasses. The unmusical, repetitious *chur-chur-chur* of the little bird perched upon a crude tombstone abruptly stopped. Beneath the morning's softer symphony of warblers and whistlers in the peaceful quiet of the cemetery was the whispering tread of sisal sandals.

She wove between the graves, marked with wood crosses crudely hand hewn and headstones of hand-chiseled limestone rock, to the edge of the cliff. Her skirts billowed like a banner over the precipice as she stared out upon the vast, open plains. From this vantage point she could see what seemed like the whole world.

In the north what looked like cloud formations she knew was a mountain range. The slopes of those faraway mountains were mantled with forests of ponderosa pine from which the vigas were made. There was a sawmill up there. And a reservation where Mescalero Apaches lived. She had learned those things from the horse soldiers and Padre Zxavian. He had come from the north, but much farther north than those mountains in view.

He had been very young then. He had put his people's needs before the mother church's greeds and consequently had been suspended from the clergy and barred from communion for heretic leanings. In retaliation, the defrocked priest and his loyal followers broke their yoke of bondage and made a pilgrimage across waterless deserts and rugged mountains to seek a new domain where they would go unmolested by the bed-partner dictatorship of the hacendados and the mother church.

Along their long journey, they had suffered many hardships—loss of people and livestock to disease, injury, and thirst. One minute the desert in front of them was barren of life for as far as the eye could see; the next minute there they were, like dusty adobe statues, as if they had taken shape from the earth itself, with spears poised and arrows nocked.

Inexplicably the gang of dust-powdered dark natives did not murder the pathetic exiles, and that miracle in itself was seen by the people as a propitious sign, without need for the padre to give it divine interpretation. Their unlikely angels of mercy guided them through the desert wilderness to the little mesa, *mesilla,* in the shadow of the great plateau mountain. At the top of the mesilla was a cuesta, a low hill with a cliff side opposite a gently sloping side, which from the desert floor was not perceivable in the mesilla's flat-topped configuration. The cuesta was roughly like a low bowl on a table, and in the bowl was water. Nobody on the desert would imagine that on top of the small mesa was a sweet-water lake in the sky.

Neither had the exiled wayfarers until their unlikely saviors had led them up to it. The padre and his followers had at last found their new domicile far enough away from the archbishop and hacendados in Santa Fe and even the mother church in Mexico City to be safely out of the reach of their oppressors' persecution. In the years that came and went, the padre and his people enjoyed an enduring peaceful coexistence with their God-sent savage saviors and did not try to convert them to Christianity. In the heretical way of the padre's thinking, why push luck?

Under the padre's patriarchal leadership, his people plodded from peon poverty to peasant prosperity. Their chief sustenance was the communal livelihood of raising sheep and goats, some beef cattle and pigs, and dairy livestock for their own use. There were craftsmen among them who knew how to work wood and leather, metal and clay, and many of them as well as the padre knew the ancient Indian arts taught by the mission monks of irrigation and making desert land yield food crops.

They remained largely self-sustaining. However, the padre, a connoisseur of fine wine and a master vintner, was a shrewd operator as well. He generated revenue by marketing his wine and the wool from the sheep and the surpluses of the people's products outside the village to copper and other mining communities and small settlements in the vast region. He also expanded trade to the large settlements of Ysleta, Socorro, and San Elizario that had grown up around the old missions of Corpus Christi de la Isleta and Nuestra Señora del Socorro, and El Paso and Ciudad Juárez, all two or three *jornadas* to the west, jornada being what the arrieros called a day's journey. This could mean any amount of miles, depending on how fast or slow one traveled. Additionally, the arrieros annually made the five- to six-months' journey down to Chihuahuan markets with the oversized-wheeled, oxen-drawn carretas loaded with barrels of wine, bundles of wool, sacks of corn, and the people's crafts for trade. They came back with sugar and coffee imported from the islands, rice imported from the Orient, spices from Spain, bolts of fine fabrics and lace from everywhere in the world, cookware, tools—a whole wealth of supplies and materials.

It had been a thriving community until El Lobo and his gang.

Dominica stared south, the wind blowing her long, chestnut hair and billowing her clothes. She looked for any sign of the dark-skinned horse soldiers. The first time she had seen them had been a fright to her. They were darker than the Indians and strange to her. If she had ever seen such black people in her other life, she could not remember. They were led by a white officer, and her impression was formed that the dark horse soldiers were more polite and respectful than even the humblest old men of the village. The dark horse soldiers had invariably been in pursuit of Apaches and had stayed only long enough to water their horses at the trough by the church and buy foodstuffs. Then they mounted up and were on their way again to chase Indians.

Carlos Valenzuela had told her the dark horse soldiers wouldn't be coming again, because the fort where they had come from was abandoned. And the other horse soldiers who came from the fort in the mountains up north, that sometimes had been seen in the distance chasing after Apaches, probably wouldn't be seen either, since the Apaches had been settled on the reservation, and the soldiers' job was to keep them there. She supposed that was why the Indians had stopped coming to the village. Still, she fantasized about having either the Indians or the horse soldiers come and do her bidding of revenge on El Lobo and his gang of *bárbaros*.

Padre Zxavian and Consuela—his housekeeper for appearance's sake, though everyone knew they lived as man and wife behind closed doors—had thought it curious that she had no fear of the Indians, considering that she presumably had seen her blood kin massacred by them. She could not remember. No Apache close up in the village had ever triggered such disturbance within her as the strange rider who had passed through the village the evening before.

Seeing no sign of the stranger this morning, her green gaze traversed the flat horizon in the southwest. She recalled the day only two months ago. Standing where she was now on the overlook, she had watched the caravan of oxen-drawn carretas, top-heavily wobbling with all the people's worldly belongings. Bringing up the rear were the pastores and young boys herding the surviving livestock. Carlos Valenzuela on his horse in front was leading the leaderless people toward the old mission towns in the Rio Grande valley for a new start in a new domicile. She watched from her vantage point until the train was a mere dark blotch on the pale landscape, moving into invisibility and forever out of existence for her. She could still hear the high screeching of the wooden wheels, the wailing of a mournful farewell.

Carlos had promised to come back to see how she fared. Maybe someday he would. But how did she know if he and the people had arrived at their destination safely? She had no way of knowing if Carlos were dead or alive. Or if he at last had realized his dream of being a vaquero and was working on some hacienda in Mexico. Or if he was in El Paso or Ciudad Juàrez, reveling in wine and women and she, Dominica, long forgotten.

After all, she had rejected Carlos's amorous attentions enough to discourage any man, let alone a worldly young handsome *caballero* as he, who could have any pretty señorita he wanted in any town or city. But she had never been able to think of Carlos as more than a big brother or friend.

Carlos loved horses and, when she had first met him, had been Padre Zxavian's stable boy. Padre Zxavian, a horse lover himself, had had a gray stallion, Jumadera (cloud of smoke), and three brood mares and on occasion took Jumadera to race in El Paso or Ciudad Juàrez. Carlos had been the jockey, and the padre's wins had gotten him customers to buy Jumadera's offspring. In the first days of her arrival at the village that she could remember, she had attached herself to the horses and the stable and in time had become Carlos's voluntary helper between her chores for Consuela. Carlos started going out with the arrieros on short trading trips and coming back to tell her about all the wonders of the places he had seen. When Carlos started going on the long trade journeys, she had become Padre Zxavian's official stable girl, although Consuela still expected her to help with the domestic chores.

The small black horse, barely fourteen hands, out of a small black mare became her favorite. Padre Zxavian had said his name was Sombra and that he was hers. As Padre Zxavian had taught Carlos how to ride, Carlos had taught her how to ride. Carlos had become a big-brother friend. Her only real friend in the village.

Not going with the people had been her choice, which repelled Carlos's persuasions. Consuela had not made any attempts to dissuade her from staying behind and had begrudgingly left what bare necessities Dominica might need. The woman had cleaned out the living quarters and the church—and no doubt would have taken all the *santos* and *retablos* if she could—but there was no more room in her wagon or the loads piled on the horses or in any of the carts, which were already top heavy with all of the people's possessions. It was a wonder the avaricious housekeeper, who had shared the padre's bed, had not grasped the nearly new Saltillo blanket from Dominica's bedroom doorway and the sheepskin off her bed.

Dominica missed Padre Zxavian and Carlos Valenzuela, and even Consuela sometimes—certainly Consuela's cooking—but more so she missed the horses. At least she had Sombra and Topetada, the nanny goat, and the laying hens. She did not miss the people. By nature or by circumstantial habit, she was a solitary creature. *La solitaria silenciosa extraña,* Consuela had called her—the strange, silent loner.

She had always been aware of not belonging. Being different. An outsider. La gringa. Had not spoken the language. She had felt more natural in the companionship of animals than with people, except for Carlos and Padre Zxavian, who spoke her language. Consequently, in the abandoned village, she was alone but not lonely.

She turned to look at the escarpments of the plateau mountain. They rose over the mesilla like a great wall, an invincible eastern barrier. The truth within herself was that the mountain's haunting power held her prisoner to this place. Somewhere within those riven escarpments, the spirits of her unremembered massacred family called to her. The mountains held the secret to herself. They possessed her memories of her other life, of the girl she had been before Dominica.

And they would not yield the memories, only taunted her with vague glimpses as elusive as the changing colors of their sheer cliffs in sunlight and shadow, in the morning, afternoon, and evening. For the most part, the mountain kept the memories hidden from her in a darkness as black as their night-time shadow against the moon-milky sky.

She knelt at Padre Zxavian's grave and crossed herself, and her prayer for his soul turned into an invocation of his seraphic consolation.

"Padre, I had a dream. Not like the others. Not of places and people I know in the dream, but I don't know when I wake up. This one . . . blood and fire. Men in high moccasins. I think . . . I think . . . my mother . . . screaming. I woke up on the ground in the moonlight next to Sombra. I was all wet with sweat and shivering cold. Sombra was lathered from hard running. I do not remember riding him. I felt so strange. Afraid. Please, please—"

Her voice halted, and chills ran up her arms and spine. She was not alone in the cemetery. She jerked her head around.

The warning buzz of a cactus wren sawed through the silence. Blinded by the sunlight bursting through a crucifixion thorn, her green eyes widened in recognition of the dark contours—

the wide-brimmed hat . . . the headset and broad shoulders . . . the jerga swinging to his saunter. . . . The dark silhouette emerged closer and larger upon her from the thorny sunburst whirling round and round, whirling, whirling . . . a maelstrom of light and shadow that sucked her into utter darkness.

Chapter Five

The darkness raged red. A bloody skull grinned gruesomely from a spinning wheel of fire. Eyeless sockets oozed yellow liquid. A naked woman thrashed on the ground. Moccasins covered the calves up to the knees of legs wedged between her widespread, pinned-back thighs. High-pitched screams . . . *Mommy! Mommy! Dadddeeee!!* . . . echoing and reverberating from canyon to canyon and swallowed up in the great silence of the indifferent mountains.

She came to, shrieking and lunging up like a wildcat. The unexpectedness of her violence knocked him clean off his haunches. He sat on the ground between graves and wiped a palm over claw-raked eyes.

"She devil," he muttered.

He sighted her fleeing downhill, zigzagging through chaparral like a rabbit. He cursed and went after her with grim determination.

What so determined him? He didn't know. He felt bound by a force that governs destinies. The thought jarred him. It was almost like feeling a twinge of the faith that had died within him a long time ago. Was the corpse coming back to life? He resisted the idea. Why was he questioning his motivations? He had stopped questioning them when he had begun living by instinct and the habits of what he had become—a machine. A killing machine. With a job yet to be done.

His existence had been reduced to a single purpose, and

anything he did was only a means to that end. He was close to the end, and the girl served no means or purpose. She was a warp in time that threw him back. A link to the past. He was a dead man responding to the invocation in her haunted, green eyes. He was not the machine. The machine had no conscience, no compassion, no concerns. The corpse was, indeed, coming back to life. The machine could not resist the will of the man it had been.

Her tracks led him through an archway in an adobe wall. In a large courtyard, gaudily painted wooden and plaster saints blankly stared from niched altars at his profane passage. Grapevine arbors, fruit and pecan trees, and rough-hewn wooden benches flew past in his vision as he quickened his steps to a sprint, pursuing the flash of white petticoat flounces and red over-skirt ruffles. He passed through the open wooden gate of another archway and saw a slip of a shadow glide around another adobe corner.

He stood in the dirt street in front of the church. He glanced up at the belfry, which faintly resounded with a phantom peal. He sensed her eyes on him, only this time not from the belfry. His gaze studied the dusty street of vacant houses. From somewhere in the village, that pissed ghost persistently banged the shutter. He dropped his gaze to the windswept, sandy ground.

The sandal tracks, spaced at a springing run, took him into the sun-speckled shade of a ramada of woven ocotillo wands. The ramada sheltered an outside kitchen typical of campesino houses, equipped with a *horno,* a beehive adobe oven for baking leavened bread, a firepit missing a comal of thin metal for cooking tortillas, and a metate stone for grinding *maíz* . . . all dust-layered from long disuse.

He ducked his head through a doorless entrance as he

normally had to in passing through the low doorways of campesino adobes. Inside, he paused and listened. The only sounds were of the blowing sand, abrasive sibilations that filled the quiet of the vacant house with ghostly whispers. And the distantly banging shutter. He cautiously moved through the few empty rooms.

Although dim with daylight coming in through cracks in closed window shutters, the interior was bright with the stark whiteness of gypsum-washed, smooth-plastered walls. *Rajas,* split vigas, framed inner doorways, one of which was closed off by a heavy plank door. He thoughtfully regarded the door.

The heavy wood slide bar was open, and he toyed with the notion of sliding it shut in its wooden brackets, then waiting for the expected response. He imagined ears on the other side alerting to the bolting sound, and in seconds loud fist pounding and shouts demanding to be let out. On the other hand, he might wait forever if there was an exit of some sort on the other side.

Slowly he pulled the door open. Swinging on wooden pivots set in carved pockets in the frame, the door, heavily grinding on long-ungreased wood, squealed and groaned a yielding complaint. Damn, he mutely mouthed. Such squealing would carry a mile. Unless she had the capability of walking through solid, two-foot walls, he would have heard the door if she had used it. Now, wherever she was, she knew where he was. As expected, the storeroom or larder was empty.

He went back out into the sun-speckled shade of the thatched roof over the portal. He rolled a cigarette with the makings from a pocket under the ragged jerga. He smoked in narrow-eyed contemplation. He had been outwitted. He laughed at himself without his hard lips showing any such expression. Good thing he was not on a paying job. He had not made his professional reputation that commanded a high price by being outwitted by anybody, let alone a mere snip of a girl.

Chapter Six

Peering through tall rushes, Dominica wondered if he was dead. He looked dead. She had dared to move in closer to detect any sign of life but could not see the most shallow rise and fall of his chest to show that he was breathing. He looked dead. Her heart thumped erratically. What was she to do? How could he just become dead?

The thought of him being dead and her having to look at his corpse every time she came to the springs to replenish her water supply was of no consolation to her fears of him alive. Her fears rose hackles of indignation. Why did he have to choose *her* water hole at which to become dead? She cringed at the idea of having to drag his body to a place where she wouldn't see it, where hopefully scavengers would dispose of the remains entirely. Padre Zxavian's scowling image in her mind tweaked her conscience. She balked and said aloud, as if he were there, "But why should I have to bury him?"

"I don't know. Why should you?"

She jumped nearly ten feet back. She peered at the corpse, not certain if she had heard it speak. It had not moved, was stone-still as before, with one arm raised under the head, and one moccasin crossed over the other at the end of long, stretched-out legs. But there was something different. Two silvery slits glinted in the darkness under the brim of the hat covering the face. The corpse had opened its eyes. Chicken flesh broke out on her arms in spite of the midday heat.

He wasn't dead. He was alive! And awake. Watching her! What had possessed her to get so close? She raised her ruffled skirts and fled.

She did nothing productive for two days. All she did was spirit around the village, up and down the belfry, like a crazy person, distracted by his presence and most frequently running up to the springs to see if he was still there.

He had built a fire and made *camp* as if he planned to root himself for a duration. Right on the ground below the floodgate. How was she to water the crops? How was she to open the gate to the acequia, the main ditch that fed the secondary irrigation ditches, with him right there? To get to the floodgate she would have to practically lift her skirts to step over him. Well, put herself within his arm's reach to pass through his camp, anyway.

Presently she watched him from the rim of the water-filled depression at the top of the cuesta. The *aguajes,* running springs, flooded the cavity and formed a pond large enough to be a small lake. Fringing a low bank of the lake on one side grew cattail, bamboo-like carrizo, and other reeds and marsh grasses. Higher ground around the bowl was a velvety border of emerald-green grass, graced by desert willow's lacy leaves and orchid-like flowers, when in bloom, and above that—just beneath her surveillance point on the rim—limestone outcrop and boulder rocks made ruggedly sloping walls sheltering the lake in the sky. It was an oasis in the desert a traveller on the dry plains below would never guess was on the mesa. But El Lobo had found it. And now the strange intruder.

Padre Zxavian had said El Lobo wanted all the savannah and yucca grasslands in the area, including and especially the mesa for the perpetually running spring water, for cattle. Carlos Valenzuela had told her there were a lot of cattlemen who would covet such land to graze cattle. She wondered if the intruder was one of those cattlemen with his designs on the springs and the land.

He had taken the poncho off. She mentally scoffed at the jerga, made from the inferior wool of the scrub churro. The pastores had raised the scrub sheep but had crossbred them with the aristocrat of sheep, the merino, which improved the quality of wool. The purebred merino was not hardy enough, like the tough churro, to thrive on the desert grasslands. The pastores had been proud of their hybrid flocks and of the wool, which had brought them good prices at the markets. It had been a tragic and traumatic loss when the El Lobo gang had herded and trapped the prized sheep in a ravine, with enough dry brush to make a living pyre. The stench of burnt wool and flesh had hung in the air for weeks, and the sight of all the burned bodies of the sheep in the defile was heartbreaking.

Dominica shuddered at the memory. Hold a little lamb in your arms, look into its delicate face and round brown eyes, hear its tiny *baa* and feel its tiny hooves . . . how could one not weep at their cries of being burned alive? Women, with terrified children clinging to their breasts and skirts, and even grown men were weeping and kneeling in prayer in the street, those not moaning and wailing in the church, beneath the pall of pathetic bleating of the flaming ewes and lambs. It seemed God would have ended their torture sooner if He were the merciful God that Padre Zxavian claimed in his church sermons. After that night, Dominica couldn't help questioning God's goodness. After Padre Zxavian was shot down by the Lobo gang, Dominica was too mad at God to give Him any thought at all. She refused to speak to God and sometimes accused Him of not existing at all.

She had challenged His existence. She ran out into the street when a thunderhead broke loose. She stood in the downpour, with lightning jabbing down all around her, and raised her fists to the wrathful heavens, challenging God to strike her dead if He were really there. The more furious the ground-trembling thunder and electrically crackling lightning, the louder she screamed her challenge to the raging heavens. Lightning struck very close; the bell resounded as if an appealing peal. Or a warning. She laughed at God's poor aim. She jumped around in the rain, beckoning a bolt to her spot. Nothing consequential happened, except she got wet to the bone and saw some horseback riders in slickers, watching her from a close distance.

The storm blew over as quickly as it had blown in. In the silvery sunshine breaking out from behind passing black clouds, she saw the riders gallop away as if spooked. She ran up to her vantage point in the belfry and recognized El Lobo and his gang galloping on the road down the mesilla toward the town. She laughed wildly, feeling wonderfully powerful. She pulled the rope and rang the bell madly, sending peals across the clearing sky.

However, afterward she felt embarrassed to think of herself having acted like a lunatic that day. In any case, El Lobo and his gang never came back up the mesa to bother her. She began to regard herself as the protector of the village and the precious lake in the sky.

Some protector, she thought, spying on the intruder. In the heat of the day he was bare chested and bare headed. The sunlight haloed his wind-tousled hair silver and gold. His naked upper torso was lean muscled, appearing smooth and creamy golden. It was odd seeing him do the woman's chore of laundering clothes and spreading them out on bushes to dry. He had the gun belt on, the holster tied to his thigh, the walnut grip curving out. Her curiosity about him was starting to get the better of her caution. Resentment of his presence gave way to fascination.

Who was he? Why had he chased her from the cemetery and

then stopped looking for her? Why was his strangeness somehow familiar? Why did he bring to the forefront of her mind the knowledge of her family's massacre without the memories? Only flashes of the horror she must have witnessed.

Chapter Seven

He was gone. As abruptly as he had appeared, he was gone.

Instead of relief, his absence intensified her aloneness. Before the stranger, she had been alone. Now she was so strangely lonely. Or, more precisely, longed for his presence. Thoughts of him continued to dominate her conscious thoughts and her unconscious dreams.

The next day she went to the springs, hoping to see him. Each day brought disappointment. She brooded and could not pull herself out of the dark depression that came over her. Was her aloneness starting to overpower the spiritual force that had held her there? Causing her to have fantasies while falling asleep at night of the strange intruder spiriting her away from the mountain and the spirits of her unremembered dead family that had held her there? What stronger power did the stranger have to break the spell of the mountain over her?

On the fourth day after his departure, she got a grip on herself. She went back to occupying her time as she had before his disrupting advent into her life. She washed and groomed her long, chestnut hair and wove it into its customary loose braid worn over one shoulder. In clean clothes on a clean body she felt alive again. As if she had been dead or had been walking in the land of the dead for the past week since his appearance.

Work gave purpose to her solitary existence. Busyness gave her no time to think beyond the moment at hand, or her next project. The longer she lived alone, the more natural it became.

The black pony and nanny and laying hens provided her warm-blooded company.

It was not as if she were totally isolated from all civilization. There was the little town down there with people if she really needed human contact. She had never been down there, but strangely she felt she had been. Perhaps she had dreamed she had been. The chimerical world in which she slept was so bizarre, often scary, more nightmares than dreams, virtually never peaceful. And now the strange gunman in them.

Carlos used to go to the town, mostly to deliver Padre Zxavian's wine to the cantina. Carlos came back with the smell of pulque on his breath. On occasion Padre Zxavian had been summoned there to give last rites. She didn't know anyone there, but that didn't mean she couldn't get to know someone there. If she really wanted to. She just didn't want to. Not yet. If ever. Not ever if the people down there were anything like El Lobo and his gang.

Their entering her thoughts engendered the fearful notion that, if she did go down there, El Lobo and his gang might take the advantage to seize control over the mesilla and the springs and keep her from returning. She was not only held captive in the ghost village by the spiritual power of the mountains but by El Lobo, too.

Nearly a week after the stranger was gone, life was back to normal. Life as it had become normal for her after Padre Zxavian was murdered and the people had gone. She had the lake in the sky back to herself.

With the hem of the back of her skirt pulled up between her legs and tucked in her waistband to form baggy pantalones, she was weeding and breaking up the dry earth before opening the wooden gate to the ditch. The acequia, the main ditch, was flooded and waiting to be released. She had closed the wooden floodgates of all the secondary ditches except the ones she wanted open to route the water to the plot of crops she kept cultivated. She paused and leaned on the long-handled hoe to appraise her work. She lifted her nose and sniffed the air.

Sometimes she suffered such longing for meat—anything—fried chicken, mutton stew, or goat meat—that the milk nanny and the laying hens grew wary of the look in her eye. But her craving for meat had not yet gotten so strong to overcome her squeamishness about chopping off a chicken's head. When they had had a pollo dish for dinner, it was Padre Zxavian who had done the neck-wringing and Consuela, the gut-cleaning. The feather-plucking had fallen to Dominica.

She paused to wiggle her nose again. She ignored her imagination's mean joke and resumed her work vigorously. The aroma of roasting meat on the air grew too real and strong for her to ignore. Figment of her imagination or not, she had to pursue it. She dropped the hoe and followed the tantalizing scent.

Her nose took her on various footpaths all the way up to her surveillance spot in the rocks at the rim overlooking the lake. He was back. Roasting something over the campfire gone cold for so many days, now once again hot.

He saw her coming out of the corner of his eye. Her windblown figure raced toward him as if she were going to barrel over him. Odd pantalones ballooned out at her sides like a clown's britches, and, long braid flying, loose strands and wisps of sun-coppered hair fanned out about the jubilance of her flushed face. At the contact of his eyes, she stopped dead in her cannonballing tracks ten feet short of colliding into him.

"You're back," she said breathlessly.

"Yes, I am back," he said.

She looked like a bashful school girl, he thought, standing

with her arms locked behind her, swinging herself slightly to and fro, staring at him shyly and saying nothing.

"You hungry? Plenty here. I was lucky. Got a buck up in the mountains."

Her mouth watered. Her belly growled. She stayed back, warily, staring hungrily at the slab of meat spitted on a whittled branch and roasting over red-hot wood coals in which little flames flared up from drips of grease.

She had intervened in his butchering of the rest of the carcass, strung up by hind legs to a low branch of the cottonwood over the fire, which sent up smoke around the carcass. She knew the reason for such arrangement; she had been to animal slaughters and butchering by the village people and knew how they did it. The smoke frustrated the flies and insects from landing on the fresh meat but didn't stop them from trying. Strips of deer meat dangled over a rack of branches erected near the fire. She knew the strips of meat were drying for charqui. She wished she could get some of that raw meat to pack in salt for storage, so that, long after he was gone, she could have some for roasting or a stew.

He furtively observed her. Outlined with lustrous lashes shades darker than her chestnut hair, which shone with copper highlights in the sunlight, her emerald-green eyes emitted a lucid shine of the perfectly sane. And intelligent. Not only sane and intelligent, but more beautiful than he had imagined she might grow up to be when he had seen her after all the dirt and blood had been washed off the terrified, half-starved, tattered and torn wild creature he had captured in the mountains seven years ago. He had lived for so long on the dark side, he had forgotten the salubrious pleasure of clean and simple sunshine. So used to painted ladies of the night, ravaged by men, drink, disease, opium, and time itself, he had to squint at Dominica's wholesome and innocent youthful splendor. So used to the fetor of sweetly perfumed decay, he got woozy on the forgotten fragrance of pure freshness. He had to take a breath deeply into his lungs.

He calculated: if seven years ago she had been nine or ten, that put her at sixteen or seventeen years old today. A nicely matured sixteen or seventeen, he noted, as the wind molded the cotton camisa and strange clown's britches to the maidenly form of her figure.

"You don't remember me, do you?" he said.

Her gaze lowered to his high moccasins. High moccasins between thrashing naked legs flashed in the darkness of her mind. She took a fearful step back.

"You don't remember Nadie? She brought you here. To the church."

She took another step back. "Nobody? I don't know what you mean."

"Nadie. That was her name."

She stared at him.

"All right," he said. "Never mind. I don't mean to frighten or confuse you. Why don't you sit over there? I promise to keep my distance." He turned the meat on the spit held up by forked branches on either side. His rigging threatened with an unstable wobble, and he quickly grabbed the meat with bare hands, yelled, "Ouch!" and dropped the meat in the coals. Using a quickly drawn seven-inch blade from a sheath at his belt, he impaled the meat and held it up toward her. "You like your meat with ashes?"

Her hand impulsively went to her mouth to smother a giggle. "*¡Espérese!*" she cried, telling him to wait, as if he were going anywhere. "I'll be back."

She left him standing there holding the slab of ash-coated, half-roasted meat on the Spanish blade.

Chapter Eight

Dominica spread the blanket from the pony's back on the grassy ground in the lacy shade of a willow, away from the carcass dangling from the cottonwood limb. From yucca-leaf-woven panniers carried by Sombra she laid out earthenware and wooden and reed-woven containers. Then she staked the black pony on higher ground to graze. The nanny was unburdened of the water jugs to be filled later.

Presently, the stranger humored Topetada and played her butting game, letting her push against his palm with her nubbed head. The sound of his low laughter enchanted Dominica. The very resonance of it wrapped her senses like a baby's flannel swathing, something totally unexpected from a man whose overall appearance looked hard and cold as stone. But even cold stone could be warmed by the sun and be soft enough to etch one's own mark on it.

"Her name is Topetada," she said.

"Topedata," he repeated.

"No. Topetada."

"—tada. Got it. I feel that means something."

"What she is doing. Pushing you with her head like that. That's all she likes to do. She thinks she is a *macho cabrío* with horns."

Topetada stopped her butting and sidled up and rubbed herself against him. Topetada never had been one to take to strangers. The goat would run away, and only when a person became familiar did she approach and butt the person. Topetada's fearless affability with the stranger lowered Dominica's guard even more than his disarming laughter. Her green eyes gleamed upon him in a new way.

His amusement by the goat seemed to linger somewhere in his stony face as he said, "It's been a long time since I've been on a picnic with a girl."

Glints of light danced in Dominica's lash-shadowed eyes. "When?"

"Oh," he drawled reflectively. "Way back in another lifetime."

"Like me? You had another life, too?"

"Actually, many." Something like a chuckle emitted from his mouth, which had the vestige of a smirk.

She sat on the edge of the blanket and puttered around, arranging and rearranging the array of food she had brought, while he attended the brushed-off meat roasting over the fire.

"Use this," she said, a copper platter in her proffering hand.

"Yes. How civilized. I forget." Using the long blade of his knife as a fork, he placed the slab of roasted meat on the large oval plate.

Poncho off and jacket off, in a collarless cotton shirt, he sat with legs folded in taut, pale breeches and crossed at the ankles of the high moccasins. She sat with her legs folded to one side, tucked under her skirts, an embroidered blue cotton rebozo over her shoulders, and closer to him than he would have thought she would have allowed. Within arm's length. It appeared he was making some progress in gaining her trust.

"Do you like *chile con arroz*?" she asked and held out a tin bowl of rice speckled with chopped green chili peppers and flakes of dried red pepper. He accepted and used a cold tortilla from the small stack she had brought to scoop some onto his plate. "*Riquezón?* I made it myself, with the milk from the goat and the yellow berries of *trompillo.*"

"Those are poison," he said.

"Consuela showed me. When you boil the berries, you throw them out and keep the water. The water is not poison. Only the berries. That is what you use to make the milk lumpy. I forget in English. *Cuajada.*"

"I am guessing 'curdle.' I don't know how to make it, but I know you curdle milk, or make it lumpy, to make cheese," he said. "I'm surprised you kept any of your English."

Puzzlement furrowed her brows.

"I mean," he said, "after so many years living with Mexicans, I figured you to talk Mexican."

"Padre Zxavian was a strict teacher. He said Mexican is a people, not a language. Spanish is the language Mexicans speak. Same as American. He said the correct way to say the language of Americans is 'English.' Not 'American,' as Americans say."

The gunman's stony face developed a crack of humor as if in concession to having been duly reprimanded.

"He always spoke English with me," she continued to say as they ate with their fingers and the tortillas in lieu of forks and spoons. Although forks and spoons were not unknown to her, it was more convenient to drink soup out of a bowl than slurp it out of a spoon, and Padre Zxavian had liked to say that God gave man fingers before man invented forks. The gunman appeared to have no problem using the tortillas to scoop the food into his mouth in the way of Mexicans.

"To keep his in good working order, he said. He had many books in his library, in Spanish and English. He let me read what books I wanted. Reading the English ones came easy to me. He said I must have had some schooling in my other life and that I didn't forget. I could do my numbers, too. Many of his books were history. He said you must look into the past to find the secrets of the future. But I have no past to look into, only that my family was massacred by Indians, so they tell me. What secret of my future does that hold?"

He did not answer. She finished the wine in her cup and hiccuped and poured more in her cup. It was not long before her spirits lifted from inebriated despair to inebriated gaiety. Her engaging giggle tickled him in a deep forgotten place within himself.

"I miss the books. I often wish I had some books to read. Do you like to read?"

"I do," he said. Then corrected, "I did."

"In your other life?"

He nodded, murmuring, "Uh-huh." He reflectively added, "I still do whenever I can get a newspaper."

"Carlos Valenzuela and the arrieros brought back newspapers from their journeys for Padre Zxavian. He used to like the newspapers. Consuela took his books," she cheerfully complained. "I don't know why. She could not read in any language. She said she had enough to do, no time to learn that, for what? Carlos Valenzuela liked to practice his English on me, too. He was my only friend. I know what they said about me. *La solitaria silenciosa extraña.*"

Solitary and strange, maybe, he thought. But silent?

She hiccuped and giggled and put her fingers over her lips as if remembering something of forgotten importance. "You like vino?"

"Looks like you do," he remarked.

"I forget my manners." She squeezed some of the reddish-purple liquid from the goatskin bota into a copper mug and held it for him to take. "I think I have lived too long alone."

"Thank you," he said and was about to take her remark as a lead to a question, which he left unspoken to allow her to continue without interruption.

"This is from what is left in a cask. Consuela and the people took the full casks and the barrels. El Lobo and those men never found the way down there," she said in her newly acquired lighthearted voice, whether it was due to the wine or a natural volatility. "It is under the church, but the door is in the garden in the ground. Padre Zxavian made the wine cellar underground because he said it stays one temperature, which is good for the wine to age in the barrels. First, the wine is put in the casks, then into the barrels to age. Did you know that?"

He nodded. Something like a grin teased the corner of his sober mouth.

She squeezed more into the cup for herself and continued her soliloquy, and he wondered a bit gloomily if she was naturally so talkative. Or maybe she needed to talk after having nobody to talk to for so long. He had known a miner who preferred to live the life of a hermit in the hills even after he quit mining, but any human contact released a nonstop stream of chatter.

"El Lobo and his gang didn't go in the church. I think they are afraid to go in the church. I think they are afraid it will fall on them and bury them alive," she said as if it were more a wish than a conjecture. "Then they will know how it feels."

"They didn't bury anyone alive, did they?" he asked.

"No. But they said they would start burying the niños alive if the people didn't leave. When they rode over the crops, I screamed at them and threw stones. They laughed and called me daft. With San Isidore's help, we saved some of the crops. He is the saint that helps farmers. They destroyed the grape vines. His grapes were his life," Dominica said ruefully as she poured herself some more wine. She quickly amended, "Next to his work for God. But more for the people."

The gunman assumed she meant the dead priest, not St. Isidore.

She drank the wine and squeezed some more. "I am happy

you came back," she said, her speech somewhat slurred.

Her tipsy girlish candor warmed him in a way no boozy whore had ever warmed the tombstone coldness in his chest. He almost shuddered at the effect.

"Why didn't you go with the people, Dominica?" he at last released the question on his tongue.

Her glassy gaze receded to an entranced stare. With the wine vessel held in her lap, she swayed a little, from side to side, like a moored boat in gently rocky water in the bay at Galveston. She was about to fill the copper cup again when he said, "I think you had enough, Dominica, don't you?"

"I was filling the cup only not even half," she protested and poured. Then she shook the floppy vessel in the air and said, "All gone anyway." She subjected the goatskin, grasped in her fist by the curved neck like a dead goose, to an unfocused stare and slurred, as if accusingly, "It doesn't hold much." She squeezed the dead goose directly into her mouth for the last drop.

Her wine-drugged, unfocused green gaze perhaps by accident directly alighted on his icy gaze. "You came to take me away from here."

"Yes," he said and understood now why he was there.

Chapter Nine

Clunky and heavy, the small man-sized boots made Dominica walk like she had adobe bricks tied on her feet. "You won't be walking," he said to her complaint.

"My feet can't breathe," she complained of the heavy socks.

"Just wear them," he said.

"You don't wear hard boots like these."

He walked away from her to look at some hats.

The boots bothered her for more than being so heavy and clunky compared to her sisal sandals. She did not like that they had come off a dead man. Most of the clothes, especially the boots, the hats, and the belts—gun belts and guns for that matter, too—that the proprietor of the general store/trading post/livery had to sell or trade came off dead men in payment for the proprietor's burial services. The proprietor was also conveniently the doctor and mortician as well. He had known Padre Zxavian because the one thing he was not and didn't pretend to be was a preacher. He had sent for the priest whenever one of his customers asked for one because the patient was dying of the most common cause of death in that town, a bullet in a vital organ.

"Miss Dominica," the proprietor presently said, "do I look like a gentleman who would eat my own investment?"

Her gaze perused the long, bent stovepipe hat on top of his wild-haired head. His eyes looked like boiled eggs about to pop out of his bearded face. As she was considering an answer, he went on to say, "The eggs and the milk will prove far more profitable in a long run than if I were to make an epicurean repast out of the givers of such treasures to the palate and stomach in this godforsaken country. I give you my word your pets will be cared for as kindly as my own children. Sworn on the grave of my good friend, the padre—may the Lord rest his soul—who will be missed dearly, as will his esteemed services I regretfully will no longer be able to provide my unfortunately departed patients, whose poor souls will be the most to infernally suffer from the venerable padre's lamentable demise."

Dominica stared at the man. She turned from him to search out the gunman, who was browsing through merchandise. "Mister, are you sure we can't take my chickens and goat?"

"Only if it saves me hunting for meat," he answered without looking up from his rummaging through a jumbled heap of odds and ends on a table.

Dominica turned back to the speaker of tongues. "The hens are good layers. If you give them dry *mazorcas de maiz.*"

"Give them what?" the proprietor said.

"Corn. You don't have to take it off the mazorca, just throw them the whole mazorca, and they'll peck the dry corn off. But you can give them the grain, too."

"Where do you suppose, child, I am going to get grain, much less dry ears of corn? I have cornmeal to sell, but I shan't be giving that to any chickens."

"We brought some sacks. There is more corn to be picked in the field." Her voice quavered emotionally. "It makes me sad to go away and have nobody to pick it. The worms will get it. If you got some empty sacks, we can bring some more from the field, since there aren't any dry ones left in the *cabril.*"

A soft cackle came from somewhere.

Dominica glanced about but saw only the gunman, who was staring at her, as if—like hell he was going to be picking corn and filling sacks to haul back for chickens. It was enough she had made him clean out what was in a corn crib and carry the sacks to town as it was. Paying his look no mind, Dominica said, "There are pumpkins and frijoles and chiles . . . you can have it since I can't take it. Just take good care of my hens and Topetada."

"What's a *topetada*?" the proprietor asked as if at his wit's end under his waggling hat.

"The nanny."

"I thought that was a *cabra.*"

Again the soft, disembodied chuckle.

"She is," Dominica said impatiently. "She still gives milk. Do you have a *cabrío*?"

The sourceless soft cackle came again, accompanied by an ancient voice: "She means a he-goat."

"Good God, for what should I want a he-goat?" said the proprietor. "They stink to high heaven."

"For when it is time for Topetada to have babies, so she doesn't run out of milk."

"I know where there is a buck," came the gravelly, ancient voice.

Dominica looked around but could not find the owner of the voice. She turned back to the proprietor in the bent stovepipe hat. "How much will you pay me?"

"I will deduct it from your total bill when you are through making your selections."

She held out her palm. "I want to be paid now."

The proprietor threw a pleading look at the gunman, who was having nothing to do with Dominica's negotiation and went about looking at dry goods as if he heard nothing. The proprietor reluctantly took a stick of peppermint candy out of a jar on the counter and put it in her persistent palm.

"I don't want that," she said. "That's for niños. Do you have *piloncío*?"

The stovepipe hat waggled.

"She means panocha," came the gravelly voice from its hidden place. "Those people up there talked different."

"You are a most difficult one to bargain with." The proprietor brought out a box of small cones of brown raw sugar. "You may have two."

She took two. "I think that is not enough for my laying hens and goat." She moved to where strings of garlic and strings of red peppers hung. "I can sell *you* some ajo and chile ristras. I will have to leave too many behind."

"We might make a deal."

The gunman looked their way. The proprietor quickly turned his attention to something else.

"What are those?" she asked of the little bottles on a back shelf.

"Extract flavors: Vanilla, lemon, orange, almond, rose. And none contain poisonous oils or chemicals. Very expensive. The price of a goat."

She had a sneaky feeling he was lying. She turned to the gunman. "Mister, what else can I get?"

He shrugged, examining a hat. Then he said, "Bacon. Salt."

"Bacon," she said to the proprietor. "No salt. I got a lot of that."

"Dried peaches?"

"I have that."

"Raisins?"

"I have."

When she and the proprietor finished their transaction, she retreated to the gunman's side. She looked about the emporium of so many wares it appeared a jumbled mess. They were hanging and stacked in precarious piles so the bodily part of the disembodied ancient voice could have been out of sight anywhere. She felt a hat smashed on her head.

"Wear it," the gunman said. "No back talk." He looked at the proprietor. "That, too, for the goat."

The proprietor eyed the gunman and said, "As I would have suggested to complete the negotiation."

The hat was down below her eyebrows, and she had to tilt her head back to see him from under the wide, flat brim.

"Not like that," he said. He adjusted the hat on her head and stepped back from her to make an assessment. "A little roomy, but with all that hair you can use the extra space." He jammed the bead up to her chin on the chinstrap.

A tear rolled down her cheek.

"Now what?"

She shook her head. "Nada."

At the end of the proprietor's itemization for the purchases, the gunman muttered, "I'll need a pack mule. Or horse. So long as it's sound. And a packsaddle."

"I have a mare. Sound, tough, and agreeable."

"Let's have a look."

Dominica's watery eyes promptly dried upon the sight of a pretty red roan. The mare was well-rounded, her salted strawberry-red coat thick and healthy. No galls. Straight, sturdy legs, with white stockings and fetlocks. Hooves round and wide and well-shod. Her flaxen forelock was long and thick as her mane and tail, and her round brown eyes, rimmed with long, curled blond lashes, showed alert vigor. It was instant love for Dominica, although she did not love Sombra any less. She was glad when the gunman dropped the mare's last uplifted foot, concluding his all-over examination, and said, "She'll do."

Dominica hugged the roan's thick neck and promised that Sombra would love her, too. He did. It was instant mutual attraction. And, in the way of horses, they formed an immediate attachment to each other. The gunman's dorsal-striped dun remained aloof and above such romantic nonsense. The horse was as cold-blooded as his human.

Dominica fell in step with the gunman as he made his way out of the dim interior of the store, which was cool inside compared to the outside. They paused under the ocotillo and beargrass awning that ran the length of the front of the long adobe and cast sun-speckled shade on the hard-packed dirt walkway. The horses were hitched to the rail in front, the packhorse between Sombra and the dun. Dominica gave the gunman an inquiring look.

"Feel better?" he said, not looking down at her beside him. He was picking his teeth with a toothpick from a glass container inside the store, which buying customers got for free. She had taken one, too, sticking it in the corner of her mouth, copying him.

"No. I need holes in the toes of these botas so my feet can get air." She spat out the pick chewed by her teeth to splinters, which made it hard to talk.

"Never mind," he absently mumbled.

She looked to where he was squinting out across the desert. A dust devil whirled down the upslanting plain below the horizon in the southwest. He flicked the toothpick with his fingers out into the dusty street and lit a slender roll of tobacco purchased in the store.

"El Lobo," came the gravelly voice from behind them.

A shawled, wrinkled, brown woman puttered about baskets and other displayed wares piled, stacked, and hanging from the crooked support scrub-wood posts along the length of the *portico.* The gnome of an ancient woman met Dominica's glance with twinkling eyes between folds of crinkled skin.

"I will make sure he does not eat your chickens and goat.

Ever since the people left the village, I have missed the eggs and milk Arturo Ruiz used to bring me. I look forward to having those luxuries again. I would like to raise a few goats."

"Muchas gracias, señora," Dominica said.

The gunman stepped out from the shade of the thatch awning and exhaled tobacco smoke with the words, "Let's go."

As they started out of town, she looked back at the riders angling in from the southwest.

"You don't have to worry about them anymore," he said.

"I'm not worried about them," she said. "If I had a gun—"

"You wouldn't know how to use it," he said.

"You do."

"I get paid for using my gun. And my price is high." He looked at her. "Even if you had enough, I ain't for hire."

His silvery eyes slid over the two loafers leaning against a bullet-pocked wall. They lazily watched the gunman and the girl ride out of town toward the ghost village on the mesilla in the northeast.

Chapter Ten

The wrinkled brown face watched the riders gallop in. There were eight. The hairy gringo, said to be part man, part wolf, was in the lead, with a white cloth wrapped around his throat. Their horses slid to a stop in a cloud of dust.

"You! Ol' bitch!" the leader rasped hoarsely.

Sitting on a grass-woven mat in the shade of the awning and weaving a basket, the *viejita* softly cackled.

"Ain't nothing you don't know or don't see around here," a bearded rider next to the neck-bandaged leader said. "When and which way did that pale-eyed fast-gun on that zebra leave town?"

She shrugged and softly cackled, continuing to weave.

The bearded rider went for his holster and was stopped by the leader, whose own hairy face was triangular, with bushy brows and topaz eyes. El Lobo nodded toward the twin bores of a double-barrelled shotgun. In the interior shadows beyond the doorway of the store, wild iron-gray hair topped by a crooked stovepipe hat hovered over the long barrels.

El Lobo flipped a coin to the old crone. She picked it up off the ground with gnarled, brown fingers and inspected it closely. She pointed in a direction.

"When? Two days ago? Four days? How long?" the bearded spokesman for the sore-throated leader impatiently prodded.

"You rode over his shadow," she croaked and cackled.

"How long ago? An hour? Three hours?"

She shrugged. He tossed another coin. "Two hours, *más o menos.*"

"Looks like he's headed for El Paso."

"Damn! Let's ride!"

The viejita cackled softly as she watched the Lobo gang thunder out of town, swinging their horses west.

From the late afternoon shadows, the two loafers watched the gang. They fell into a fit of laughter. They took off their gray sombreros and slapped at each other. Their amusement spent, they got on their horses and rode northeast toward the small mesa.

Chapter Eleven

Checking the cinch on the packsaddle and the ropes around the pack, he muttered, "Should've gotten two mules."

With serious worry, Dominica said, "Is it too heavy for the mare, Mister?"

"You wanna leave something behind?"

"If I have to. I don't know what."

"She'll do fine." His voice took on a relenting tone. He patted the roan's round rump. "You might want to give her a last drink if she'll want it. First water hole we'll come to is ten or so hours. And it might be dry."

"I can fill the wine bota. Carry it on Sombra."

"Make sure it's water, though, not wine. Rinse it good. *¿Comprende?*"

"*Entiendo.* I will look for others. We had many *tecomates.* I know Consuela didn't take them all. I will fill as many as I can find." His look had her quickly saying, "Not so many, too hard to carry all."

He nodded. "Glad you catch on fast. You'll have to."

Appearing flat, the beige-colored grassland into which they rode imperceptibly rolled into hollows capable of swallowing two riders and a packhorse out of sight from any eyes on the plain. Yucca trees, with green, round, spiked heads, shaggy trunks, and brown, dead, lance-shaped leaves in variously bent shapes, began to appear and eventually marched across the grassy landscape like straggling, ragged survivors of a defeated army regiment. The vast grassland was interspersed with cholla, mesquite, creosote, tarbush, and other cacti and brush. Always ahead of them was the great plateau mountain, which appeared to swell larger and higher each mile they trekked, yet at the same time seemed to keep receding farther away, as if they could ride forever and never reach it. Sometimes it seemed they were going straight east, or going north, or going northwest, but always the mountain was in front.

Dominica's only sense of time's slow passage came from the sun's traversing positions and short shadows growing longer. Crossing an edge of white salt flats, she was amazed to see a pond, harbored by low mounds of the white sand and lush, green reeds, rushes, and tall marsh grasses. Lacy mesquite bushes and desert willow fringed the sparkling clear water. The water-magnified pebbled bottom could be seen with crystal clarity. Its invitation was too strong for Dominica to resist. The tissues of her mouth felt like dry paper and her tongue like a dry corncob from the parching wind and blowing dust. She got off Sombra and stumbled in her impatience to wet her mouth with clean, cool moisture.

"Take a small sip first." She heard the admonition. "You don't want to gulp and get sick."

She squatted and dipped her hand in. It was cool as anticipated. She sucked in a palmful and promptly spat it out. She frowned at the gunman. "You coulda told me."

"I coulda," he agreed. "Figured to let you find out for yourself."

Lesson number one, he thought. The clearest, coldest looking water in the desert often was too briny for man or beast. Having been twice tested by the rigors of self-survival—initially orphaned in the mountain wilderness and recently left to fend for herself in the ghost village—did not make her less vulnerable than a brand-new initiate to the desert trail. Maybe it was enough for the peasant mind to attribute her chance survival to "the saints who watched over her," but in his way of thinking, only the very ignorant or a plain fool would leave any matter of fate to the saints or to chance.

The mountain seemed to breathe, to have a life, a consciousness, like a great beast lying in wait to consume her as it had swallowed the life and the identity of the girl she had been into nonexistence.

They crossed the end border of a salt flat, where great *playas,* shallow hollows, were filled with rainwater that had fallen in the rainy season still not quite over, forming large and small lakes. Those they bypassed, being too salty for even the horses to drink. She had been aware of the vastness of the land, having seen it from her lookouts on the mesilla. But her perspective of herself was in relation to the everyday features of her life that were nearby—the village, the casas, the church, the people, her little world where she had a proportionate sense of herself. Riding on the desert where everything—the sky, the land, the mountains—was so overwhelmingly huge, she felt as tiny as a grain of sand.

At long last she got the courage to ask, "Mister, are we going right into the mountain?"

"Right up those cliffs," he said.

She looked at him. A queer warmth flushed through her under the teasing twinkle of his icy eyes. In that instant a concrete conviction was formed within her: he was as invincible as the mountain; she would be protected and safe with him anywhere. Even in the mountain's bowels.

"We'll be staying to the foothills. We'll be going into the high country in those mountains ahead."

She didn't question her destiny in his hands. He had saved

her once from the wilderness. He was saving her again, this time from the mountain's hold on her.

They rode into the early darkness and stopped in the ink of night. He made a small campfire. She got her bedroll, with the sheepskin from her bed rolled up in a wool blanket, and was so tired that she fell asleep without eating as soon as she dropped on her pallet. The night was cool and silent, the crackling of the fire a lullaby, and, snugged up in the warm, wool poncho, sheepskin, and blanket, using her clothes sack for a pillow, she fell into a sound, dreamless slumber.

In the morning, she washed her face and under her blouse with a wet cloth, using all the water in one full gourd. The underground water, which emerged in a bubbly flow that only stayed above ground a short way before it went under again, provided good-tasting cold water to refill all their water containers. She brushed and re-braided her hair while the gunman shaved. Then they got out the fixings: chicken eggs protectively packed in the cornmeal, smoked bacon from the emporium, tortillas to use as edible scoops, and coffee. After a good breakfast, they packed up and started out all over again. She felt freshly renewed and rested and enthusiastically looked forward to another day on the trail as an adventure.

Soon the burning rays beat down from overhead. Dominica felt stifled in the clothes the gunman made her wear. Her feet sweltered in the socks and boots. Her hot, sweaty toes longed to be bare and free to wiggle in the drying, arid breeze. The hatband was a forehead torture band. Her head stewed under the hat that shaded her face, which streamed with perspiration. Her hair-saturated head begged for the wind to cool its steamy scalp.

Making matters worse was the blanket. He had pulled the rectangular blanket down from where it served as a privacy door to her bedroom in the living quarters behind the church. Using the knife from the sheath on his belt, he had cut a slit in the fine, colorfully striped wool not long ago carried by the arrieros all the way from Chihuahua. He had placed her former soft door about her and pushed her head through the slit, and now she had a poncho such as his, only his was the lowly jerga, and hers, a fine Saltillo wool. Despite its quality, her makeshift poncho was bulky, stiff, and heavy. It might have kept her warm during the chilly night, but during the day, riding under the hot rays of the sun, it became insufferable. Enduring the burden of the cumbersome clothes strange to her body made her weary in the saddle.

"I am sweating," she said. "I am all wet."

"That's good," he said.

"It's stupid to wear these heavy things when the sun is so hot."

"The desert's a bitch," he agreed.

She looked up at him from the saddle on her black pony, and he met her lower stare from his tall dun. She had to bend her head back to see him from under the hat brim.

"Persuaded many a man to peel off layer by layer," he said in his certain voice that was becoming familiar to her, which triggered an eager anticipation of a story to follow. Even if she gained nothing out of the gunman's stories, she liked to listen to the sound of his voice. As cold and steely and stony as he appeared, his voice on the trail had become, paradoxically, as if of another man, another man whose voice wrapped her doubts and uncertainties and anxieties in reassuring warmth.

"After peeling off all the layers," he continued, "and he's down to being naked, that's a sure sign of the final stage of an awful death. The tongue swells up and turns black." He brought the icy slits of his eyes from the trail to her. "Do you want your tongue to swell up and turn black?"

She frowned at him. "No." She didn't like that story at all.

"Contrary to what seems common sense," he said, "wool makes the best desert clothing. It insulates the body from the roasting rays of the sun and the wind's drying effects. Yet it lets the skin breathe and at the same time retards evaporation of perspiration. It keeps the body vitally moist in the dry air and slows down dehydration. The Arabian desert-dwellers discovered that a long time ago. They live in a country that is all sand. Very little water. They learned wool clothes helped keep them alive in that hot, dry place they live. Now do you understand?"

"I would like to know more about those desert dwellers. Are they always hot and sweaty like me?"

"You'll get used to it."

He thought that she would learn what had to be learned, hard and fast, with him as a teacher. The desert wilderness showed no mercy for the soft and slow student. He might bring tears to her eyes, and she might come to hate him, but she would be a lot wiser than she was now in the ways of survival in the wilderness. He wanted her to be equipped with the knowledge of how to survive should anything happen to him. A mere day in the wilderness can mean death for a novice.

Chapter Twelve

He looked back over his shoulder. They were still coming. In this higher, open area, he could see them plainly, two dots churning a wake of dust on their back trail, pacing themselves to steadily stay a few miles behind. He slid his gaze over the girl, bringing it back to the trail ahead. She was unaware. Better that way.

The rough-rolling foothills, liberally strewn with low-growing shinnery and coyote willow thickets among various cacti, offered no cover other than the arroyos. Some were rocky gullies hard to negotiate, risky on a horse's feet. Others, sandy channels cleanly carved by swift mountain runoff, were deep enough to offer cover, but the laborious trudge in deep sand could wear on a horse's stamina. Besides, a distant rainstorm could turn any one of the arroyos into a roaring rapids at once and with no warning, especially in the wet monsoon season, even at the end of it. Thunderheads marched across parched blue skies like foreign invaders looking for arroyos to turn into roiling rivers and drown unsuspecting victims, beast and human. That was a paradox of the waterless desert: drowned victims. Best to stay to the trail as he had been and keep the eye in the back of his head on their followers.

"We'll rest here awhile," he said two miles farther up the hills.

Dominica stumbled off the black pony, perspiring profusely, heat flushed, dusty, and exhausted. Only the second day, he dismally thought. With luck he hoped to get to the Corvalan ranch in no more than a week, when he had anticipated already being there before his impulsive notion that took him up the mesa and through the ghost village. Good thing he was not on a paying job with a deadline. He was in no hurry to get to the Corvalan ranch, but he really did not want to take a year to get there.

She scrambled up a sandy mound to the scant shade of a creosote bush. They were in a thriving stand. The plants grew large and bushy and were widely spaced apart as if their tarry smell made the creosote bush socially unacceptable in the plant world. No other vegetation liked to grow near them, therefore its roots had no competition for ground space or precious underground moisture.

He sat on a heel in the shadows of the dun and the packhorse and uncapped his canteen. Her eyes moved to his gesture, then to the goatskins and gourds hanging by their straps from the saddle horn of her saddle. She appeared to lack the energy to get up from where she was slumped. She listlessly stared at her pony, which had wandered to munch on some bunch grasses more palatable than the stink bush. The knotted reins had been carelessly dropped on its neck, allowing the pony freedom to roam. The gunman did not get up to offer her his canteen or to retrieve her straying pony.

The lesson was learned. The next time they paused to rest, she held on to the pony's reins, since it apparently hadn't been trained to ground tie or was one of those headstrong critters with a will of its own. She promptly lifted the uncorked water gourd and carelessly guzzled for approximately five seconds before the goosenecked vessel was pulled from her surprised, then chagrined, face.

"Too much at once will make you sick. Drink slowly. Don't be so wasteful, drooling it all over."

She guiltily wiped the dripping wetness from her chin with a palm and dragged her palm down on the wool blanket, where it smeared the moisture. She resented being treated as if she were a child, but she was at a loss as to how to verbalize her feelings when she felt so guilty.

"Don't forget your horse. He's thirsty, too," he said, impervious to the daggers of her scowl. "Even if you just wet his tongue."

She held a contrite silence. Her gaze slid to Sombra. How could she be so neglectful of him? She never had been.

"Keep a stone in your mouth to help retard thirst."

"A stone?"

He picked up a smooth round pebble for her to do what he had said. "Under the tongue. Just don't swallow it."

He left her with the horses in the evening shade of an outcrop and a prickly pear the size of a small tree. Most conscientiously putting the horses before herself, she dug into the sack of grain and gave each one a palmful. As the pebble worked up the saliva in her mouth to keep it moist, the corn kernels worked up the saliva in their mouths as they ground them between their teeth, and they slobbered all over her hand.

Even though they had been keeping a steady pace at an easy walk, except when the horses themselves wanted to jog, it seemed sometimes Sombra's shorter legs had to labor to keep up with the longer-legged horses. Padre Zxavian had told her corn was a hot feed and to give Sombra corn only when she exercised him to use the energy, otherwise he would become too full of unused energy and a nervous pacer back and forth in the corral and hard to manage on a lead. On this journey he needed all the extra energy she might provide, she thought, and let him nibble an extra handful of corn out of her palm.

She had not imagined this trek to be so grueling; had to the contrary thought it would be fun, as any horseback ride had been exploring the mesilla and its gullies. Horseback riding had always been a pleasure for her, not a punishment. She had envied Carlos Valenzuela for "seeing the world" on horseback. She had imagined this journey would be as exciting as she had enviously imagined Carlos's faraway travels with the arrieros. She had been in for a rude awakening.

The gunman had said it would take five or six days—he hoped not seven—to get where they were going at the pace they were going. Only the second day and not even two full days away from the village, yet it felt like two weeks. She was longing for the comforts of home—what had been her home for the last seven years. She longed for a dip in the lake in the sky. A really good drink of the fresh, cold spring water cascading from the founts in the rock. And a juicy, sweet peach right off the tree and a cluster of grapes right off the vine. She had begun to crave and grieve for what had been left behind and to which she could never go back.

From her saddlebag, she took out the kitchen knife wrapped in a kitchen linen she had thought to keep there for quick finding. She cut off a few of the thicker, smaller prickly pear pads and de-thorned them. She was good at that, having helped Consuela prepare nopalitos, the nopal pads cut into strips, for boiling and mixing in rice. The horses did not need them cooked. When the gunman came back, he found her feeding the nopalitos to the horses, whose slobbering mess slimed her feeding hand and gave the horses green, foamy mustaches.

"Let's go. Are you fit to ride after dark without stopping to make camp?"

"We rode after dark yesterday," she said, wiping her hand in her washcloth, which would have to wait to be laundered at the next water hole. Living on the trail she was finding not so hard to learn.

"We started out late and didn't ride all day. I mean all night until sunup."

"I can do it," she said stoutly, even though her body craved rest. She worried more about Sombra than herself and said so.

He checked Sombra out and said, "He seems fit." He scratched her black pony behind the ear. "We'll be coming to a stream that should be running full this time of year. We can rest up there. Did you give him some grain?"

"Yes. I gave them all, but Sombra a little more."

"Bueno. Let's ride."

She glanced back as they rode on, looked at his stony profile, and decided not to ask.

Chapter Thirteen

It was another nice starry night. Rather than ride until sunup, as he had said, they stopped to make a cold camp well before dawn. Dominica felt he stopped only because of her and Sombra, and possibly the roan, which seemed more fit than Sombra, but neither were so indefatigable as the dun and its human. The gunman and his horse were cut from the same super-normal fabric. If not for the excess baggage of herself and the two horses lesser than his own, she thought, he and his dun would have kept riding until they got to where they were going, nonstop. She would have argued to go on, but she worried about Sombra.

It could not have been more than ten minutes that she had been sleeping when she bolted upright at the clap of thunder, bewildered by the floodwater swirling around her. Before she was fully awake, the water rose. She placed her hand on a fat, mushy, sodden softness and screamed, flinging the drowned rat away. She was on her feet quicker than the next lightning flash. But too late. It began to pour, and in less than a minute her boots were ankle deep. The wind howled and furiously slammed sheets of rain against one another. What felt like a bucketful of water splashed into Dominica's face. That spurred her out of her transfixed state.

She bumped into the gunman. He already had the pack on the roan and the tarp over the pack. He shouted at her. She couldn't hear him in the deafening din, but she read his gestures. He was easy to see. Consecutive bolts of lightning ripped open the night's blackness to long-lasting flares of eerie daylight. She saw water sluicing down from his hat brim through the sluicing down of her own. He had a slicker on. She rushed to put hers on, but it was under the sheepskin and blanket, already saturated. She didn't bother pulling the oiled canvas poncho over her already sodden woolen poncho but rather used it to tie over the tarp on the packsaddle for double waterproof protection.

She followed the gunman's instructions like a frenzied zombie. She went from one thing to another until they got the frantically dancing horses bridled and saddled, and then they were riding into the worst of the storm. He led the way, with the roan's lead tied to his saddle, and Sombra staying up close to the roan.

Dominica didn't know how the gunman knew where he was going. Most of the time she rode with her eyes squeezed shut against the stabbing needles of rain, which the wind blew under her hat brim. She put her faith in Sombra to stay close to the roan and let him have full rein. Her leg was periodically crushed between the two horses, Sombra stayed so close to the roan. The blind contact was a reassuring discomfort that was sure to leave a bruise on her leg.

Through squinting peeks, she saw lightning flashes of turbulent torrents where dry washes had been. Every crease and crevice in earth and rock made fast-running streams. The intermittent flashes of angry heavenly light froze features of the topsy-turvy night in suspended animation all around, above, and below. Wind-bent trees. Floodwater-rushing debris. Steamy ridges. Glistening boulders. All an unearthly pandemonium.

The ground under them quaked as if in terror at heaven's awful wrath against hell's unleashed fury. She would dare not challenge God's existence now, too sure she would be struck dead. She truly feared it was the end of the world.

Suddenly, she became aware of not having had contact with the packhorse for she didn't know how long. Seconds? Minutes? She had no sense of time. She kicked out her foot in the stirrup to feel for the pack, or the roan's tail, or something. She squeezed Sombra to make him go faster. She flailed her heels against him. Her eyes were fearfully wide in the skin-prickling rain. A series of lightning flashes revealed nothing. The gunman and the packhorse were gone!

Panic slammed open the heavy door to the hidden chamber in her mind, freeing the horrors so long locked within. The night's stormy blackness flashed red. A bloody skull grinned gruesomely from a spinning wheel of fire. Eyeless sockets oozed yellow liquid. A naked woman thrashed on the ground. Moccasins covered the calves up to the knees of legs wedged between her wide-spread, pinned-back thighs. High-pitched screams . . . *Mommy! Mommy! Dadddeeee!!* . . . echoing and re-echoing and swallowed up in the great silence of the indifferent mountains.

She screamed at the sight of the bloodless face in the flash of cold light. The pale horse set back on its powerful haunches, sidling, half-rearing sooty legs in the Stygian waters, its sleek-wet, powerful, pale body glistening like steel in the lightning flashes, sooty nostrils squared, white fire gleaming in its sooty eyes. A satanic steed!

The gunman danced the dun around to bring it alongside the black pony, pushing the roan on the other side of the dun into compliance with the movement that was no doubt confusing and frightening to the packhorse. She was a mare willing to comply and with some difficulty got herself out of the way and alongside the dun as the black pony was jostled to the other side.

Dominica was unaware of the reins sliding out of her yielding hands. The black pony followed at the length of the reins on one side of the dun as the roan mare on the other side of the dun followed on the lead tied to the saddle. By natural inclination rather than conscious intent to keep from falling out of the saddle, both her hands clutched the saddle horn as she stared out of a black region within herself.

Like a great arm flinging out of the storm, a low-hanging tree limb caught her across the shoulders and pulled her from the pony. As she hit ground sideways, not so much pain as a flashing light, like another lightning bolt in the black night, crashed through her skull.

Then there was nothing. Not even blackness. Only a void.

Chapter Fourteen

He didn't know how long it had been that her saddle was empty. He had been so absorbed in concentrating on picking the way through the worst part of the storm that he hadn't looked back until the thunderheads had passed from directly overhead and the punishing bluster had eased up. The torrent had turned into a steady drizzle.

Glistening wet inkiness swallowed the back trail. She could have been anywhere back there. Searching in that ink, he could come within three feet of her and never know it. If she had moved from where she had fallen, he might never find her. Finding her seemed an impossible feat. But impossible feats had never stopped him before.

For four years he had not deviated, each paid job that he had taken in one way or another leading to his next quarry. Each knowing the death kiss of the Spanish blade as Nadie had felt on her throat before being disemboweled, their unborn infant boy, still in the sac, impaled on their cabin door. He had never broken the methodical stride of his sheer dedication to his avenging cause.

For four years he had searched for six unknown men. He supposed he should have been perversely flattered that not one or two but *six* men had been recruited to go against one man and one pregnant woman. Only he had not been there. It had been six men against one woman swollen with child. If it had been fewer men, they might not have had a chance against her with his Spanish blade in her hand. It had been her favorite fleshing knife. Before he had left with the horses to deliver to the army fort, she had confiscated it from him to do her chore on some new pelts he had brought her to turn into skins to sew into garments.

"I will be plenty busy and not even know you are gone," she had teased him, and he had teased back, "Then I will take my time and not hurry back." But he had hurried back, though still not fast enough.

He had painfully wrested from the ruins of his home and his life signs that painted him a picture: one had a peculiar dragging limp by the spoor of his flat-heeled plainsman's boot; another, identified by a narrow-heeled boot of the vaquero variety, with huge spiked rowels; another left a calling card of wooden matches broken into a V and many twisted ends of corn-shuck butts of evidently chain-smoked cigaritos; the other three left no distinctive marks but were distinctive enough to make out six murderers. One of the fiends had long, frizzy, red hair, from the pulled-out strands entangled in Nadie's fingers. One of the bastards had the silver and turquoise bracelet gone from her wrist, a Zuni-made trinket he had gotten for her at the pueblos and that she had always worn.

They had stampeded his stock down into the desert, where he had tracked the horses of the six killers back up into La Luz Canyon. They had gone into Puma Canyon, the side gorge settled by Don Corvalan. Then he had lost the tracks in the high country of the Indian reservation. The Corvalan family had been horrified by what had happened. Don Ramón had offered whatever services he could from his political influences in Santa Fe to his many influential connections throughout the territory, but he himself knew his was a futile, however noble, gesture. Don Ramón was not above taking matters into his own hands when the situation on his land demanded justice that his own force of vaqueros could deliver more swiftly and effectively than any ineffectual arm of civil or military law. His son Raul had wanted to take a dozen vaqueros and go with him to find and gun down the fiends. Raul's sister Encarnación had cornered him alone to confess her undying love for him, had vowed to get a divorce from Frutozo if he would stay and not go on his suicidal mission of revenge. He had never had more than a fondness for the sweet Encarnación, had expected no justice from the law, and, consequently, had taken up the vengeance trail alone, as it had to be.

Day by day, week by week, month by month, year by year, through the contacts he had made and by the caliber of men he had encountered in his work, by the underground channels of society he had traveled, by the scum and the dregs of humanity he had infiltrated—the very lowest, the very dirtiest, the very meanest—one by one he had gotten his man until the last one. The impossible had been accomplished, except for a seventh man he had not expected. The seventh who in proper context was the first, the mastermind behind the fiendish plot to destroy him.

Finding the last man on his list was not an impossibility. To the contrary, it would be the easiest—a certainty to find at the Corvalan ranch. The key man had not actually surprised him. The man had had a grudge against him from the minute they met, compounded a few years later by his hatred for white men who consorted with heathen women. The man had no notion that he was a marked man. He would not go anywhere. He had been entrenched at the Corvalan ranch for years and expected to die there. He didn't realize how soon that would be.

He was impatient to get there, yes. It had taken him over four years to get this far and close to the end. Another delay of a day or two would not matter. The girl could be dead, but he could not leave that uncertainty without closure. Leaving her to fate would be leaving her to a certain death if she was not dead, a cruel death, and in any case would make his whole effort of taking her from the abandoned village pointless.

Leading the riderless black pony by the reins, the packhorse on the lead tied to the saddle ring, he squeezed the dun into the wet blackness out of which they had come. He could only hope *this* impossible feat did not take four years.

CHAPTER FIFTEEN

When she regained consciousness, she moved strictly on motor reflexes. She flapped around in the muddy water on her belly and chest until a gasping face full impelled her to her hands and knees. She crawled around in circles until she came to an obstruction with thorns. She felt no pain as she grabbed a thorny limb and then another and another until she was on her feet.

Like a blind person she groped with outstretched arms. The mud sucked one of the oversized man's boots off her foot. Then it sucked off the other. She didn't notice. She stumbled in her stocking feet through the sucking mud with outstretched arms toward a ledge over roiling waters.

The wet night was as black as her mind.

He spent the night going mostly on the dun's one-track mind, which gave the dun his remarkable horse memory. Horses had a habit of backtracking to where they had been. He allowed the dun full rein to take him back to their campsite. With misty grayness of early morning came visibility. The features of the landscape took on a new perspective in the early light, different if even recognizable from the impressions made by his glimpses in the lightning flashes of the night before. The floodwaters had gone down, their tracks of the night before washed away.

The one most salient feature that stood out in his memory was the turbulent water of an arroyo. He hadn't stayed with the arroyo for long because its rim was wooded and grew too broadly dense for passage. He remembered lightning flashes on a high outcrop, with a jumble of balanced boulders at the top, where he had turned away from the impenetrable thicket along the arroyo. He moved to higher ground and through the binoculars looked for a brush-bordered arroyo and a high outcrop with a jumble of balanced boulder rocks.

Spotting the arroyo, he scanned the entire area along the fast-moving flooded channel within his visual range. Nothing. His vision in the twin lenses held against his eyes blurred as he passed them along the ground looking for something he thought he had seen. *There.* He focused in on the object, adjusting the field glasses to their highest power.

Her black sombrero was hung up by the chin strap in the thorny branches of a dead mesquite bush in the vicinity of a low box-elder limb. He recalled the low limb. Just waiting to knock two riders out of their saddles in a stormy night. The limb had nearly gotten him. Before reining the dun out of its path, he had glanced back and issued her a warning. Now he cursed himself for not having looked back to make sure she was okay after passing the menace. Still, for all he knew, she could have merely lost her hat there, and, knowing how she had hated wearing the hat, he wouldn't put it past her to have been glad it was gone. He searched around the area for other signs before ruling out the place as the one where she had left the saddle.

Under a ceiling that was lifting and fast breaking up and casting a pink light on the saturated world, he came upon her boot almost buried in the mud. The subsided floodwaters had left brown silt mounds as smooth and unmarked as new velveteen. Water-filled indentations of one booted and one stockinged foot were plainly distinguishable.

Staying mounted to spare his moccasins the hock-deep squishy ground, he followed the tracks to her second boot.

Hanging sideways from the saddle, he pried the boot out of the mud's tenacious grip. He poured water from the boot and held it along with its mate by the mule-ear pull-up straps. Footprints in the otherwise unmarked silty wash zigzagged toward the brushy rim of the arroyo.

Her tracks led into a clearing of the brush. The area was matted with an entanglement of tall, bent grasses. The soggy grasses made a trackless mat along the bank of the arroyo. He sat the dun at the grassy edge, with the muddy boots hanging from his hand at his side. He watched dead wood and whole living, uprooted, small trees rush by. He envisioned her body lodged among the debris being carried downstream by the rapids.

Topsoil rapidly dried in the returned heat of the sun. By the height of the afternoon parched surfaces began to shrink and crack where only hours ago they had been underwater. The drying process was hastened by the southwesterly winds. Flooded dry washes were on their way to being dry again as the waters receded almost as rapidly as they had risen.

Dominica opened her eyes in an entanglement of brush and tree roots. Her gaze was clouded and unfocused. Instinctively she tried clawing her way out of the snare. The agitation disturbed her nest of leafy branches caught in exposed tree roots at the top of the bank, and she and the branches went crashing down eight feet. The impact with the ground knocked the breath out of her.

She lay still for long minutes. She moaned and stirred and pushed herself up to her hands and knees. Her drying hair was tangled with twigs and other detritus of the floodwaters. A reopened head injury released a stream of blood down the side of her forehead into her eyebrow, where it broke into bright crimson rivulets down her cheek, along the side of her nose, into the corner of her mouth, and down her chin. She struggled to her feet. She staggered like a drunkard in the wet wool blanket coated with sandy mud and stickered with twigs, pieces of tree bark, and other debris.

The bed of the arroyo was veined with a myriad of thin streamlets and littered with steamy small boulders, tree limbs, and dead and dying brush piled in heaps where the mighty currents had swept and deposited them.

She blindly walked into obstacles. Time and again she became ensnared by tangles of brushy driftwood, which she struggled out of, around, and even through and over to free herself with stuporous persistence. Every time she fell down, she picked herself up as she doggedly trudged onward without any conscious sense of direction and on sheer survival instincts that dictated forward movement.

Chapter Sixteen

The two riders came to a dead end and confusion. For several minutes they circled around, looking for sign. Not watching where they were going, they bumped horses. The fat one nearly lost his sombrero. Following a short tirade of Spanish oaths, he demanded, "What do you think, estúpido? If you are so capable to do that with the bird shit you have for a brain."

The other grinned foolishly. "*No sé,* Esquivel."

"You don't know! You don't know!" Esquivel's jowls shook. Their disgusted quiver was punctuated with the ungroomed ends of long mustachios. "It's plain as the stupid look on your face, Sanchez. We lost them! The storm washed out all their sign."

"I think they went the other way, Esquivel."

"Now you think, Sanchez! What other way?"

"The arroyo."

"Why did we come this way, Sanchez?"

"It was your idea, Esquivel."

"Because you did not have one, Sanchez."

"We go back."

"You go back. I will rest now while you go, and don't come back until you find which way they went. You are supposed to be the expert tracker, can find a man by the smell of his asshole with your nose, you stupid Indian. Don't take too long. I don't want to have to go look for you."

With that, Esquivel dismounted with much grunting and

could not get his foot dislodged from the stirrup in time to get his balance on the ground, so he fell over backwards.

Solemnly, Sanchez observed and evaluated the performance. "I think, Esquivel, you are too fat."

Esquivel lumbered to his feet before he replied. The other continued to sit his horse like a wooden statue wearing a broad-brimmed sombrero cinched squarely down on the head by the chin strap hooked under the nose and a dagger impaling the hat's sugar-loaf crown dead center.

"¡Ay! Fat but still fast, eh, Sanchez?"

"Sí, Esquivel, you are still fast," Sanchez conceded solemnly.

"And I still have the delicate touch, eh? Not so bad on the aim either."

"I am glad for that, Esquivel."

"What are you waiting for?"

"I am going, Esquivel."

"First, return my knife, *chupadero.*"

"It is not nice for you to call me a cattle tick, Esquivel."

"Yeah, yeah. Give me the knife."

For a moment, Esquivel thought Sanchez was going to give him the knife not where Esquivel wanted it in his extended palm. He had to be careful with that *cholo.* Couldn't trust him anymore than you could trust an Apache.

Esquivel settled himself in the shade, of which there was plenty in the cottonwood bosque. He was no fool to leave this place when the sun was at its hottest. He built himself a cigarito with a corn shuck from a bundle of *hojas* and powdered *punche* from a little tin carried in a rawhide pouch kept tucked under the narrow sash of red cotton girding his paunch. His gun belt loosely rode over the sash, which was weighed down by the pistola in the holster. Following his smoke, he dozed. He came out of the *siesta* with a snort and a start.

He glanced about in a slightly disoriented daze. Then he narrowed his eyes suspiciously. His horse was still where he had left it, calmly browsing on branches, although the rangy mustang had one ear turned watchfully, with the respective eye looking in the direction of an outcrop.

Esquivel stifled an urge to call out Sanchez's name. He acted on delayed impulse to see if his pistola was still in the holster, as if somebody might have sneaked up on him in his sleep and unarmed him. He kept one hand on the butt, ready to draw, as he slowly pushed his paunchy weight up from the ground. Slowly, because he didn't want to make any noise, and because he couldn't have gotten up from the ground any faster if he had to.

The stupid cholo was right. He had gotten too fat. It grieved Esquivel to think of the forever-gone time when he had cut a trim and dashing figure who dazzled the *chiquilinas.* Now, added to the injury of time's thievery of his handsome youth was the insult of having to sink to paid services. And then one silver *peso* for a *puta* not worth *cincuenta centavos.*

Well, that would soon change. When he rode into the brilliant white streets of Chihuahua and flung coins to the beggar children and old hags, he would be sought after by the classiest bitches in all the city. No inferior mescal or pulque either. Tequila for Esquivel. He envisioned himself going to Pichachos, bearing gifts, of course, to show what a devoted husband and father he was. After that he might make the long ride to Piedras Negras to reconcile the affections of his wife and children over there. When she saw the gold and silver coins he had, her reconciled affections would turn to passion. How he missed them all. The pain of it in his breast was almost too much to bear. It made him anxious to get this job over with and done.

Where was that cholo? Stupid son of a flea-bitten Yaqui bitch. *Chupadero!*

Chapter Seventeen

Esquivel looked at the empty trail Sanchez had taken. It curved around a limestone outcrop that resembled a group of candlesticks that had melted in a clump at the base, the tapered tips forming a sawtooth rim. Like some mountains. Esquivel found humor in that and laughed. The outcrop looked like a miniature sawtooth mountain.

These mountains they were in had crazy rock formations. Hidden caves with stone hanging from the ceiling like icicles dripping water. They had taken refuge in one from the storm. The crazy cholo knew his way around the mountains. Sanchez had lived with the Apaches for how long Esquivel did not know. The red dogs owned the mountains, which was what worried Esquivel. He did not want to go too far into them and be caught trespassing. They might make allowance for Sanchez, since he had lived with them, but not for Esquivel, who was pure Mexican.

This was not turning out so simple as they had planned. By now they were supposed to have been halfway to Chihuahua with the *hombre's* sacks of money. There was no doubt about what the two heavy sacks contained. Any idiot could see they were not grain for the horse. The way the gringo pistolero dropped a gold coin on the bar in the cantina supported Esquivel's theory. Visions of gold coins danced in his head. A bonanza for him and Sanchez. They had unequivocally agreed that the hombre was not one likely to be easily relieved of anything in his possession, certainly not sacks containing any size fortune. Thus, the hombre's death was imperative to their imminent wealth.

To accomplish their mission with minimal jeopardy on their own lives, it would have to be done silently while the hombre slept. That was, silently until they got up close enough to perforate his sleeping body with both barrels of their pistolas. One could not be overly cautious with a pistolero like him.

They had not followed him up to the ghost village because they didn't want to do anything to upset the sacred dead up there. The girl said to be loca, who lived up there with the ghosts, added to that deterrent. They were not ones to bother those with afflictions of the mind. They had not expected the pistolero to take the *chica loca* with him.

After getting some good looks at her themselves in town, they had decided she didn't look so crazy like the Lobo gang wanted people to believe. They concluded El Lobo wanted people to believe she was not right in the head to keep people from going to the abandoned village and taking things for themselves, or even claiming the village to live in it.

After the pistolero and the girl left the village, he and Sanchez had braved an investigation, crossing themselves to appease the holy spirits and to ward off any unholy ones that haunted the village. They found the deserted *paisano* houses emptied of everything. Inside the church, Sanchez, who was more superstitious than worshipful, did not cross himself like Esquivel, who made the sign of the cross many times. He genuflected before the altar and, in passing the *santos,* in their niches. The church had a feeling of a ghostly presence, as if the padre's spirit were watching them, which made Esquivel edgy.

Esquivel did not feel irreverent ransacking the wine cellar under the church. Disappointingly, there was only one mostly empty wine cask among the empty barrels left behind. The cask was too cumbersome to be hauled around on a saddle horse, so they filled their goatskins and smashed the cask so nobody else could have what little wine was left. They smashed all the empty barrels, too, for good measure.

What they were going to do with the girl after they dispatched the pistolero, they hadn't decided yet. Not that they didn't have some good ideas. If she cooperated with them and gave them no trouble, they would be nice to her. She was one pretty young thing. Esquivel had never had a gringa, not even that disease-infected whore in town, whom he would not have had even if *she* had paid *him*. Anyway, she was found dead the day the pistolero gringo arrived and made a laughingstock of El Lobo. Anticipation about the *chiquilina americana* after dispatching the pistolero hard boiled Esquivel's *huevos,* but there were too many other important matters on his mind to give himself a fast hand job.

Nevertheless, he fondled his privates with one hand and the butt of his holstered pistol with the other as he thought about the other reason he had wanted to make this business with the pistolero short. The longer it took, the more time the Lobo gang had to catch up to them once they realized the trick the old hag had played on them. Of course, if worse came to worst, there was the idea of trying to negotiate a partnership with the competition. Esquivel would rather it not come to that, especially when he could not put much faith in his last-ditch idea. It was best to get this business with the pistolero over soon and not have to share the coins in those sacks with anyone. Maybe not even Sanchez.

Where was that cholo wasting so much precious time?

There was a distinct sound of an iron horseshoe striking stone. The mustang's head was up and alert. Esquivel drew his pistol. It wasn't an Indian; Indians didn't put iron on their horses' feet. On the other hand, it could be an Indian on a stolen iron-shod horse. It could be one of the El Lobo gang coming in advance. And, who was to say it wasn't the pistolero himself come to get Esquivel after having killed Sanchez? In that case, surely Esquivel would have heard gunshots. Maybe not. Maybe the pistolero had not used a gun to kill Sanchez.

Esquivel's pondering put him in a sweat. He recalled how the pistolero had used no gun to put El Lobo out of commission. How he had walked his horse right into El Lobo's gunfire. The hombre was not human. *La máquina.* A machine impervious to bullets.

Esquivel cursed his horse for being so far from him. He could swear he had not tied his horse to bushes so far. It was too late to make a run for the horse. Besides, he was too fat to run.

The approaching horse was coming around the bend. The stupid mustang greeted it. Esquivel paid no attention to the reciprocal call of the approaching horse. He was too intent upon what he expected. He raised his pistol. He saw himself backing away like El Lobo, blasting both barrels, only he had just one barrel, and the hombre, *la máquina,* impervious to bullets, was coming at him to end his miserable, pathetic, wasted, fat life.

"My children!" he cried.

"It is only me," the stupid cholo-son-of-a-Yaqui-bitch who was familiar with Esquivel's death cry announced. "I found his tracks. And look what else I found!"

At the end of Sanchez's *reata* was a *novilla.* Only not a heifer, but a *chica* in the noose being pulled along like a heifer. And not just any *chiquilina.*

Sanchez took the binoculars down from his face and came down the rocky slope to where Esquivel waited with the horses and the girl.

"He is coming this way."

Esquivel looked at the girl. Bedraggled, she stood in a stupor, with little if any awareness about her. Esquivel wondered how she stayed on her feet at all. *Bestia.* Crazy or not, the girl had been reduced to no more than a docile dumb beast who had learned to respond by the jerk of the rope. Her impassive condition had snuffed out any lust in his loins. She had no *chispa,* no spark to lend some excitement to the activity.

"My little heifer," Esquivel addressed her, though he knew he might as well be talking to a real cow, "maybe you will serve a purpose after all."

Chapter Eighteen

Even though he had gone up and down the arroyo looking for any sign of her body—anything, a shred of clothing—and had come up with no more than the hat and the boots, he had to go back. Maybe it was only a mechanical deed driven by some mystical force to fulfill a commitment made by the man he had been to a dying man. Or maybe a particle of moral sense that the man he had been possessed still remained in the machine. By commitment or by conscience, perhaps by the combined power of both, he was compelled to go back.

By the time he got back to the arroyo, in what little daylight was left, he saw the water had gone completely down. He rode the grassy rim to where Apache plume, burro brush, and scrub sumac got taller than his head and impenetrable as a brambly entanglement. Circumventing the scrub thicket, he came back to the rim, where a knotted jumble of large tree roots protruded from the bank. Gnarled and snarled branches of scrub oak and desert willow hung over the rim of the arroyo. At the bottom was a pile of broken limbs and branches. There he saw them. Footprints.

It was too steep of an eight- to ten-foot drop for the horses to jump. He let himself down by the rope looped about the saddle horn. The dun stood rigid, keeping the rope taut, as if holding a wild horse on the other end. He examined the prints more closely in the failing light, followed her stumbling, meandering tracks to where he came to see she was in more trouble than he had imagined.

A rider had met up with her. The rider did not take her up on the horse. She continued to stumble and stagger, only now in a more deliberate pattern behind the horse. At one point, it appeared she had fallen and was dragged a couple of yards before the rider stopped. The horse's hoofprints indicated that. The tracks continued, showed her back on stumbling feet.

The evening light faded too fast. The bottom of the dry wash became puddled with the black ink of night. Not having night vision, he had to go back to the horses. He would have to wait until daylight.

The sign that she was alive affected him strangely. He thought he had lost his capability to have emotions. The emotion radiated from his chest where for the past four years he had felt not the beating of a warm heart but a stone of cold indifference to life and to death. Now, by the sign that Dominica lived, he felt the emotional warmth of caring.

Leaving the horses hobbled and grinding grain inside nose bags, he climbed to an overlook of the landscape that was as velvety black as the deep black of the starry sky. He saw no sign of a campfire in the great well of inky blackness. She was out there somewhere.

Beneath his hat shoved over his face to shut out the world, he slept the light sleep of a man whose only constant bed partner was danger, but still as a rock. Even when he slept, his unconscious perceptions were keenly tuned to the pulsations of his surroundings.

In his light sleep, his dreams were more conscious recollections than unconscious illusions. A man lashed upside down to a wagon wheel . . . the rope not burned through to release his incredibly still-living charred remains . . . more incredible, still coherently conscious . . . begging for his girl to be saved . . .

whispering that she lives, feels her near, hears her . . . pleads for her to be found, to be saved . . . begs for mercy, to end his agony. The girl was nowhere in the devastated camp. He and Nadie searched the nearby area outside the camp, and Nadie spotted her. Watching them, as wary and elusive as a wild creature, staying close to the campsite and her massacred family, but running off at his approach. She had fought him and screamed in such terror when he caught her that she passed out. She collapsed in his arms so lifelessly, he thought her heart had stopped.

He had initially intended to take her with him and Nadie, and to Fort Stanton in the vicinity of their destination, his valley purchased from Don Corvalan so many years before. But the girl had fallen to fever and had become too ill for long travel. Nadie's Indian remedies had gotten her over the fever, but it was apparent the girl needed medical attention they could not provide. It was Nadie's idea to take her to the church in the village, having seen the cross skylined on the little mesa from the higher point they were in the mountains. Because the sight of him agitated the girl, Nadie carried the girl in front of her on her horse to the church. They expected there she would get the help she needed, and the priest would get word to the authorities in those parts. He had kept his word to the dying man. He completed his moral obligation by reporting the massacre and the girl's location to both Fort Stanton and the county sheriff some months later after he and Nadie had gotten settled in his valley. Hence the girl's fate was in the authorities' hands and out of his. So he had thought. Then, after so many years gone by, when he had learned of the white girl living in the abandoned Mexican village alone, it was as if a commitment long buried had been exhumed.

As the constellations slowly moved over the mountains and canyons, he fell faraway in another place, and there he and Nadie were together again, and they made love as they had never made love, and her ebony eyes had the vitreous shine of emeralds, and her heavy, straight raven hair felt like wispy silk threads in his fingers and glistened reddish-brown, and he awoke abruptly to a viscous wetness between his thighs.

In the canyon quiet of early morning's lavender dimness, the raspy chirrups of a cactus wren distantly mocked his abject loneliness.

He saw the Mexican spying on him from a craggy ridge up ahead. Then the tall crown of the sombrero dropped out of sight below the ridge.

The gunman paused to roll and light a quirly. He sat quietly, leaning an arm across the pommel of the saddle, and smoked. He narrowed his gaze on the trail ahead. He knew it. The trail descended to a boulder-crowded corridor of bluffs. The gunman thought that if he wanted to waylay a lone man carrying two sacks of American gold, that narrow stretch between the bluffs, with all those boulders for cover, would be an ideal place to do it.

He sat smoking the cigarette down to a stub, thinking about it, how easy it had been in the new early light to come upon their tracks. As if the tracks had been laid for him to follow. The two loafers had obviously taken the girl up on one of their horses to make better time in keeping ahead of him. Intending to lead him into an ambush.

The gunman pinched the hot tip out before flicking the butt away. He reined the smoky dun away from the well-trodden old Indian trail and laid his own track. The roan packhorse and the riderless black pony followed, the black sombrero hanging by the chinstrap from the pony's saddle horn and the boots lashed together by the pull-up straps hanging on the other side.

★ ★ ★ ★ ★

From each one's side behind balanced boulders, they watched the empty trail. *"Pues, donde está?"* Esquivel said from his side of their cover.

"No sé," Sanchez replied, peeking from his side.

"You don't know! You don't know! That's all you know!" Esquivel stepped over to Sanchez's side and gave his partner's bony shoulder a hard shove. "Go see. Before the girl dies and we have to go back to our original plan. I don't want to spend one more night in these mountains. We have been lucky so far not to meet up with any Apache. And the weather is no better, as unpredictable as the Apache."

It took Sanchez nearly a half hour to go see. Esquivel started to get nervous. Sanchez at long last came back. He shrugged. "He is not there."

"What do you mean he is not there?"

"He is not coming like he was before."

"Where did he go?"

"Another way."

"Why is he doing that?"

"He was too far away for me to ask him."

Esquivel's jowls quivered. "Let's go before we lose him."

"We won't lose him. He is not covering his tracks."

"You mean he wants us to follow him?"

"Maybe he got tired of following us. So now wants us to follow him for a while."

"What is this? Some silly game? What do you suppose he is up to, you fool?"

A wise fool, Sanchez grinned to himself behind the chinstrap knotted under his nose. He shrugged his shoulders and kept his lips sealed against saying the words.

"Do you think he knows we know he was following us?" Esquivel asked.

Sanchez shrugged his shoulders, stubbornly refusing to say the words.

"Meaning," Esquivel calculated aloud, more to himself, the mental effort making his eyes squint as Sanchez imagined they must when the fat slob strained the other end of him in a constipated squat, "if he knows, then he figured out we were laying an ambush and now is leading us into a trap."

Sanchez shrugged his shoulders.

Esquivel punched him. "Will you stop doing that? Like an idiot!"

Sanchez frowned and rubbed his arm.

"Listen, idiot. We will follow him and let him think we are not on to him, eh? We got the girl. We still got the edge, eh?"

Sanchez almost shrugged and thought better of it. He evasively said, "You put the girl up behind you now."

"Oh, but I am too fat; you said so yourself. You are skinny. Your horse don't have to work so hard carrying you as my horse works carrying me. It is better you keep the girl up behind you. *¡Vamos!*"

Chapter Nineteen

Resembling a wide bottleneck entrance to a gorge in the rocky slopes of a ridge, the short passageway led into a cove-like chamber, a dead end. The gunman sat the dun in the cul-de-sac and moved his gaze around the surrounding low walls of stratified, variegated limestone that formed ledges at various heights. Juniper, twisted into exquisitely grotesque shapes, projected gnarled limbs from the higher ledges and the rim. Cliff-clinging sotol shot sawtooth blades out of the ruggedly layered rock at the lower levels. A variety of brush, prickly pear, and other cacti, interspersed with mesquite, maple, oak, and locust trees, formed a thicket around the base of the circular walls. The wind swirled. Little dust devils chased one another around the largely barren central floor.

It was reassuring to find his memory still sharp, with the way the insentient machine's capacities were malfunctioning at an emotional level. His gaze picked out a mineral deposit of a much darker shade than the varied tones of gray limestone. The different coloration high in the rock wall marked the spot below where trees and brush concealed a defile. He released the black pony, urging him ahead to lead the single file through the narrow serpentine passageway, he on the dun following close behind to keep the reluctant pony moving, the roan on the lead tied to the dun's saddle ring bringing up the rear.

The sinuous rock corridor let out into a secluded meadow. The meadow, of good graze from mixed gramas to needle grasses, was enclosed by steep, broken slopes made more hazardous to climb or descend by spiky and bristly colonies of cactus and brush. Only a mountain goat or puma would attempt to negotiate the rugged scarps, or an Apache. It was a perfect natural corral if one wanted to keep livestock without building fences, which was exactly what the Apaches used the place for—a secret hideout for stolen horses.

At one side of this inner sanctum, a seepage of springwater mistily sprayed down rock and formed a marshy place of cattails and reeds and a puddle for the horses to drink. He left them saddled in case of need for a quick departure. Turned loose, with mouths freed of iron bits, the dun and black impatiently broke into trots to join the roan, whose halter was of no hindrance to her faster start at cropping off mouthfuls of the grasses and flowering forbs. He dragged some dead brush to block the opening to the passageway to discourage the horses from wandering out, which was unlikely, for their rich feast would keep them content for many hours, if not days.

Taking the canteen and Winchester, he returned on foot, in shirtsleeves, to the main chamber. Unencumbered by any outer garments, he had more freedom of movement for climbing rocks.

For a minute he listened to the quiet, haunted by echoes of death-fall screams of naked warriors toppling from the upper reaches under cavalry fire. It was also a favorite place for Apaches to lure bluecoats and rain down on them rocks and arrows from the heights. Bitter intimacies interwoven with sweet made up the tapestry of his memories rising like ghosts from their graves in the desolate desert of his mind.

They entered the entrance of the cul-de-sac, cautiously.

He got on a knee, brought the Winchester's sights up, and his hands shook. An unnatural chill prickled his skin under the sweat-soaked shirt. Beads of perspiration rolled over the brown-gold hairs of his brows and splashed into his gilt-tipped eyelashes, stinging his eyes with his own brine. He had known it to happen to other gunmen, better than himself. Sharpshooters and marksmen in the army. But it had happened to *others,* not to him. Even when he had lost control of a situation, temporarily, he had always kept in control of himself.

The girl. Her effect on him was worse than he had thought. Visiting him in his dreams in the form of a succubus . . . stirring up ghosts of the past . . . memories of old desires . . . of old hopes . . . of irrevocable losses . . . of irreversible regrets . . . making him long to live again . . . to be a living, fallible man, not an emotionally dead machine. But even machines were not infallible and had breakdowns, and, if he kept this up, he would be useless as a man or a machine.Succeeding to will a steady bead on one target, he could not take the shot, could not risk the sound startling the mustang. The skinny loafer was leading the girl on the end of his lasso. The noose was about her upper arms and torso. The other end dallied around the saddle horn. All the horse had to do was bolt by a gunshot, and she could suffer serious injury by being dragged and kicked under hooves.

"Hombre!"

He didn't answer.

"Hombre, we know you are here!" The fat one's voice reverberated off the rock walls.

Narrowing his eyes on the girl, the gunman tried to judge her condition. Her head was fallen forward. Hair hung like a stringy curtain concealing her face. She still wore the blanket he had improvised into a poncho for her, cinched by the rope around her chest and arms, no longer colorfully bright, rather dingy with dried, caked mud, its frayed raggedness reflecting the wear and tear of the body it shabbily covered.

"Hombre!"

The fat one, with long mustachios hanging like Spanish moss

below fatty jowls, was squinting beneath the awning of a palm as he scanned the encircling rock ledges.

"Hombre, leesen!"

Echoes got lost in silence.

"We gar sumtheeng of yore as you can see!"

Silence.

"We theenk maybe you lose somehow and maybe you like back, eh?"

He mutely waited.

"Hombre, the sun, she ees get hot! You no theenk?"

Silence.

"Maybe you like to know sumtheeng, eh?"

Silence.

"The señorita, she have a accidente! War no fault of our, of course! She war hurt when we find her! We rescue her for you. We theenk maybe you geeve us a reward for rescuing her for you, eh? Hombre?"

Following several minutes of a living and breathing silence from the cul-de-sac's walls, Esquivel amiably said, "Okay, hombre! You no wan talk now! We wait! We gar lotsa time! *Pero* the girl I no theenk so much. She need some water. You theenk about that." The fat one raised his water container and made a show of taking a long swallow. The loafers moved into shade, the fat one riding his horse and the skinny one following on foot, leaving Dominica standing in the sun beside the ground-tied horse she was still tied to. The gunman could feel the promise of the mid-afternoon heat yet to come radiating off the walls not in shadow. The floor of the cove had already begun baking at the noon oven temperature. Dominica dropped to her knees, disturbing the horse from its hipshot stance. Luckily the sorrowful looking bony critter appeared too listless to move from the spot, its head continuing to hang in abject lethargy. Despite the two buzzards in clear range of his sights, he still could not risk a shot until Dominica was detached from the horse.

She was on her knees, slumped back on her hips. The only motion of her still form was that of the wind blowing long strands of hair. It seemed the only thing keeping her from toppling over was the line stretched taut from her torso to the mustang's saddle horn, the tension possibly keeping the horse from moving in the likelihood it had been trained to roping cattle in its lifetime and to holding the rope taut with a cow on the other end. More likely, in its miserable, captive life it knew little more comfort than standing and waiting in the hot sun. The broom-tailed creature docilely stood lazily dozing, with its much-abused ugly head hanging low, indifferent to the flies eating at the mucous drainage from its nose and heavy-lidded eyes, and periodically flicking one listless ear.

"Listen, Esquivel."

"I don't hear anything."

"That is what I mean. The quiet. It is empty."

Esquivel listened. The wide, curled brim of his sombrero waggled to his nodding head. "But how could he be gone?"

"Maybe he was never here. Maybe you were talking to yourself."

"Idiot. The horses' tracks lead right into this dead end."

"But where are they?"

"You are the expert tracker," Esquivel retorted. "Go see where they went."

Esquivel mopped the sweat from his brow with the back of a hand. He wished he were back in town where, right now, he would be taking a siesta in a shady place. That stupid cholo son-of-a-Yaqui-bitch and his get-rich-quick schemes. Esquivel thought that Sanchez even walked like the *indio* half of him, with that slow, low-slung, long-armed ape swing. He watched

Sanchez move across the floor of the cul-de-sac, reading the ground. Sanchez came back, looking like the noon heat did not bother him one bit, his terra-cotta skin appearing as dry as the drab dust that coated his boots and clothes.

"They don't go no place. They just stop."

"You loco. What do you mean they 'just stop'? How can they just stop?"

Sanchez shrugged. "Esquivel," he said sadly, "I tell you what I see. I am thinking, Esquivel, the hombre tricked us. He come in here, then he covered his tracks going back out. He is gone."

"You mean this was all for nothing? We lost him and the gold?"

"We don't really know it is gold in those sacks."

"You said you were sure it was gold."

"I said it looked like sacks of gold coins. Could be silver."

"Oh, you . . . !" Esquivel's jowls quivered with too much exasperation to think of a word to fit his partner's stupidity. "Shut up! Think about what we will do now. All we got is the girl, who is good for nothing to us. Not even the Comancheros would buy her! Not even the Apaches would want her! In her condition."

"She is good for something, Esquivel. Even in her condition. She is not dead."

Esquivel grunted disgustedly, his jowls and mustachios quivering. "You would do it to a dead woman. Anything with a hole in it."

"Then she is mine."

Esquivel had second thoughts. The talk about it worked up his juices. "*Pues,* for all our trouble, we should get something, eh?"

Esquivel and Sanchez froze.

The hombre had somehow sneaked up behind them. The

hombre issued instructions in clipped Spanish that was universally understood no matter what corrupt dialect of Castilian a person spoke. Esquivel and Sanchez obeyed. They unbuckled their gun belts and tossed the belts out onto the wind-whirling sand. Then they placed their hands behind their necks and dropped down to their knees. Then, as they were peculiarly instructed, they took off their charro sombreros and held them against their chests with both hands, so—as the hombre concluded—they could say their prayers and ask God's forgiveness so their souls can go to Heaven.

At that announcement Esquivel good-humoredly whined, "Aaameeego, you would not shoot two men on their knees sayeeng their prayers een the back, would you?"

The hombre's reply came swiftly, with hard taps of the butt of the revolver. Quietly, one after the other slumped to the ground.

"That'll keep you for a while," the gunman said, spinning the revolver back into the holster on his thigh.

Restraining himself from rushing, he proceeded to ease his way up to the horse, murmuring in soothing tones to keep it calm at his unfamiliar approach. Patting the neck of the miserably abused, raw-boned beast, which turned doleful, fly-bitten eyes at him, the gunman undallied the rope from around the pie-plate saddle horn. Then he rushed to the girl.

At his touch she collapsed but was conscious. He held her in one arm while loosening the slipknot of the noose around her torso with the other hand. Her lips were parched white in a scald-red face, smeared with dirt and caked with dried blood. She was dehydrated, no doubt suffering from exposure, lack of nourishment and heat prostration, the head injury, and what other injuries she had sustained that were not as apparent in his diagnostic glance. In his cursory analysis, water was the most vital thing she immediately needed.

He was hunched over the girl in shade where he had carried her, applying a wet kerchief over her flushed face, when he sensed his error before hearing the click of a gun's hammer. Staying on one knee, he straightened.

"You wouldn't shoot a man on his knee in the back?" he said.

Esquivel laughed out of equal good humor. "Ameego, I tell you, you geeve Esquivel one beeg ache een the cabeza. Sanchez, I theenk you keel. He no wake up. Ees too bad, amigo. Now I gar no choice, pero first I like to know the treek you do weeth the caballos."

"Kill me and you'll never know. But, even if you find the horses, it doesn't mean that's where you'll find what you're after."

"Why don't we make eet easy then? You geeve me what I am after, and I weel let you and the girl go."

"I will have to get up off my knee and take you to it."

"Why don't you just tell me?"

"Do you think I am a fool?"

"No," Esquivel unhappily said. "Maybe eef I shoot the girl een the leg, you weel tell me. And eef that don't work, then maybe I weel shoot her in the other leg. And eef that don't work, then—"

Esquivel abruptly stopped talking. His mouth became fixed as a tooth-decayed cavern between long, unwaxed mustaches in a fleshy face that acquired a blank look as a hole appeared between his beady eyes. The gunman pivoted himself around on his knee to see the result of his blind side-shoulder shot and replaced the Remington in the holster as he stood up to better examine his work. The machine was back in optimal operation.

He picked up Esquivel's pistol and went over to the mestizo, who was lying where he had fallen from the blow on the head. The fat buzzard had spoken the truth. Or a half truth. The

Mexican half-breed was dead all right, but not by any blow on the head. His compañero had apparently cut him out of the deal. Literally cut. The mestizo's throat had been slit by a razor-sharp instrument.

After the gunman tended to Dominica, he unbridled and unsaddled the mustangs, which slowly and uncertainly tested their freedom. Eventually, they wandered out into the desert foothills. Their neighs and whinnies could be heard like happy horse laughter at their realized liberation.

Chapter Twenty

The copper half moon came and went out of the blackness . . . hovered at long intervals . . . its half glow a soft, comforting light in the blackness . . . beckoning, drawing her into a gray light away from the bloody horrors . . . in the grayness moved around shadowy images . . . fuzzy halos dimmed, and the images came into sharper focus . . . the copper half moon took on the features of a face—one side hidden behind a curtain of polished-jet hair . . . the unconcealed side lustrous and smooth as burnished copper, prominent, high cheekbone, ebony eye rimmed with thick, shiny black lashes, a dimple at the curved-up corner of a soft, fleshy mouth . . . the black curtain fell forward revealing in shadow a milked-over black marble peering through an eyehole in a grotesque mask . . . a blurred figure in the grayness, a man in high moccasins. . . .

She woke up flinging her arms about but quieted to the soothing voice and lay still under the damp cloth placed over her eyes and forehead. She hoarsely asked, "Mister, did you kill my father?"

He became still, hunkered beside her where she lay on the pallet of blankets. "Another dream?"

"Yes."

"A dream I killed your father?"

"I don't know it was you. He wore high moccasins like you. They all wore high moccasins."

"The Indians?"

"No. I don't see their faces. Only you. Your face. And his."

"In your dream? Or in your memory? What are we talking about, Dominica?"

She pulled the cloth away from her face. "I don't need this anymore. I think I am better. I feel like I should get up." She pushed the blanket away and tried to stand up, settled on sitting.

"Maybe not yet," he said.

"I think I am dizzy from sleeping too much."

She put her fingers up to rub her forehead. He took her hand away.

"Don't do that."

"It itches."

"That's good. It's healing. Leave it alone, or you'll start it bleeding again."

Her lucid green eyes beseeched his glacial blue eyes, and it seemed the ice in them melted a bit.

"Dominica, he begged me."

"To put him on fire?"

"Jesus Christ, no. That's what you dreamed?"

"No. Yes." The bemused expression in her eyes was imploring. "How do I know a dream from a memory?"

After what seemed a stumped moment, he said, "I think what comes to you while you are awake we can safely say is a memory, not a dream. You are remembering, not dreaming awake."

She raised her knees and leaned her forehead against them, with her arms wrapped around her legs. "I remember," her voice came muffled from the hidden well under her bowed head, "you put your gun to his head and shot him."

He sucked in a deep breath before saying, "He begged me to, Dominica."

"I saw you kneeling by him. You put your face down close to

his, and she was standing over you, with her hand on your shoulder."

"It was too late when Nadie and I came on your folks' camp. He was suffering badly."

"I know. I heard him. I didn't know what to do. All I could do was cry and beg God."

"I don't know how he stayed alive. Nadie said it was because he was aware you were still alive. So long as he felt you near, he couldn't die. When we came, he felt you would be safe. He felt free to die and begged me to do it fast. Put him out of his agony. I promised your father I would see you to safety. We would have saved him if we could. Nadie understood his pain better than me."

"Her face?"

"You do remember then."

"I remember she made me feel . . . as my mother made me feel. When I was sick. Like my mother, she made me feel I would be okay. Always her face was covered by her long, black hair on one side. The side I saw was beautiful. Smiling at me. Comforting me, like my mother. When the hidden side of her face came out of the shadow, it did not look like a face. Made me faint to see. So terrible. But I was not afraid. I kept myself looking only at the beautiful side, and I was not afraid. Her closeness, her smile, the soft touches of her hands . . . I closed my eyes and felt she was my mother. I remember that." She brought her face out of hiding and looked at him, dry eyed and composed. "How did her face get like that, Mister?"

"She was young, a girl your age. Maybe younger. A slave in Mexico."

"What is that?"

"A slave?"

"I never heard of such thing."

"You never heard of slavery? Esclavo?"

"Oh. That. Consuelo used to say all the time, *'Trabajo como un esclavo por aquí.'* She liked to complain and feel sorry for herself and let everybody know the work she did—washing the clothes, cooking, cleaning, as if no other woman in the village did the same things and she didn't have me to help her. I thought esclavo meant that. Women's work. She had to work like other women when she would like to be sitting like Señora Reina Consuela and talking to people about other people. She liked to do that."

He had no remark for that. He tried to explain what a slave was in the simplest terms without elaborating. "I believe it began when strong men discovered they can control weaker men and make them do work they themselves didn't want to do and without paying them for their labor."

"Ah-ha! Then I was a slave to Consuela!"

He almost laughed. "You helped Consuela do her chores, but you weren't her slave."

"Well, sometimes I felt like it."

"How could you feel like something you never heard of? You just learned what a slave is now."

"Well, I am a fast learner."

He shook his head. "A slave is owned by another person as an animal is owned. Consuela didn't own you as if you were an animal, did she?"

"No." She frowned. "Your wife was owned by somebody?"

"Yes. Her owner was jealous of the way her husband looked at Nadie. Nadie told me he never did anything but look. His wife threw hot wax they were pouring for candles into Nadie's face."

"That is terrible. But why?"

"I suppose to stop him from looking at her."

"Did you save Nadie from that mean woman?"

"No. The hot wax happened years before I met her."

He moved from her to the campfire to stir something he had cooking.

"That smell makes me hungry. What is it?"

"That's good. Means you're better. My specialty. Rabbit stew," he said.

She saw he had pulled out her little copper cauldron kettle to cook in. She saw many of her kitchen wares out. And he had complained about all she had packed on the roan, had bragged all he needed was his one dented tin pan to make up his whole camp kitchen.

"Can I use your knife?" she asked. "To cut this meat off the bone."

"Why can't you use your teeth?"

"Why can't I use your knife?"

He was using it to pick the meat out of the stew on his plate and surrendered it to her, handle first. "Be careful. It's very sharp on both sides."

"I never saw a knife like this," she said, admiring the fancy grip of silver, etched with designs, the small pommel inlaid with a lavender gemstone on either side. "The stone changes colors."

"Jade," he said. "At least that's what the vendor in Mexico told me."

"You got it in Mexico?"

"Uh-huh. A silversmith who learned his trade in Spain made it. His son makes the blades out of Toledo steel. Most knives you find in Mexico are *navajas.* All daggers are called that, as all fixed fighting or hunting knives today are called bowies. That one is double-edged like a dagger, but its broad blade, with that clipped tip, makes it a bowie. I got the whole story I'm sure to make the sale. Whether true or not, I bought it because I liked it. The feel of it."

"What is the whole story?"

"The silversmith said Cortez found that kind of jade of many colors among the Aztecs and called it *piedra de hijada,* stone of the loins."

"What does that mean? Stone of the loins."

"Don't ask me."

"You didn't tell me," she said, as they ate his stew off the copper plates from her supplies, "how you met Nadie. And why was she called that? I never heard such a name."

Sitting in his usual sitting position, legs crossed Indian style, with his plate held over his lap in one hand, he said, "Long story."

"I like long stories."

"I don't think it was meant to be a name. But she got so used to being called that, she thought it was her name. She was a slave. A nobody to the people who owned her. I met her after I quit the cavalry."

"You were a horse soldier?"

"A career officer. An Indian fighter. I began to see the Indian's side. It was different in the War Between the States. I was on the side of freeing a people from another slave system."

"Again slavery?"

"I reckon every corner of the human race you will find one people enslaving another. Makes you wonder what kind of human race the Creator created. Makes you wonder about the Creator. The Indian wars were a different matter. I quit because I didn't make a good army officer when I didn't believe what I was doing was right. I started thinking it was like a stranger forcing himself into somebody's house and chasing the family of the house out and the stranger telling the family their house was now his. They no longer had a home."

"Like the Lobo gang did to Padre Zxavian and the people of the village."

"You can say that."

"Nobody ever told it to me that way about the Indians. You were an Indian fighter when you met your Indian wife?"

"No. When I left the army, I got into freighting from Santa Fe to Mexico and back again. I met her in Mexico."

"A slave to that mean woman?"

"No. But you might say still a slave. It was not a nice place, Dominica. Where a lot of Indian slave women end up. For the pleasure of men." He kept his hatless head bowed over the plate of stew balanced in the lap of his crossed moccasins.

"You were there for that pleasure?"

"A man needs that pleasure. It is the way of nature. I was not married, never had any special woman in my life, never wanted any. Never had any desire to settle down with one woman. Then I met her." He raised his head and met her intrigued green gaze directly with his desolate, cold stare.

"Then what? I know. You fell in love with her and took her away from that place," she said perhaps more romantically than perceptively.

His hard mouth could not resist the impulse to smile. He kind of shook his head as if not believing he was having this whole conversation. Yet, he found himself readily admitting, "Yes. That's about what happened."

"Did you see the bad side of her face?"

"It didn't make me blind to the beautiful side. Nor to the inner beauty of her. Maybe I loved her more for it."

"Then what?"

"The first padre I could find I had marry us. Then she was my wife. So now you have the story. Satisfied?"

After a small musing silence, Dominica murmured, "She was lucky to know such love of a man like you."

"I was the lucky one," he said. "She changed me. Gave me purpose. She was my purpose. We had a good life together. I saw us together until old age. We had a whole lifetime together to look forward to ahead of us. We had only three years."

"I am so sorry, Mister," Dominica said sorrowfully.

He stood up and got busy about the campfire with kitchen cleaning.

She watched him wistfully.

Women with brimmed bonnets covering their bowed heads and faces, strange cloaks, and billowing skirts, men with stiff, white collars and peculiar bows tied at their throats, children no less oddly dressed than the women and men, all holding open little books . . . singing in a church . . . a milch cow's silken tongue licking her face . . . a boy helping her pull a fish caught on her line out of a pond . . . kneading dough and forming it into loaves and putting them in a strange kitchen stove . . . an elderly, smiling woman, patting her aproned lap, beckoning her to come sit on it, and she snugging up against her grandmother . . . "Aleah . . . Aleah! . . . Aleah, wake up! It is getting late! Aleah, come eat your breakfast . . . Aleah! Aleah! Aleah! Aleah! . . ."

She sat up in the blankets and looked from the overhang shelter at the horses grazing in the meadow. She brought her gaze to the gunman hunkered at the campfire, trying to pat masa into tortillas.

She got up and in her white cotton nightdress went over there and said, "Let me do that. You make a mess. You waste the masa harina. It is much work to make. Looks like you put too much water in again. Might as well make pinole." She wiggled the tecomate to see how much water was left in the gourd and sniffed the steam coming out of the copper kettle held up over the fire bed by an arrangement of rock blocks within the firepit. "What did you put in this time? I never heard of letting something cook for so long. And every day making it into something new."

"The stew doesn't spoil that way," he said. "Indians do that.

Always have something over the cook fire and keep adding to the pot."

"How do you know about Indians?"

"I was married to one."

"Oh." She had forgotten. "There must be no rabbit meat left."

"But the flavor is still there."

"So what did you add this time? Frijoles and wild onion and cattail yesterday."

"Figured more of the jerky and chile peppers would perk it up. Some more garlic."

"Did you put in more salt?"

"Yes, ma'am."

She finished patting the masa between her palms into round, flat pancakes and cooking them on the hot tin pan that was part of his few cooking utensils.

"Did you check the eggs when you made us scrambled ones for breakfast?"

"I did."

"Are there many left?"

"I didn't count them," he said sheepishly.

"That's how we kept the eggs from the hens for many weeks, even months. Packed in cornmeal."

"I have learned from you," he said. Dropped back off his haunches onto his side, legs extended, and propped up on an elbow, submissively observing her takeover of his kitchen work, he remarked, "I think you're ready to hit the trail, Miss Dominica."

"Aleah."

"Aleah?"

"I dreamed it. I heard it . . . someone calling me. I didn't see her. Only heard her voice. Her voice sounding so real. The dream so real. I knew the voice was my mother calling me. I woke up with the name so clear in my mind. Aleah Nicholson. I knew it was my name in my other life."

"Aleah Nicholson."

"Yes."

He went quiet, trying to remember what the dying man had called her, but all he recalled was "my girl." *Save my girl. I feel her near. I hear her crying my name . . . my girl.*

"Then I should call you Aleah?"

"I don't know. I think I would feel strange. I think I have been too long Dominica."

Chapter Twenty-One

"When I couldn't remember, when only I saw things like bad dreams, pieces of bad dreams . . . I think, Mister, it was your soft boots. Made me mix you up with them."

"With the Indians that did that to your family?"

"They weren't Indians. They were white men. They were wearing high soft boots like Indians. Now I know why it seemed I saw El Lobo before. The first time he came to the village, I felt I knew him from somewhere but could not remember. Every time he came, I got the feeling I saw that hairy face in some other place. I thought maybe my other life. And the way he looked at me. Like he knew me. Now I remember."

"You saying it was El Lobo and his gang who murdered your family and made it look like Indians?"

"The other faces I don't know. All dark beards like his gang. Maybe they were. But El Lobo for sure." Her gaze went into a remote stare. "Remember him tearing my mother's clothes off . . . pushing her on the ground, getting on top of her . . . she screaming . . . and then he cut her throat . . . she stopped moving . . . blood . . ."

"All right, Dominica," he said. "You remember. I would like to know how you got away from them."

"I was in the woods," she said, staring as if seeing it in her mind. "I could see down into our camp from the trees. I was looking for berries and went maybe too far. I heard shouts and screams. And laughing and yelling. I sneaked back as close as I could and watched. I wanted to . . . I wanted so much to stop it."

She put her face in her hands and her shoulders convulsed until the dam burst and she wept uncontrollably hard. He broke his own dispassionate restraints and held her against his chest, sitting on the ground among broken boulders at a thin stream where they had stopped to rest beneath a canopy of oak and maple and other autumn-turning trees.

At length, she wiped the tears with a heel of her wrist. He produced a handkerchief and wiped the moisture from her cheeks.

"Better?"

She nodded her head *yes,* then shook it *no.* "I . . . it . . . me watching and doing nothing. Letting that happen. Me doing nothing. Just watching. So scared. Wanting to stop them, but just watching, not helping my family. How could I? How could I just hide and watch . . . watch them kill and take the hair of my little brothers and sister, do that to my mother and burn my father?"

"What could you have done, Dominica? You were only, what? Ten years old? You would not have been able to do anything. Just get yourself killed, too."

"I should have died with them. The dog, too."

"The dog?"

"We had a dog. I remember now. Our dog. They shot him."

He said nothing. He did remember there had been a dead dog among the carnage.

"Dominica, your folks would not have wanted you to die too. Your father begged me to save you. That was his dying wish. For you to live. Don't feel guilty that you escaped their fate. I am sure where they are now, they are glad you are alive."

"Do you believe there is a life after this one, Mister?"

He stood up and retrieved the horses from where they were

grazing on bunch grasses. He tightened the cinches and checked the ropes on the packhorse.

"Time to go."

"You were lucky they didn't see you," the gunman remarked as they walked the horses side by side.

"They did. Two came after me. I ran up into high rocks and hid. I couldn't see them. Only heard them. I heard one say, 'Let her go. She won't live out here long.' "

"You can't remember what they looked like?"

"Only they had dark beards. They all wore high, soft boots. And the horses. They had soft boots. Leather tied on their feet." She pulled the chinstrap away from its choking tightness against her throat and pulled the hat up from where it had fallen on her back and put it back on her head. "I remember only El Lobo's face and hair. It was him. I know it."

"You had me mixed up with those men who attacked your family. Do you think maybe your memory, which you didn't have for so many years, is mixing El Lobo up with them, too? Maybe putting him in your dreams you think are memories?"

"No. I know now it was him," she said. "He violated and killed my mother. The others got mad at him for killing her. I think they wanted—"

"All right," he said and then looked at her as if out of a sudden, new thought. "Do you think El Lobo knows you are the girl he left to die in the mountains?"

"I didn't know I was the girl he left to die in the mountains. Until now."

"Did he ever give you reason to think that? Say anything?"

"He always made me feel strange the way he looked at me. Like I was familiar to him as he was familiar to me. When he killed Padre Zxavian, this other man looked like he was going to shoot me. El Lobo told him let me be. He said, 'She's daft.

Ain't got no memory. Anyway, that was seven years ago.' "

"He said that? Exactly that? He mentioned seven years ago?"

"Now that I'm thinking about it. I was on my knees trying to help Padre Zxavian. When I looked up, I saw the other man's gun pointed at me. I thought I was dead, too. But El Lobo told him leave me be. That's what he said."

"What did the man look like who had the gun pointed at you?"

"Mean, like all of them. They all look the same. Dark beards. Only El Lobo has hair the color of wet straw. Not just a beard. All over his face. But the boy . . ."

"There's a boy?"

"He had no hair on his face."

"I don't have any on mine. I'm not a boy."

She giggled. "But you don't look like a boy. You have a nice, clean man's face."

Ignoring her remark, he said, "How young a boy?"

"I don't know. I think younger than me. But as rough and mean as the men. They called him 'kid.' He liked to shoot at people's feet and make them run. He chased down one girl. Played with her like she was a goat on the end of the rope. But the only one killed was Padre Zxavian by the one called El Lobo."

They rode a long way in silence. They rode a narrow shelf covered by a forest of juniper and piñon trees. They rode along an eyebrow trail, scary to her. She looked only once at the drop down to a vast desert plateau, its flat surface way down there riven with twisting and turning arroyos, and still another drop to the desert floor.

When they got back on safe ground with no dizzying drops, she said, "I never saw anything so far down. I never knew how it looked to look down from the top of a mountain. How far was that, Mister?"

"About two thousand feet would be my guess."

"Was there no other way?"

"That took us less than an hour. The other way would have taken us down on the desert and around that plateau you saw, and we'd have to come back up through a few different canyons and not be too far ahead from where we are now. That would have taken about three days."

"How do you know that?"

"I've done it."

"Oh." After a while of thinking about it, she said, "I am glad you know the ways to take in these mountains."

"There was a time I had to rely on army maps. But they didn't cover the ways I learned from the Indians."

"Oh."

They rode the bottom of a narrow canyon shaggy with green grasses, speckled with early autumn, or late summer, wildflowers. The narrow meadow was between slopes snarled and tangled with a mixture of deciduous and evergreen trees of all heights and sizes from giant ponderosa to twiggy dogwood thickets, living, dead, and dying. The grassy floor was mushy in spots and periodically puddled where springs surfaced. They rode the higher dry ground along the ragged edge of the trees.

He looked at her and said, "Dominica, did any of them . . . hurt you in any way? El Lobo or any of his gang?"

"No. Only that one time it seemed the one was going to shoot me. None of them ever came near me. I think because they thought I was like El Lobo said—daft. I know what some people called me. *La loca santa.* The holy crazy one. Holy because they said the saints kept me alive when my family was massacred. Crazy because I could not remember. I was not the same as them; I know that. Consuela, I know, did not like me, but she liked I helped her do her work. Padre Zxavian made me feel special, not like others, which too made me feel different. Only Carlos Valenzuela did not make me feel different or somebody to be afraid of."

The gunman kept a thoughtful silence. He had known soldiers in combat who suffered memory loss and ended up in a government facility for the insane. Any mental disorder was equated with insanity. Insanity was like leprosy—people normally shunned the afflicted, as if the affliction might be contagious or the afflicted person was spooky, as the unnatural was eerie. He supposed a girl not being able to remember who she was or where she came from or the people from whom she came would be regarded as not normal, therefore insane.

Could be El Lobo had his own superstitious fears of the insane. Could be, if he was one of the killers of her family, her loss of memory was what had saved her from the fate of the priest. In that case, if El Lobo were to find out or even suspect she had recovered her memory, it would very likely put her in his crosshairs.

They rode in silence for many miles. They passed vistas of rugged descents, broken gullies, and dry washes filled with jumbles of boulder rock falling to lower hills as monotonously clad in the same juniper and piñon pine trees as they rode through. The open vistas reaching far below and across the vast desert to distant mountains broke the monotony of the juniper-piñon woodland. The landscape gradually changed, and she asked what were the trees that stood so tall and straight with branches spaced apart showing large patches of sky through them.

"Ponderosa pine," he said.

Then they were in a pure ponderosa stand until other pines began to mix in. The breathing of Sombra and the roan was labored. The gunman said, "The climb was fast. We gained a thousand feet in a short time. The horses need a rest."

"Does your horse not get tired?"

"I reckon he's an old trouper. He has endurance."

"Endurance," she tried under her breath. "What does that mean?"

"It takes a lot to wear him down."

Endurance, she repeated silently, liking to learn new words. And she had learned more on this excursion than she would have learned reading a book.

They came to a rest in another meadow, or a nearly treeless low spot between the convoluted hills. This meadow was not soggy. The ground was thick with grass and forbs and sedges appearing cropped as if recently pastured, although there were no cow flops or other animal droppings visible to support that appearance. The canyon floor stretched out like a long, narrow green carpet between wooded hillsides, blazing with the reds of maple and gold of oak and yellow of aspen, as well as the turning leaves of locust, box elder, and ash mixed in with evergreens.

"It is so beautiful," she said, lying on her stomach on the woolen poncho, which she had taken off and used as the blanket it used to be. It was much cooler up in the trees than in the desert hills below, so much cooler that her bare arms in the short-sleeved cotton blouse ran with chills periodically even with the thin woolen shawl draped over her shoulders. Still the mosquitos bothered in the cool air, and she used the shawl to flap them away. "I think I would like to stay here always."

She brought her eyes down from the trees to him beside her. He was in the jerga, lying on his back, one raised moccasin supported across the other raised knee, his arms raised behind his head, hat pushed forward but not totally shielding his face. There was a long stem sticking out of the corner of his mouth.

"What are you thinking, so quiet?"

"How it used to be."

"What used to be?"

"Living in a canyon like this."

"With Nadie?"

"Uh-huh."

"In these mountains?"

"Uh-huh."

"Close to here?"

"Not too far."

"It has been a long time since you have been there? Where you lived with her?"

"Over four years. Since she was killed."

They were lying so leisurely close together, she could move her hand only inches and be touching him. A strong urge to touch him came over her; however, timidity overcame the desire.

"Will you take me there?"

He didn't answer.

She looked at him. His eyes were open under the hat, but he kept them from looking at her.

"You don't want to go there," she said.

"I wasn't plannin' on it."

She stared at her fingers playing with the blades of grass along the edge of the blanket. "I thought they were holding my memories and the spirits of my family." She felt his eyes slide to her. "I thought when you took me away from there, my memories and the spirits of my family were left behind in the mountain. But I have my memories back."

She turned her head, her hair free of the braid falling along one side of her face turned to him. The breeze lifted long coppery filaments from the darker cascade of it and tossed them about her face and head. His gaze held hers. His eyes wetly shone as if the ice were melting.

"I think the mountain wasn't holding them. They were always inside me. In the dark of me. All they had to do was come into the light." She turned her profile to his wordless stare. "I mean, my family, my father and mother, my two little brothers and sister, and even our dog, will always be with me in my memory. They will be with me no matter where I go. The mountain didn't hold them. I don't feel lost from them anymore. Or they lost from me. I carry them in my memory." She turned her gaze back into his.

He was so quietly staring at her, she felt a strange magnetic pull between them. If he had not moved, had not gotten up, she thought their mouths would have come together.

Chapter Twenty-Two

"A couple dozen or a hundred Mesky-leera broke off the reservation," the horse soldier said. "They be all scattered throughout the mountains the way Patchie like to do to confuse the issue, suh."

"What issue, Sergeant?" the gunman asked, noting the three chevron stripes, the lemon-yellow color of the stripe down the trouser legs, a bit wider than the corporal's.

The sergeant rubbed a stubbly jaw and spat tobacco juice. "The issue of roundin' 'em all up and bringin' 'em back."

"What, might I ask, sent them running, Sergeant?"

The gunman noticed the horses of mixed colors, what, when he was in the cavalry, was called a calico troop. Having subsequently provided horses for the army, he was aware that the cavalry went through hundreds of thousands of horses a year, due to disease, misuse, abuse, over-use, combat and other injury, and a variety of mishaps, as well as poor veterinarian practices when there even was an army veterinarian to provide medical care. The army regulators instilled the ideal for troops to have horses in uniform color—dark bays or light bays or sorrels—and only when one color for a troop was not obtainable would they allow a mixture of colors, called a calico troop.

The horses of different colors were restlessly shuffling, pawing, snorting, foaming at the bits, conceivably agitated by the scent of the nearby stream water. The sergeant signaled for the corporal to advance ahead to let the horses drink. The sergeant waited until the dust settled and the noise of the moving unit receded from their immediate hearing range.

"They been without water for almost two days," he said. "I reckon it be time for us to rest up awhile."

"You were saying what got the Indians running."

"Ahh, ackshully, I wasn't. But some bonehead ranchers stole into the reservation and killed a family or two of redskins whilst they was asleep. They said that was fer their hosses bein' stolen. The Injuns as usual claim they dint steal no hosses, it was bad white men or Meskins, and they was gettin' the blame."

"As usual," the gunman muttered.

"Yes, suh, as usual," the sergeant said, more sarcastically than sympathetically. "So now we gotten usselfs a passel of heapin' mad Injuns gone on a warpath. Hit one white settler in the Fresnal Canyon and two Meskin ranchos in Labrocita Canyon up near the reservation. Where you and the missy headed, mighten I ast, suh?"

"La Luz Canyon. Corvalan Ranch in Puma Canyon."

"That's up by the border of the reservation." The cavalryman, although field dusty, was spiffy in a felt campaign hat with one side of the folding brim smartly pinned up and a yellow kerchief knotted about the neck. He eyed the gunman up and down, from wide-brimmed pale hat and coarse wool poncho to high moccasins, then shifted his silent inquiry to Dominica, as if trying to figure out what she was—daughter, child wife, or what?

"Most civilians travel the civilian roads, not the back trails," the sergeant said. "Let it be a fair warning: ain't no place safe in these mountains for any white folks much less where you're headed. Keep yer eyes peeled and watch yer backs."

"Much obliged, Sergeant."

The sergeant tossed a smart farewell salute.

★ ★ ★ ★ ★

Wolves howled in the bright light of the full moon.

"I hate that sound. I druther it be coyotes."

"I ain't never been partial to the mountains neither. I understand they be painters up in these rocks. And bears in the timber. Iffen he goes up into the high timber, I gotta tell you boys—"

"Shh!"

"What *shh*?"

"SHHH!"

A total hush fell on the cold camp. Several metallic clicks of pistol hammers resounded in the silence as loud as a tomahawk-wielding Comanche's yell.

"Hold it!" a gruff voice shot out of the dark. "Put yer damn irons away. It's me. Boyles."

"If it ain't you, it's a billy goat," a reedy voice piped, evoking some laughter, which relaxed the overall tension and encouraged the reedy voice to add, "I swear, Boyles, you don't have to announce when it's you. A body could smell ya a mile away."

"Give him an inch and he's gotta go for the mile. Shoulda quit whilst ya was ahead, kid. We should send him back home to mama."

"Yeah, sheddup, sis."

"I told you don't be calling me that, chivo!"

"Who you calling chivo, snot-nose?"

"Drop it! Just *drop it*!" a hoarse voice painfully strained to a raspily whispered shout. "Alla yooz. So whadja find, Boyles?"

"Ain't them. Ain't their campfire. Army. Hunting Patchies that broke from the reservation."

"That's all we need. Patchies on the loose."

"So you went in and talked with 'em?"

"I did. Palavered a bit. Acted all non-challant. A outline rider searchin' fer strays fer the outfit I work fer."

"Criminey. What outfit, Pete?"

"I don't rightly recall. Cross Timber or sumthun like that. They dint question it, so figure they bought it."

"Where'd you come up with that moniker?"

"I don't know. Maybe I heard it somewhere."

"What if they questioned it?"

"Well, they dint. So shet yer grillin'. The sergeant was chatty enough. Mentioned he hadda warn some other folks they come acrost, a man and a girl. I made out I come acrost them, too, kinda gave a description in a way of friendly conversation, you know? It's them awright. He mentioned they was headin' fer the La Luz Canyon in its high headwaters, some Puma Canyon there. I remember that cuz I can't stand painters. Some ranch . . . don't remember the name. Korlin? Kavo? Or something like that."

"Good. Good work, Boyles."

"So now we gotta watch out for redskins on a warpath crawlin' these hills," came a dry remark. "Just wunnerful."

"You want out, Leaman?"

"And do what, Poke? Me, all alone," Emett Leaman said, "with a bunch of gut-eaters loose in these hills. I don't rightly cotton to bein' roasted alive nekked."

"The Corvalan ranch, huh?"

"You know it, Al?"

"Me'n Poke rode acrost the range oncet. It's in the Puma Canyon. Them Corvalan greezers is no pee-ownies. A rich lot. Got themselfs a big layout. Hacienda. I heard a hunnert bah-kay-row."

"A hunnert? That's an army."

"Well, maybe it ain't a hunnert. You know how things get stretched."

"Me'n Al nearly had a run-in with them bean-eaters," Lenard Poke said. "But we outrun 'em. Hadda been two dozen chasin' us. I reckon they mistooken us for rustlers as we was lookin' at the cattle. Got one a dem fancy Meskin brands hard to read. Curly q's and wigglies."

"Yeah, just lookin' at their purty brand, Poke." The gibe aroused laughter.

"Well, they do got themselfs one wild bunch of bah-kay-rows guard the place."

"If we're aimin' to start out at daybreak, I'm turnin' in."

Mutters and mumbles in agreement broke up the assemblage in the pewter light of the moon.

After all were bedded down in the fireless camp, Lenard Poke consulted with the leader in a confidential huddle away from the snoring others.

"Al, you shoulda not stopped me from takin' care of that loony gal when I wanted to. Even if she was daft."

"I reckon yer right. But how was I to know that snake-eyed devil was to come along and take her away? I figgered so long she was where she was at, bein' not all there, no threat to us. Fer the time bein'. You know how the others feel about harmin' women and younguns. You'd think all women was their mothers."

"How you think they react if they found out about us partakin' in that what happened to her folks seven years ago?"

"Yeah, well, we wasn't plannin' on goin' to such extremes."

"Shit, Al. I thought all that was buried in the past long forgot. Then she hasta turn up alive in that Meskin village. Al, d'ya think when a person loses their memory like that they ever can get it back?"

"I don't know. I hadda uncle oncet, got kicked in the head by a hoss. He was out don't know how long. When he come to, he couldn't remember nuthun. Not hisself, not nobody. His memory was gone fer, I don't know, two, three weeks, I think.

Then one day, he remembered who he was and everybody. Just like that. He was back to actin' normal. Even remembered pickin' the hooves of that damn hoss that kicked him. So I don't know, Poke. With her, it's been years. I'll tell ya this, though, the way she acted up on the mesa that day of the storm proved to me she was daft. Jumpin' around like that in the rain pourin' down and lightnin' hittin' ground so close. No wonder she was left behind by the pelados, not wantin' nuthun to do with such a loco gal."

"It's really queer, don't ya think? How we make it look like injun work on her folks, and it's a injun woman brings the girl to the church. Really queer."

"I reckon."

"That was one wild bunch back then, huh? Wanna know sumthun, Al?"

"What?"

"When they strung that poor soul up, head down to boil his brains first, I hadda swaller my own puke back down."

"Best to leave that buried in the past, Poke. We don't want none of the boys to find out about that. Sure wouldn't set right with any of 'em atall."

"Don't set right with me thinkin' back on it. That bunch scalpin' them little boys and little gal. That really drew the line fer me. I was glad to have sumthun else to do, going through the wagon. We dint even get nuthun out of it. Them settlers had nothun worth takin'. What was it? Five hundred dollars? Split six ways. Wasn't worth it. I'm glad we decided not to bother with pilgrims no more."

"I'm glad we broke off from that bunch, too, Lenard. But what good's talkin' about it?"

"It jes been preyin' on my mind since that gal turned up alive in that village. Al, can I ask ya sumthun?"

"What?"

"Why you cut that woman's throat how you did? I dint see it; I was busy rummaging in the wagon."

"Shit, Lenard. I dint like none of it no more'n you. But I reckon we hadda go along to prove usselfs or be on the other end of that bunch's scalpin' knives. You ask me they was more injun than injuns. Since we're bein' so open and honest with each other, I'll tell ya. I couldn't even complete the act. The old prick jes wouldn't get up stiff nuff. The woman was throwin' sucha holy fit . . . she was gonna die anyway. I just made it quick so she wouldn't hafta suffer like the others."

"Why, Al. I dint know you had such mercy in you."

"Lenard, me'n you go a long ways back. Have we never showed mercy where mercy was due?"

"That bunch was damn mad at you. Then they couldn't catch the gal to get what you cheated them outta. I was damn glad when we quit that place."

"I'm glad we quit that bunch. I reckon it bothers me, too. That gal could put the finger on us even if not fer that but the padray and sheep burnin' and all."

"I tell myself who's gonna give a damn about a Meskin priest and a bunch of pelados? Shit, ever'one of them Meskins in that village could put a finger on us if there was any law to lissen to 'em. But her bein' white is what I'm thinkin' it be better fer us if she wasn't able to tell nobody nuthun."

"I'll tell you what keeps pesterin' me, Lenard. The way that snake-eyed bastard left those greezers. Like jes fer us to find. Laid out like that, their sombrayos on their faces, and their saddle blankets laid over their carcasses and a gold coin on top a each one a them. Like them gold pieces was a token a what them sad asses wanted, so he give it to 'em. But a sign fer us."

"Yeah, I got that same feelin'. Lettin' us know fer sure it's gold in them sacks. And them gold coins on top of them dead bean-eaters tellin' us to come and get it."

"Well, we're comin', and we're gonna get it," the wolf-faced leader vowed, touching the cloth around his throat.

Chapter Twenty-Three

The gunman listened to the imitated wolf calls as he regarded the full moon in a sky light as washed-out blue denim. The moon's bright light would last throughout the night as it had for the past few nights and would for the next few nights. He brought his attention to the muffled sounds coming from the humped blanket beside him. He placed his hand on the hump and massaged soothingly. She woke up, feeling for him, where he had been lying beside her. Not that he had put himself there. She had crawled from her sleeping place to his and cuddled up against him, which was what had awakened him.

"Mister?"

"I'm here."

She sat up and leaned against him, hugging his arm. Then, in her innocence, at least he thought it was innocence, one of her hands found its way under his poncho and onto the inner thigh of his leg crossed Indian-style. As he had earlier massaged her hip to appease her troubled dreams, she massaged his thigh in a sleepy way. He believed she had no idea of what she was doing to him. Or did she? He had known putas younger than she. Married señoras younger than she with children. She was no child, yet in the frame of his mind he kept her the girl she had been when he and Nadie had rescued her. He believed her to be a decent girl, but how did he know what she had done with that Carlos Valenzuela she spoke of so fondly, which might have made her not so innocent as he liked to think.

He found her hand and captured it with his, putting a stop to her unwitting torment. At least he hoped *unwitting.* He held her hand under his and brought it out from under the jerga into the chilled mountain air. She nestled up to him closer and murmured, "I would like to know how it is to be a woman with you."

That did it. He got himself disengaged and stood up. "Let's ride."

She was instantly wide awake. "Now? At night?"

He was already bridling and saddling the horses. "Best time to travel. Cool for the horses. And us. Besides, I heard Apaches. Not safe to stay here." His voice was tight, words clipped.

She was up and making the bedrolls in a hurry. The night was invigoratingly chilly, with only a small breeze. She decided he was right, it was a good time to ride rather than in the heat of the day. She took the advantage to let her head breathe and hooked her hat by the chinstrap around the saddle horn. She looked forward to the night ride and decided not to re-weave her hair into a braid but leave it loose and let it be free.

Before they mounted up, he said, "Listen to me. I want you to know that I had the love of my life. She is gone. I'll never get her back. There will never be another. The day will come when you will meet the love of your life. What you feel for me is not love. You must save yourself for the right man, Dominica."

"You are the right man."

Her green eyes glistened like colorless wet glass in the lunar light. With her long hair loose and shiny with moonlight, taking on a night hue nearly black, she resembled Nadie in his mind, although they looked nothing alike in reality. What was the matter with him? This girl was doing things to his brain so he couldn't see straight.

"You call me 'Mister.' "

"What else should I call you?"

"What I mean is, you don't even know my name. You don't know who I am. Where I've been, what I've done, where I come from, where I am going."

"You told all what I need to know."

"Dominica, I am the most wrong man for you."

"Because you are older?"

"Because, for the most important thing, I don't feel for you what you think you feel for me." He quickly looked away from the damage he had done, seen in her face as luminous in the nocturnal light as its source. "Mount up. Let's go."

As they rode, she proved herself too persistent for his own good. At length, he said, with involuntary affection he resisted acknowledging, "Darlin', it's true. You brought pieces of a dead man back to life. But it's too late for the whole man."

His term of endearment, as unexpected as his knife stabbing her in the gut, felt as piercing, but the pain was rapturous and emotionally liquefied her bones. She murmured, "I don't understand that."

"My soul's already in hell."

"Don't say that." Her voice quavered.

"It's true, Dominica. Your idea of me doesn't change the truth of what I've become. A killer of men. A killing machine."

"You can stop. You don't have to keep being that. You can be like you were when you were with Nadie. I can be what she was to you."

"I don't doubt that you can, sweetheart," he reluctantly murmured.

He indicated for her to veer left at a fork in the narrow animal trace they had been following. The juniper-piñon brakes were dark in the trees' own shadows, and the moonlight was so bright, the open clearings had such phosphorescent glow, that the meadows appeared like floating islands in the darkness of the surrounding forests. They presently rode, single file, along nothing more than a narrow grassy groove in steep hillsides thinly wooded and messily cluttered with pine forest debris, fallen logs, and broken branches and twigs.

"Try to understand it this way," he said once they got to ground wide enough to walk the horses side by side. "You said you've been Dominica too long to go back to being Aleah. Well, I've been a hired killer too long to go back to being the man I was before." He added for emphasis, "When a tame dog tastes the raw meat of a lamb, the blood of a fresh kill, he turns into a killer of sheep as bad as a wolf."

"But you are not like El Lobo and those men. You are not a killer of sheep. You kill only bad men."

"A killer is a killer. And I still have one last man to go."

"The last man of those who killed your wife and unborn child, who is at this Corvalan ranch?" she asked, with a perceptiveness that continued to dismay him.

He didn't answer.

"God understands. God forgives even a killer if the killer asks God's forgiveness."

"You told me you were once so mad at God, you questioned His existence."

"I hated Him letting the El Lobo gang do what they did. I hated Him for allowing what happened to my family."

"Then you understand why I must do what I do." Out of a remote place, a place where entombed was the memory of finding the only woman he had ever loved more than life itself brutally disembowled and their unborn son still in its sac impaled by the seven-inch blade of his Spanish knife to the door of their cabin, he added, "Maybe I don't want God's forgiveness because I can't forgive God."

The gunman fell into deep thought. His existence was coming to an end. He was near the end of the long trail. Consummating the avenging of the murder of his wife and child by killing the key instigator would have the Corvalan family against him, he knew. The man's good friends would be bound by honor, by the blood and flesh code, to stand up against the gunman for their own redemption. If it was a direct confrontation by Don Ramón himself or Raul, his draw would be slow, his bullet purposely high. If given the choice, he would rather be gunned down by their force of vaqueros. In his mind, he planned it that way, if it had to be that way. But plans did not always work out the way they were planned. Ideally, for the sake of Dominica most of all, it would be best if he were able to slip in unseen, get the job done, and vanish without a trace. This was what his modus operandi had become as a professional gun.

In a self-punitive way, the gunman wearily looked forward to any end. To the end when he at long last might lie at rest.

Chapter Twenty-Four

In orange firelight, dark shadows worked in wordless diligence. After slitting the frightened horse's throat and throwing it to the ground, within minutes the Apaches were ravenously sinking their teeth into the bloody horseflesh.

The hapless cowboy, who had drawn the lonely range job of backcountry line riding, lay sprawled spread-eagled, no more mercifully nor dignifiedly than his butchered horse, his severed testicles stuffed into his gaping mouth beneath a lifeless stare of blank horror.

The Apaches finished their hasty meal, snatched up the corpse's weapons and ammunition, and slunk into the night-cloaked sotol grassland, angling on foot into the high country south of the reservation.

All were, in general, squat, square, and well-muscled, with bronze skin and somewhat mongoloid features—dark almond-shaped eyes, low, triangular noses, broad cheekbones, and thin, tight lips. They wore trade-cloth breechclouts under full, white shirts, cinched at the waist with wide, red, cloth sashes, and high-cuffed moccasins, the cuffs able to be turned up over the knee for better leg protection from thorns and brittle brush. Their raven hair hung long and loose, except for a couple cut bluntly at the shoulder, a sign of mourning the loss of someone. All wore rawhide or cloth forehead bands. To a casual observer, certainly to a hysterical victim, it was conceivable they all looked fearsomely alike.

A more discerning eye might make finer distinctions, such as that one warrior had breasts that moved and swung heavily like those of a woman beneath the cotton camisa. Indeed, he was a she. Her features were femininely fine. Even in the moonlight, her complexion was lighter—in daylight, honey gold—and one might suspect she was of mixed blood. She stood tallest among them. Lean, well-muscled in limb and loin, broad in shoulders, narrow in hips, she was built like her brothers, more for running than for child bearing. The savage intensity of her dark eyes was matched only by the leader's, but hers were even more charged with a vindictive ferocity and an impetuosity of youth. Her leader's look was of a controlled vitality that came with the thoughtful wisdom of age and tested experience.

It was she, the woman warrior, who had castrated the pale cowboy and had held up her grisly trophy to Ussen in exultation before interring the bloody glands in their ghastly tomb. Her tribal brothers stood back and watched as if in horror. Mescaleros, for religious reasons, were loath to touch a corpse. They therefore did not customarily mutilate dead victims, preferring to do such work while the victims were alive. She also hung the cowboy's scalp on her belt. It was usual for Mescaleros who might take the scalp of a dead victim to quickly toss it away and perform rites to ward off any evil medicine from having touched the dead. If the victim was alive while scalped, that was different. Consequently, the woman warrior's bold irreverence, her contemptuous disrespect for the vengeful spirits surrounding the dead, inspired a mixture of awe, anxiety, apprehension, and admiration in her male companions.

Several miles from the carnage they had left behind, they paused on a ridge overlooking hills serrated with pine treetops at various elevations forming the western skyline in the lunar bright sky. The leader gestured, indicating a particular constellation of stars in the west, and brought his hand down, spreading it over a faraway, unseen land, a land where he, as a young warrior, had fought against the Mexican and American enemies under the leadership of Victorio, then in alliance with Shi-ka-she, whom the whites called Cochise.

That was twelve moons of the falling leaves ago. Shi-ka-she had been walking on the Other Side for many winter moons. Victorio had left reservation life and was raiding again full force in Mexico, New Mexico, and Texas. Their own chief, Zhee-ah-nat-tsa, had been murdered by the Mexican enemy for having testified against Mexican bootleggers who sold firewater to Indians against the Mescaleros' own law prohibiting any and all intoxicating beverages. There was the newly fast-rising Chiricahua leader Goyahkla (One Who Yawns), whom the Mexicans called Geronimo.

The leader of the small band made a vicious jab with his thumb at himself: "I, N'ii, am through living the way the white chiefs tell us how to live! We live by their rules and only suffer for it in many ways. We go hungry and cold and die from their sickness. They steal land from us and then give a little of it back to us and say it is our land, as if it is a gift from them and not ours to freely live and hunt on to begin with from the days of our great ancestors, and then they steal it from us again. They give, take, give, take. They give-take what is ours to begin with. They steal our horses, they murder us, and no soldiers go after them. If one bad man among us steals from them, a hundred soldiers are sent out after him, and the soldiers attack our camps and kill our babies, dishonor our women and leave them for dead. And that is all right by their rules. Their rules for us are only like the strychnine-laced carcasses and the iron jaws that they set for our brother the wolf. Like our brother the wolf, we are poisoned and crippled by the baits and the traps of their forked tongues. Like our brother the wolf, we must learn to be clever and sly and defecate on their poisoned meat and iron jaws! I, N'ii, may never know the fame of a great war chief. But I will know the glory of an honorable death of a warrior!"

He gave the six braves a last chance to decide whether they would go with him or go back and surrender to the bluecoats who were combing the mountains for runaways like themselves. Unanimously they took their leader's blood oath, the woman warrior most vehemently.

Chapter Twenty-Five

They rode under closed canopies of sunless forest shadows alternating with sun-dappled dimness and across open, grassy clearings between hillsides of mountain oak, maple, aspen, and other deciduous trees mixed with tall conifers. They rode past travertine outcrops, craggy bluffs carved by spring water into odd formations, such as a gargoyle face pushing through green curtains of evergreen foliage, a cave orifice resembling an open mouth, and other oddly shaped calcareous rock forms, arched, looped, and upright like castle towers.

At an open gap on a divide beneath an enormous turquoise-blue dome of cloudless sky, Dominica was awed by the small hollow nestled in the heights of the mountains. A relatively tiny hidden valley pocketed in the dark piney hills, it was enclosed by a limestone cliff on one side, a narrow ribbon of water shining in the sunlight threaded down the craggy face, and steep, pine-wooded slopes with bands and splotches of pale yellow and deep gold of oaks and aspens in early autumn dress. A peregrine falcon glided on air currents low over the valley. Distant mountain slopes folding into one another formed a backdrop beyond the close piney ridges. The valley below exuded a mystique both eerie and enchanting at once.

Dominica saw a log cabin and fencing, but there was a quietness to the place that conveyed a sense of lonely abandonment. The gunman gazed at the valley in remote silence. She regarded his look and intuitively said, "That was where you and your wife lived. The valley you told me about."

He nodded.

"You want to go down there?" she asked.

He vaguely shook his head negatively.

At once the dun let out a vibrating, shrill scream that reverberated wide and far across the sawtooth ridges from canyon to canyon. It scared the daylights out of Dominica. Sombra and the roan packhorse shook their heads and manes and blew as if clearing the lingering ringing out of their ears. Patting the side of his neck, the gunman muttered something to the pale dun, which kept looking into the valley as if expectantly until they moved on and the upslope closed the view.

A sadness lowered over Dominica as an invisible shroud.

"Your horse remembers it was home," she said.

The gunman did not answer.

They soon came to an open overlook. He pointed out. "That's Puma Canyon."

Sweeping her gaze over the hills dotted with piñon and juniper trees, roundly stubby in comparison to the tall, pointed pines at the higher elevations, yucca and spindly ocotillo spiking rocky terrain beneath them within closer view, she asked, "Where?"

"See that white cliff?"

She did. It stood out at the top of a roughly dome-shaped hill indistinct from the rest, except it was darker in the foreground against more distant ridges lighter in varying hues of blue and gray.

"Piedra Blanca it's called. Old-timers say 'Pierda.' Many in these mountains still speak the old Spanish of the conquistadores."

"White rock," she said.

"It landmarks Puma Mountain. Here." He handed her his field glasses. "Look down there."

Looking through the magnifying lenses, she saw pale block shapes that she made out to be a long, rectangular adobe compound.

"The Corvalan ranch. We're on Corvalan land now."

"We are that close?" Her voice slightly wavered with apprehension. It was as if she did not want this journey to end. Going to a strange place with strange people filled her with anxiety. Knowing what he was going there for compounded her anxiety with dread. She was on the threshold of her uncertain future, and it was frightening.

"There's a way down from here, but it's too steep and rugged. We'll come to a sheep trail and take that down into the canyon."

Several yards ahead, she said, "I need to stop."

She got her personal sack from her saddlebag and as soon as she dismounted disappeared in the brushy understory of the mixed conifers. She was gone for so long he started watching for her with some uneasiness. At last she reappeared, and he watched her come out of the trees and down the gently sloping apron of grass, not looking well, her face pasty. Her shy evasiveness clued him.

He built a small fire on barren ground bordering a low wall of layered rock exposed by erosion at the foot of the grassy slope. A while later, he went to where she was sitting against the outcrop, her head bowed over arms around raised knees.

"Here," he said, at which her hat came up to reveal a blanched face. She looked at the copper mug in his hand held for her to take. "Sip on this. Warm whiskey used to help Nadie. We don't have whiskey, but I figure the wine might do. Just warm enough to take the chill out."

Color flushed her cheeks. Avoiding his seemingly too-knowing blue eyes, she took the warm cup and murmured, "Thank you."

"It's a good place to let the horses graze a spell."

It seemed to her there was no place in these mountains that wasn't a good place for grazing animals to graze. He had only said that as an excuse to stay there for her. Or did he not want to leave the place now that they were there? Was it because of his memories of living there with his Indian wife? Or was it because he wished to prolong getting to where they were going? And why did he bring her here when he had indicated he had not wished to come here in the first place?

He unsaddled the horses and set the saddles near her, unloaded the packsaddle from the roan, and hobbled the horses on the broad sweep of grass at the open bottom of the forested slope hiding the valley.

"I'll be back," he said, as if to assure her he was not deserting her, and, carrying rifle and binoculars, he sauntered away, in jacket and snug-fitting breeches tucked in high, cuffed moccasins. She watched until he was gone around a bend.

His jerga was where he had flung it over the saddles near her. She dragged the coarse woolen garment to her and wrapped it about the front of her, shoulder to shoulder, and snugged it up to her chin. Its rough warmth was as comforting as the leathery, smoky, ripe, manly smell of him. Behind closed eyes, she dreamily wished he would bring back something to boil or roast, if not a rabbit, a bird. They had seen quail in some numbers—any bird good to eat would do—but she knew he hadn't gone hunting.

He always took the rifle when he went afoot, scouting either their back trail or the trail ahead. Since the episode with the two Mexican scoundrels, the gunman's invisible antennae were always up and feeling the air. She believed, though, that he wasn't watching out for any more Mexican varmints as much as for the bronco Apaches on the loose that the horse soldier sergeant had warned them about.

He was gone a long time. She began to worry. Her worry

grew tentacles that flailed about in different directions. What if he was hurt? What if he didn't come back? What if she went looking for him and could not find him? What if she found him and he was unconscious and badly injured and bleeding? What if Indians killed him, and she was left all alone in this mountain wilderness?

She had been here before in another time, other mountains. For several minutes, fear stirred up old terrors. Her fists squeezing bunches of the jerga, she snugged the wool tightly up against her chin, trying to stem the tremors of her body.

"He'll be back," she said aloud. "He'll be back," she reiterated like a chant to concentrate on to keep from thinking the worst.

Where did he go? Why wasn't he coming back? The wine must have clouded her fears, fortified her courage to go after him.

She did not have to go far before sighting him. She followed his moccasin tracks to a natural path between rocks and boulders and spacings of shrubs and cacti that descended the slope into the valley. She came to a halt and stood halfway down the slope, regarding him uncertainly. He was down on one knee, hunched over, arm on the raised knee with hat in hand, head bowed low.

Praying? Was he praying? It seemed such an intimate thing, to find him like that, such a private thing, an embarrassing thing. She thought to sneak back in retreat, but a will not her own compelled her to continue down.

She stopped a few yards from him. There was a low mound of rocks, nearly completely covered with overgrown grass and weeds, marking what her intuition strongly suggested was the grave of his wife and unborn child. He was weeping. She heard him. She saw his shoulders convulse. A weakening sensation started in the pit of her stomach and spread hotly through her.

A whole mixture of undefinable emotions engulfed her. She wanted to collapse beside him and weep, too.

"I want you to love me the way you loved her," she said in all her ingenuous sincerity that was more crippling to him than buckshot in the knees.

"I could never love you or anyone as I loved her," he said, deliberately calloused.

In the silence that followed only the crackling of wood burning was heard. Then her sniffle. He stood up from his hunker by the small fire.

She watched him through a watery blur amble in the way he did, sans jerga, of a prowling cat, to the horses where they grazed. He inspected the soles and hooves of each one's feet and their legs and gave them an overall examination for galls and such. He didn't carry much beyond bare necessities in his saddlebags and grub sack inside his bedroll, but he did carry a curry comb and a brush and momentarily used them to give all three horses a grooming.

She had been in the process of disassembling the supply sacks carried on the packhorse but had no desire to cook, much less eat. Her lack of appetite despite hunger was from a sickness not in her lower parts, due to the unmentionable, but rather in her heart. A heart sickness as she had never known and knew not how to remedy or endure.

He came back and sat on the ground against the outcrop, next to the saddles and gear, and commenced to clean his weapons. "You might wanna get yourself some shuteye," he said, keeping his gaze on his occupation. "It'll be an hour or two before we move on again." A minute or two passed. He added, "Someday, Dominica, you'll thank me when you look back on these days from a time yet to come."

She wasn't speaking to him. It hurt too much.

Chapter Twenty-Six

The black pony and the smoky dun emitted alarmed whinnies at the roan's shrill cry as it reared before falling with feathered shafts sticking out of its neck and side.

The gunman had the rifle trained on a target before Dominica stood straight up from her blanket and screamed. He did not shoot. He lowered the weapon and placed it aside. Raising a palm from his side as both a calming gesture and warning signal for Dominica to silence herself and to stay put, he lifted a moccasined foot to make the step up the low limestone-lined cut bank. He walked up the grassy slope to meet the Indian, who had shouted angry reprimands and commands, emphasized by arm gesticulations, at his comrades in the trees.

The Indian halted squarely in front of the gunman with a space of six feet between them. Coffee-colored eyes and glacier-blue eyes looked deeply into each other as if scrutinizing the very depths of emptiness within them from whence their souls had departed to become lost and wandering spirits.

The Indian said, "Shee-lah-aash."

"Shee-lah-aash," said the gunman in kind.

They stepped forward and embraced. Separated. Looked each other over.

"Shee-lah-aash. My friend. It has been a long time," said the Apache.

"Too many winters have passed between us, my brother," said the gunman.

"I have been watching you. I was not sure it was you. There have been many stories about your disappearance from these mountains. My heart drags on the ground with heavy sorrow at the loss of your wife and child. I thought of her as my own blood sister. Some say you were killed in a gun fight. Others say you died looking for your horses they stampeded into the desert. The stories are many, my friend. But most say your spirit rides your pale horse, with your Spanish blade in the back, in your high valley."

"I am glad I recognized you before I shot you."

"I am glad for that, too."

"I have heard that things are not good for your people again."

"My brother, things never were good for my people, and they never will be. I am sorry about the horse. My braves are young and impulsive. And hungry. Hunting is not good as it was in the old days. The days you and I went hunting together."

"Yes. Those were good days. There is a saying among whites, 'all good things must come to an end.' "

"That is a true saying. I would question why *must* they?"

"The horse cannot be brought back to this life. Its spirit is free." The gunman made a deferential gesture with his hand.

"My braves and I thank you," said the Indian even though there was no word in their language to express gratitude. When an Apache wanted to express appreciation of receiving a gift, it was customary for him to reciprocate with a gift of his own. Besides, the gunman didn't figure the braves considered the roan packhorse a gift.

The Indian lifted a signaling hand. The braves came down from the trees and promptly began butchering the roan mare.

In a flying outrage and with flying skirts, Dominica went at them with bare fists. The gunman sprang, literally knocking her out of the way of a brave who had been in the act of turning his bloody knife on her.

The gunman's knife from the sheath at his belt was in his hand. He and the Apache faced each other, crouched, eye to eye. Glints of late sunlight glanced off the blade's razor edge as he tossed the weapon back and forth from one hand to the other, catching it by the silver grip inlaid with polished pieces of jadeite of the odd green-shaded lavender hue. The fast-shifting tactic worked on the Apache's nerves, his blinking eyes trying to resist the distracting motion. The gunman discerned he was not a *he*.

The gunman dropped his knife hand and brought himself into an erect stance and side-stepped the flying leap of his opponent, who continued to fly past him into a belly-flopped sprawl on the ground, which evoked guffaws from the leader and the whole pack. The leader put a moccasined foot on the wrist of the brave's knife hand to pin her until he issued a softly spoken command, then he released her hand and stepped back. She rose, belligerently scowling at the gunman, and made a resentful retreat to resume butchering the packhorse.

The gunman faced the leader. "You must forgive the girl, Chago. The horse was her friend. Let me speak with her."

The Apache gestured assent. He added, "I shed my Mexican name in the agency books. It is N'ii."

"N'ii," the gunman said.

"The One Who Was."

Dominica was frozen in a stance of consternation, with her hands clamped over the lower part of her face. He put his arm around her, stemming her trembling body with his support, and walked her away from the butchering going on.

"That could have been Sombra," she wept.

"It could have been my horse, a companion of many years as well, and I would have been obliged to do the same," he quietly said as he navigated her back to their campfire. "I'm going to ask you to do something."

"What?" she sniffled against the back of her hand. She found one of many hems under the makeshift poncho and used it to wipe the moisture from her nose and face. "They don't scare me," she said in a quavering voice. "They used to come to the village. Padre Zxavian said don't act afraid and they won't harm you."

"I want you to get out your nixtamal stuff and make the big copper pot of pinole."

"Why?" she said huffily. "They got a whole horse."

"Sweeten it with that pickoloni stuff."

"What pickaloni stuff?"

"That brown sugar."

"Piloncío."

"Whatever. They like sweet."

"You sound like Padre Zxavian. He kept telling everybody to feed them. They're just hungry. Once their bellies are full, they'll go away."

"That's the idea. Make a pot of coffee."

"We only have the two copper mugs I brought and your tin one."

"Chago"—he corrected himself—"N'ii and I will have the mugs. He likes coffee strong. Make it strong. The others can share out of one of the tin pots or whatever will serve. They're used to that."

"How do you know them?"

"Only him. Let's not keep them waiting. Sooner they're fed, sooner they'll be gone."

She begrudgingly did as he said.

One Indian came over and made hand signs, which she deciphered as a request for permission to roast his piece of meat at the fire. At least he's got civilized manners, she thought, to politely ask. And a civilized taste to want his meat cooked. She gestured for him to go ahead. She tried not to think of his meat as a piece of what had been the sweet roan mare nickering gratefully to have her back rubbed upon removal of the packsaddle for a rest only two hours ago.

Her anxiety was a mixture of fear, fury, and frustration, as she had felt when the Lobo gang killed Padre Zxavian and set the sheep on fire. She had to take consolation in the fact that the Indians had not killed the roan out of meanness, though. And the roan didn't suffer the way the poor sheep and lambs had, burning alive. By the way the Indians ate, it appeared they were really hungry. They didn't have to kill the horse, though. She could have made them something to eat as she was doing anyway.

So emotionally battered by all the events and circumstances that seemed to have kept piling up and colliding in her life for the past six months, she wanted to bury herself in a hole and hide for fear of what more trials and tribulations might lie in wait ahead to assail her. She thought if the gunman loved her as she him, then she would not feel so despairing and could overcome any calamity thrown in their path. But how could she make him feel for her what she felt for him?

"Muchas gracias, señorita," the Indian said.

She was startled out of her wistful musing. That the Indian spoke Spanish did not surprise her. Many of the wild tribe that came into the village had spoken better Spanish than she. She frowned at him. He smiled at her. His smile was brilliant white in a face not any darker than that of Carlos Valenzuela. She thought he might be better looking than even Carlos, whom the women of the village, from young girls to wrinkled *viejas,* and especially Consuela, thought *guapo.* She guessed the Indian might be her age, maybe a little younger, maybe a little older. When he looked at her, she looked away. She felt his eyes on her. She darted a resentful glance. His liquid, dark-brown eyes shined with good humor. His manner was friendly, not frightening. In spite of his musky smell, his nearness made her shaky not from fright.

He squatted at her cook fire, roasting his piece of her former horse. Well, the gunman's horse, since he had paid for the mare, but she had grown as fond of the roan as she was of Sombra. The Indian's close proximity put her in a fluster. Confusion mixed up her already mixed-up emotions. How could she love the gunman and of a sudden, without warning, without an inkling of an idea before it happened, like a lightning bolt out of the blue, be so flustered by a strange Apache boy? No doubt she was fascinated by his savage charm.

She stole stealthy glances at the gunman, who was in conversation with the leader, both sitting Indian style. For the first time she became aware of how *old* the gunman must be. He and the Indian leader were of another generation. The Indian brave and his companions appeared more of her generation.

The brave's companions came around the fire to join him, with pieces of the poor packhorse speared on cooking sticks. They were grinning and laughing and having a good time at what Dominica resentfully felt was her emotional expense. They all but one squatted around the fire pit, careful not to get in her way as she stirred the cornmeal mush in the pot. She had to concede they were considerate wild Injuns, careful not to bump her or touch her.

She furtively studied the one that held back—the one who would have cut her up into pieces like the roan horse if not for the gunman's intervention. He had a pretty face, could have done justice on a girl, skin lighter than the others, glossy dark hair longer than the others. However, he was dressed the same: full, white, cotton blouse cinched at the waist with a wide, red sash, Apache boots, bare legs, breechclout, and red headband, as if the costume were a uniform like what the horse soldiers wore, all nearly alike. Among the furry animal pelts dangling from a belt around the sash was one that looked too much like hair, not fur—curly blondish locks. She had to look away lest she be sick. A human scalp. She didn't trust that one at all.

Chapter Twenty-Seven

The gunman said, "I grieve my brother's loss of his loved ones. I agree that the men who killed the innocent families of your people in their sleep should be punished justly. But only them, not innocent families who had nothing to do with the murders."

The Apache looked up at the patch of bright, dusky sky bordered by treetops, then brought his eyes down to meet those of the gunman.

"My brother has spoken his heart. N'ii will speak his. It is all the *innocent* white families who are moving on the land and pushing my people off. Land that we have lived and hunted on freely as our ancestors have done before us. The white man herds us like he does his sheep and cattle and moves us from one place to another, *allowing* us to live between boundaries and making it a law as bad as murder for us to go outside of the boundaries to hunt for food for our starving families. The white man promises us food we too often don't get, and, when we do, it is not enough, and it is rotten and wormy and makes my people sick. The white man breaks his promises and blames my people for not keeping their word. My heart has been blackened by the poisons of the white man's peace. My broken heart bleeds the white man's own poison back out on him and on all of his women and children and old ones and babies with no more mercy than he has for my people's women and children and old ones and babies. And I say this for the Mexicans, too. In their own way, they have been worse than the whites for the many hundreds of years more that they have deceived us with their double-dealing and put our women and young, as well as the men, in the mines and worse. They collect bounties on our scalps. So, I say, it is too bad if so many of our enemies are innocent and have no blood of my people on their hands; they are guilty by being white or brown as it is with my people, who are innocent and have no blood of white or brown people on their hands but are guilty simply for being *ndee* and are killed by the Americans and the Mexicans in many more ways than with their bullets."

The gunman held an acquiescent silence.

"My brother has his path to follow to the end," the Apache said, studying his friend's features, as expressionless as if carved out of stone. "N'ii has his path to follow. We each have our own battles to fight. *To the end.* So be it."

The gunman nodded.

They walked back to the campsite.

"This is a sign, meeting you like this," the Apache said. "I must call my personal spirit to understand what it means. You and the girl will stay with my warriors until I get back."

"And should we leave?" the gunman asked.

"I cannot be responsible for what my young and impulsive braves might do against my wishes."

So be it, the gunman wryly thought.

She looked at the gunman and wondered how he could sleep like that—in the same position he invariably slept in, lying flat on his back on the ground, head flat on the ground, too, except when he had it propped against the saddle, hat covering his face, fingers of one hand, except for his thumb, slipped in the waistband of his breeches, high moccasins crossed at the ankles. Whenever they paused to let the horses rest or make camp, which could be any time of day or night with him, he could take that position and in seconds be sound asleep, looking dead. But, quicker than a lizard's tongue snatching an insect, he could be instantly awake and on his feet. With pistol drawn.

At first, she thought it was the ululation of a timber wolf in the ponderosa. Then the blood-chilling howls broke into a series of high-pitched cries that trailed on a mournful wail through the evening silence of the woods. She had asked the gunman why the Apache leader was doing that. He had said, "For the same reason Christian people pray to their saints or God."

She sat down beside the gunman, arranging her skirts so they covered even the boots from the eyes of the Indians, especially that one. But he had lost his initial allure. It seemed she had lost her allure for him, too. Could be her evasive tactics worked, gave him a sense of rejection, so he rejected her. She glimpsed the silvery slits under the hat brim. The gunman's lifeless form had conscious life in it after all.

"How long is he going to do that?"

"However long it takes."

"However long it takes for what?"

"To get his answers."

"I hope he has better luck than me. The saints never give me answers."

"Maybe not the answers you want."

She sneered down at him. Too often she didn't get the answers she wanted from him either.

The shadows grew deeper. The dusky dome overhead grew darker. Trees turned to black silhouettes. The long-lasting September full moon ascended in a milky indigo sky behind a scalloped screen of deciduous leaves near the top of the hill. And still the lonely chants haunted the high woods.

Dominica stirred and lifted a drowsy-eyed face behind a stringy curtain of tousled hair. Her hat had come off and hung from her neck by the long chinstrap. She found herself half-lying on top of the gunman's chest. She quickly sat up, shoved hair out of her face, and put the black sombrero back on her head.

A rhythmic, sonorous breathing, a soft, steady snoring, hinted but did not make certain that the gunman was asleep. She bent her head to see under the hat brim. No gleams. Eyelids appeared closed. She tried to disentangle herself from her twisted poncho and skirts without disturbing him.

"What're you doing?"

She quit trying to be delicate about it and stood up and shook her garments out of disorder. "I have to go in the bushes," she whispered, not wanting to awaken the sleeping Indians.

Then neither talked. It was still. The only sound the chirping of crickets.

"His singing stopped," she whispered.

He sat up, pushing his hat up on his head. "Well, go ahead if you have to."

One of the dark lumps of the sleeping Indians lifted into a tall, slender figure from the ground. The gunman waited a moment, the feelers of his senses probing the remaining prone figures of the Apaches. Assured they were sleeping, he strode as soundlessly as a shadow up the slope into the woods.

He paused. Listened to Dominica muffling a sneezing spasm far to his left. The night shrouded woods were patterned with reticulated moonlight. He jerked his head at a rustle of branches close by on his right. No Indian worth his salt rustled branches. Unless she did so with intended purpose.

At once it occurred to him. She had counted on him following her into the woods. Slyly used the pretense of following Dominica to lure him. He withdrew the knife from the sheath at his belt. Holding his breath, he listened to the faint whispers of moccasins bending coarse grasses. They stopped.

One laboriously slow step after another he headed in the direction he was certain the Apache waited in more solid shadow. He paused, knife poised in hand.

The screeching peep of a bat, low hoots of an owl, flutter of winged insects, chirping of crickets . . . secretive sounds loud in the ears listening to and trying to interpret the nature of the intense silence beneath the nocturnal voices of the forest.

He smelled her before he sensed her closeness. The rankness of dried blood and unwashed filth. A musky smell of animals that ate their prey raw.

"Indah."

He turned to face her.

"White man, I knew you would come. I intended no harm to the girl," she said.

"You speak American well."

"I went to a mission school and had a brother who liked to talk it better than ndee."

"A blood brother?"

"We came from the same ndee woman by the same white father."

Well, that satisfied his curiosity about her mixed look. "Your brother no longer lives?"

"He took our white father's way."

"What do you want?"

"To finish what started."

He understood. He had humiliated her by elusively sidestepping her attempted attack that had sent her belly flopping on the ground, eliciting laughter from her leader and peers. Apaches liked to laugh but, as with anyone, not to be laughed at unless intended to be a buffoon. Her solemn demeanor and manner were not those of a buffoon.

"Mister?" came Dominica's voice from close behind him.

His arm shot out to bar her from advancing. "Go back to camp."

"What—?"

"Go, I said. Now."

"No."

Between a rock and a hard place was how he felt with a stubborn girl behind him and a sinister one in front.

"K'ai!"

Saved by the leader's call. The gunman quickly called back, "Over here, Chago!" He quickly corrected, "N'ii!"

In the short time it took the Apache leader to appear in the shadow-dappled moonlight, the Apache girl had slipped into the darkness and was gone.

"K'ai is not one to be controlled," N'ii said, as they walked together down the slope toward the camp. "You must understand. She was taken by two white men, eight or nine years ago. She was about twelve or thirteen. One raped her, the other did worse. He cut her. For a man it would be castration. She managed to crawl into hiding. They could not find her. They left her to die in the desert. Some sisters foraging in the foothills found her. She has a deep hatred for white men."

"I didn't mean for her to lose face. Seems lately I've been doing that. Now I reckon I'll have to watch my back for an arrow as well as a bullet."

The gunman answered the question in the Apache's face by briefly recounting the El Lobo incident. The Apache raised his head in a half-nod of comprehension. They came to the campfire.

"We will be leaving. You are free to go your way."

"Have you divined the sign of our meeting?"

"I can only say, my brother, we share the same fate not far

ahead. Yours won't be by any arrow of K'ai. Soon we will be far from here."

The gunman made no comment on the prophecy he perceived in the Apache's reply to his question. He had already divined his own prophecy of his impending end.

Since the Apaches had no words for goodbye, and parted company by saying they would see one another again whether in this life or the afterlife, the gunman said, *"Nah-dathleeth-tseh doh-leeth, shee-lah-aash."*

"Yes. We will meet again, my brother." They clasped arms, with each one's hand grasping the other's shoulder.

The Apache band rapidly dissolved and blended in with the deepening darkness of the forest.

Chapter Twenty-Eight

She made ready to mount Sombra when the gunman took her by the arm, gently, and as gently forced her to face him. His crooked finger under her chin, he tilted her face up to his. Her gaze met the silvery slits of his in the lunar light. She tried to hold it back, but a tear slid out over the rim of her eye. He wiped the tear away with a heart-melting tenderness. Her black sombrero fell back off her head to hang on her back by the chinstrap as she bent her head back to receive his mouth on hers, but the cold flesh of his lips pressed on the warmth of her forehead.

"You are making it very difficult for me," he said, his voice husky.

"I love you."

"You only think you do."

"Don't tell me what I think. I know what I feel." Her voice lowered with more uncertainty than conviction and came out shakily. "I feel you feel something for me more than you say."

"Dominica, you're a beautiful and sweet girl that any man would be hard put to resist. I am sure there are many men in the world who would lay their hearts out at your feet. It is true. You made me feel again. I was a dead man. The affection I have come to have for you breathed life back into me. What I feel, Dominica, is affection. Not the kind of love you want me to have for you. What I feel is what a father feels for a daughter."

"You are not so old to be my father."

"But I am."

"Not like Ignacio Pedilla, whose youngest daughter was my age and his oldest daughter was as old as Consuela, who said she was thirty-six and Padre Zxavian told me more like forty-six. That made Ignacio an old man. You are not an old man."

"I didn't say I was an old man. But old enough to be your father. Age is not the problem. Even if I were as young as your Carlos Valenzuela—"

"He is not *my* Carlos. He never was. I never wanted him to be. He was like my older brother."

"Then you can understand you to me are like my little sister."

"First daughter. Now sister." She pushed herself away from him and climbed up on Sombra. "I am ready to go, Mister."

They rode north, and the Apache band rode south. The bronco band came upon the night camp of some soldiers. They slit the throats of all and took their horses, equipment, supplies, and weapons.

The landscape began to reassemble from dark shadow to visible forms like a great tribe awakening and lifting itself out of night's slumber. The bronco band came upon another camp, presumably vigilantes like those who had sneaked onto the reservation and murdered the sleeping Indian families. Unlike the soldiers, all eight were awake and hunkered down or moving about a fire.

Hair faces of the same ilk, but a young one with no more than fuzz on the chin, they all wore holsters strapped snugly about the waist or loosely about the hips, with heavy revolvers weighing them down. And a couple had revolvers stuck inside their waistbands exposed under open jackets in movement.

The broncos could not duplicate a sneak attack as they had done on the sleeping soldiers' camp. From their cover close enough to hear the men talking, the leader of the band and the girl warrior, both understanding the white language well, observed and listened for awhile to devise a strategy.

The one who seemed to be the leader of the vigilante group had the hairy visage of a wolf. The Apache leader reckoned him to be the one called El Lobo, whom he had learned about some miles ago from his white friend. He had a cloth wrapped around his throat and neck, which he fingered frequently as he spoke raspily and with obvious difficulty. They were not hunting Apaches. They were hunters all right, but their quarry was the Apache leader's good friend and the girl, as his friend had said he was aware.

Armed with army weapons, the young warriors felt immortally powerful and grew impatient with their leader's old man's dilly-dallying precautions. In spite of none ever having fired a handgun and the single-shot, breech-loading Springfield carbines being as unfamiliar in their hands, the young warriors' blood-thirsty appetites had been whetted by their previous, virtually unchallenged triumphs. They were hungry for real battle, primed by the maniacal zeal of the female member of the band, who took over leadership simply by her behavior and her peers following her.

They followed her reckless lead right into the enemy's bullets. N'ii held back, watching them rush in and drop one by one under the white gunmen's counterattack. The white gunmen had the expertise with the weapons that the young warriors did not. They should have used their bows and arrows, which would have better matched the gunmen's accuracy, the displaced leader thought unhappily.

Knowing defeat when he saw it, N'ii made a fast retreat. It would not be dying the honorable death of a warrior this way. It would be dying the useless death of a fool. If he was to die at this point in time, as the divine visitation of his personal spirit had foretold, it had to have more purpose than suicidal abandonment of reason. He vaulted upon the cavalry horse, whose nose he turned back north with the single thought in mind: he had to warn his friend.

The sound of hoofbeats pursued him. He did not look back. He concentrated fully on beating his heels on the sides of his mount and outdistancing his pursuer. Soon the pursuing horse was no longer behind. Feeling he had safely outdistanced the enemy, N'ii brought the lathered horse down to a trot under the livid sky of a new dawn.

The last thing he expected was an arrow in the back. Slumped on the horse's neck, N'ii did not know of the warrior behind. Satisfied that her arrow had flown true, the warrior on the stolen cavalry horse reined it around toward a destination in the west where she would find truly great war chiefs, such as Geronimo and Victorio, or maybe in the far south, where Alsate, in her childhood memories, still reigned.

CHAPTER TWENTY-NINE

Gunshots came from behind them. The gunman pointed at a steep descent. "I'll catch up."

"Where are you going?"

"Just go, Dominica. Get off this trail. I'll catch up."

She watched him rein the smoky dun around and lope into the southern direction from which they had come. Beneath a clear, azure early morning sky, she started the descent. It appeared to her too steep to ride down. She dismounted and led Sombra on foot.

Halfway down, Sombra jerked and yanked the reins nearly out of her grasp at the startling loud and too-near trumpet of an elk. She froze where she was, hanging onto the black pony, who stood still and listened with ears and nose pointed at the direction from which the sound of heavy crashing through trees came. But there was no sight of the animal obviously startled by their intrusive presence. Once it got quiet and seemed the beast was not going to come charging at them, her heart stopped pounding practically out of her chest, and she urged Sombra down to the bottom. They came out into a meadow that yawned widely between hills.

There was a single, tall oak in the broad grassy opening at which she took up her vigil, allowing Sombra to drop his head to immediately start sampling the grass. Once again familiar anxiety grew tentacles of fear. Wait for how long? What if he didn't appear? She watched the morning sun rise above the eastern rim of the evergreen-wooded canyon.

She relaxed at the sight of the gunman coming down through the trees. He was leading another horse by the reins, a dark bay with a slouched rider.

Under the shady oak, N'ii came out of his semiconscious stupor and fluttered a hand to wave away their attempts to make him comfortable. There was no time for futile efforts. His chiseled lips were ashen in his coppery face, tallowed with oily perspiration. He accepted the drink of water from a canteen held to his parched lips. Then he waved it away with frail impatience, needing to speak while he still could. His glazed eyes searched for the gunman, as if he could not see him, though he was right there in his view.

"I'm here, shee-lah-aash," the gunman said and grasped the Apache's hand with his.

Dominica worried about the arrow imbedded in N'ii's back. The gunman had broken the feathered shaft off at the point of entry rather than pull it out, which would have caused unnecessary pain while doing more internal damage.

N'ii had seen all in his band go down under the white gang's counterattack, except for one. The feathered shaft the gunman had broken off N'ii identified it as hers. Dominica silently felt her distrust for that girl warrior justified, but not without remorse for the gunman's loss of his friend and for his friend as well, being betrayed like that by one of his own. The mystery never to be solved was why? Why had she killed her own leader?

Dominica left the gunman alone with his dying friend. Her anxiety turned to the shooters they had heard, which had had the gunman turning back on their trail. N'ii's description of the men pointed to the El Lobo gang. After dispatching most of the Indian band, the gang had chased N'ii but were too far behind to catch up before the gunman had met up with the wounded

Apache and driven the gang back.

She brought her hand up to the brim of the hat to better shade her eyes against the sun-glare slanting from its midmorning height. She thought she saw movement in the trees around the crest of the long, narrow hilltop. Her heart jumped to her throat.

Her first impulse was to lunge for the gunman's rifle. But to what good? She had never shot a weapon of any kind. And the gunman had told her the Winchester was only good at so many yards. You had to know when and how to use it. You had to wait until you or your target were in the right range. It was a close-range rifle—a gunman's rifle, not a hunter's rifle. She had no knowledge of such things.

She got the field glasses from the gunman's saddlebag. The dun gave her a look as if he were going to bite her. He probably would have if she had been a stranger to him, but the aloof horse had gotten used to her presence, so he even tolerated her stroking his sooty mane. If she kept it up for too long, though, he would swing his pale face with dark-rimmed eyes around and feign a nip at her, as if to say, that was enough, so quit it. The horse was as emotionally inaccessible as his human.

She focused the lenses on the slope and spotted flashes of light color moving through patches of sunlight against the darker colors of the trees. They were only beginning the precarious descent. The alarm that formed on her lips went mute upon seeing the gunman on his knee, his head bowed over the Apache. He placed his fingers over the unseeing eyes and brought their lids down.

"Mister! Up there! Riders!"

He worked swiftly, untying the blanket roll in front of the cavalry saddle and using it to roll N'ii's body in. He slung the wrapped corpse over the wood saddle on the dark bay and tied the body down. She was on Sombra and ready when he yelled, "Ride!"

"I don't die the honorable death of a warrior."

"You die the honorable death of a good friend."

"Do you think that is better?"

"What do you think?"

"I think it is not so lonely."

The gunman put his old friend's last dying words to rest in his memory and focused his mind on the current dilemma. Over hill and valley they rode, and their pursuers stayed on their heels like long shadows in late evening.

Chapter Thirty

In a hollow between oak-juniper hills, the gunman stood beside the horses as they drank at a small pool where an underground spring surfaced from a hole beneath tree roots. He idly fiddled with the reins of the bay horse, knotted them on the end, and looped the knotted reins over the horse's head, then checked the security of the blanketed body. As soon as the girl emerged from a closely packed clump of juniper and piñon, a hand signal on the gentle rise was silently given. The gunman helped the surprised girl up into the saddle with a boost of such swift force, it was apparent he was aware of the silent stalkers. A pistol shot rang out.

"Goddamn it, kid!"

"They gonna get away!"

"And all you done was warn 'em at this range!"

The gunman slapped the black pony into a gallop and followed that with a slap on the bay's rump. The bay needed no further urging to lunge into a gallop on the tail of the black pony, its grim burden bouncing across the open stretch of tawny grassland.

"Fire! Fire!" a panicky voice shouted, setting off a barrage of rifle and pistol shots.

The gunman systematically levered and unloaded the magazine of seventeen shells like a machine gun. A hand waved. A voice shouted, "Back! Get back! Hold up!"

The gunman rode with the reins dallied around the saddle

horn, while half standing in the stirrups, and reloaded the rifle with shells from his belt. The dun stretched his head into the wind, sooty-rimmed eyes slanted in his smoky beige face, sooty-lined ears laid back, and bellied flat out, skimming the feathery, seedy tips of tall grasses to catch up with the black pony and bay.

The black pony had not so much lung as the horses out-matching his size but had heart in his laboring effort to keep up with the bay's longer strides. The gunman saw the black pony frothing at the mouth and stumble as the dun shot past. He pulled rein, rolled the dun back on powerful haunches, and heeled him into a lunge back toward the fallen black pony. Sombra's head arched up, his black face a ghastly walleyed grimace. He squealed his pain and terror. The froth was bloody. His lungs, already exhausted from the arduous mountain trails, had labored too hard in his eager effort to meet the challenge.

Dominica had been thrown forward as the pony went down. The gunman saw her thrust herself up to her feet, and he knew she was all right. Before she got to her pony, he placed a precise shot in its head and put an arm out for her to grab onto, which she did on frantic reflex and was pulled up onto the dun behind the gunman as the dun leaped into a gallop.

The gang had gained on them enough to send missiles whizzing in the air past their heads. The gunman felt the hot singe of a grazing bullet on the side of his cheekbone.

The loose reins dallied around the saddle horn, the dun took the bit and galloped with no cues. The gunman twisted himself in the saddle to take aim with the rifle. Dominica hunched herself low, pressed against his spine, her arms clutched tightly around his waist and her hat flapping on her back. He held off shooting until the pursuer in the lead got within the Winchester's accurate range of two hundred yards. The Winchester boomed. The target flew from the saddle. The rifle roared again. A second rider fell. *Boom!* Another down. The remaining five pulled back and picked up their fallen.

He heeled and squeezed the dun into a puma pounce, landing him not quite directly beside the bay, which had dropped down to an aimless trot. Dominica's arms around him to stay herself behind the saddle lent support to keep him in the saddle as he leaned out to grasp the knotted reins and pull them forward over the bay's head. He set the dun at an easy lope, the bay matching the pace closely alongside. They left the open land and blended in with the midafternoon's shadows of the dense juniper and piñon trees on the higher slopes.

The cavalry horse followed the dun's lead without hesitation, and they boldly crashed through the brush-choked gully, plunging through a snaggle of entangled vines and broken, brittle scrub. They had covered a good ten miles down into broken, lower hills, with no sign of pursuers.

He brought the horses down to a cooling walk. The canyon trail took them through broken, hilly brush land, desert vegetation predominating, and then dust, sand, rock . . . rock, dust, sand. The shadows gradually grew long in the yellow sunlight deepening to gold and slanting from the west over vastly rolling ridges. Dominica had thought they were out of the mountains and in the desert until she saw what looked like a great patch of snow on the pale beige sprawl of desert far below.

"Those white sand hills—what did you call them?" she asked his back.

"Gypsum dunes," he said.

"They are the same what we saw from the high forest?"

"The same ones."

The coarse wool jerga was tied to his bedroll, but the canvas fabric of his jacket was no less rough against the skin of her cheek when she had pressed her face against his back holding on for dear life in their galloping flight. Even his clothes repelled her closeness. Presently, the one side of her face feeling hotly chafed, she kept herself erect with space between them and said, "I think you shot two. I saw two fall."

She got no reply.

"Do you think you got El Lobo?" she said hopefully.

"No. The white throat rag fell back with the rest when the third went down. I winged another one earlier in the morning."

She silently pondered upon not so much the reality of his shooting men with no more compunction than shooting cans off a wall and keeping score, as her own elation at his hits and desire for them all to die. Most of all El Lobo, especially now that her memory had been recovered that he had not only been one of the brutes who had murdered her family but had committed the heinous act on her mother. But was she *really* sure? That had been over seven years ago. Could she be misremembering El Lobo as one of the accomplices of the massacre of her family, as she had the gunman?

Still, the indisputable fact remained that El Lobo had cold bloodedly killed Padre Zxavian, and that was as clear in her memory as if it were yesterday. No doubt about that. No doubt about he and his gang barbarically terrorizing a village of people who had done nothing to deserve such treatment, and ruthlessly burning the sheep alive. And no doubt they would kill her and the gunman if the gunman didn't kill them first. And if she could, she would.

She felt lucky to have the gunman, who possessed the practiced skill to fight evil. If he had not come back into her life, there was no telling how long it would have been before the El Lobo gang would have come to eradicate her from the abandoned village, and she would have been defenseless against them. In her most heartfelt conviction, the gunman was her savior. Not once, but twice. If anything happened to him, she would die. Literally.

Nevertheless, her conscience could not help being bothered by the wrong of it—being glad at the possibility of men's deaths and feeling no remorse even if she herself hadn't shot them. Did that make her as guilty as the gunman, in spirit if not deed? Her emotional confusion continued to become a more entangled snarl of ambivalent feelings.

Chapter Thirty-One

The horses whickered at the smell of water, a damp scent detectable to even human noses. It was prominent among powdery-dry canyon smells of sun-baked rock, crusty clay, and parched plant life, with small leaves folded even smaller and looking dead. He let the horses choose the way through a stretch of ocotillo wands and snakeweed.

The horses climbed a gentle grade to where cottonwood and willow trees made a shady grove along the base of a low bluff. The horses' heads bobbed vigorously in an eager fast walk, straining at the bits. He let them have their heads, and they broke into a jog for a short distance to a colony of mesquite trees crowding around a rock formation sculpted by erosion into a fantastical shape that only nature could create. Beneath the wide umbrellas of lacy mesquite branches was a deep pool of underground spring water. The horses sloshed their noses, clearing surface debris, before sucking in drooling mouthfuls.

"Here," the gunman said. She looked up at the back of his head as he turned it, giving her a back view of his profile over his shoulder. "We'll bury him here."

She got down from the rump of the dun with the help of his hand. He roped a fallen dead cottonwood limb thick as the trunk of a mature oak, and the dun dragged it a couple of yards. The cavity the heavy log left in the ground was shallow but deep enough to hold the army blanket–wrapped body of the dead Indian. They used large pieces of thick tree bark that littered the ground around the cottonwoods as scoops to shovel gravelly dirt until the mound of blanketed corpse was banked all around. Then they gathered rocks and stones plentiful for the picking around the broken area of the weathered rock formation. Dominica stood over the finished cairn in appraisal of their work.

"Should we pray?" she asked.

The gunman was already getting the horses settled where they could graze on bunch grasses. "If you know any Indian ones," he answered.

"Padre Zxavian said they believe in a God like we believe, but I can't remember what he said they call their God."

"Eyata," he said.

"Eyata? That's what all Indians call God?"

"Mescalero. The ones I knew. Different Indians have different names for what they think of as Something Above, or a creator of all things," he said, muttering, "or something like that. You can call it God."

"Padre Zxavian said they believe in different creators of different things, not just one God."

"The ones I knew believed there was one creator of all things. And, yes, other creators of different things."

"Like what?"

"Gan, for one. A mountain spirit. Isdzanatleeshe' or mother earth or changing woman. Not much different from your God and saints, I reckon."

"Why do you say *my* God and saints? Do you not believe?"

"I'm gonna go take a leak," he said, leaving her with a feeling that was a statement on his beliefs. He took his rifle and binoculars with him.

She bowed her head and silently said a prayer to Eyata over

the Apache's cairn. And, said one to the civilized God, which in her mind was the Big One over all uncivilized ones.

The gunman inspected the contents of the cavalry saddlebags as he sat on the ground under the mesquite. Dominica sat beside him and studied his stubbled face. Usually he at least broke out his shaving kit and dry scraped the stubble with a straight razor, if not giving himself a soapy-wet clean shave whenever they rested, even if for only an hour.

It was a peculiar habit of his that appealed to her. She thought he had nice looking clean features, however hard set, that should not be covered with hair that made a face look dirty and unwholesome as the El Lobo gang. The only other white men she had seen in her life as Dominica had been the army officers in command of the black troops that occasionally came to the village. And they had mustaches not so appealing to her either. She liked clean faces such as Padre Zxavian's and Carlos Valenzuela's that were easier to trust, maybe because the hair on the face was like a bush behind which the owner hid his real self. In any case, the gunman's clean-shaven face might have been what had encouraged her to trust him.

Padre Zxavian used to say, "Cleanliness is next to Godliness." Well, she thought, it was not so easy trying to stay next to God on this expedition in any way. It was a task to keep her hair brushed clean and free of tangles, even when she wove her customarily loose braid into a tight weave. Long strands still escaped, and the fugitives flogged her face, and the tight weave came loose. Her grubbiness alone wearied her. She feared she would never know a tub bath again, let alone a clean body.

"You are bleeding," she said and lifted a finger to touch his cheekbone.

"It's okay," he said, flinching away from her touch. He moved to fetch his own saddlebags and sure enough broke out his shaving kit. In the tin mirror, he examined his face where the bullet grazed the cheekbone.

"Are we going to stay here until dark and travel at night again?"

"That's why you should get some sleep."

"I can build a fire. Heat water for you. Aren't you hungry?"

"No fire. Cold water will do." He went to the pool to fill the tin mug.

"It's still light. A small fire can't be seen like at night."

He resumed his former place, seated cross-legged, and proceeded to lather his face and scrape suds and stubble off with the straight razor.

"The smell of burning wood carries far. Besides, what you got to cook?"

They had each hastily jammed what they could into their own grub sack, leaving most of their provisions and supplies with the packsaddle and the half-eaten carcass of the packhorse. Suddenly she remembered. They didn't even have her grub sack anymore, as it was left with her saddle, which was lost with Sombra. She had to get up and walk away from him so he wouldn't see her tears.

"Are you crying?"

"I put the cornmeal in your grubsack. I can make pinole. I can sweeten it with raisins."

"I'm sorry about Sombra. I couldn't leave him to die slow, Dominica. He was bleeding from the lungs."

"The raisins and other dry fruit were in my grubsack, but look." She pulled her hand out from under the blanket poncho, which was not so colorfully bright as it had been hanging in her bedroom doorway what seemed in another lifetime already. In her hand was a small round tin. She undid the lid for him to see the raisins inside. "I forgot I put these in my pocket. I can use them to sweeten the pinole."

"No fire," he sternly reiterated and used the remaining soapy water in the shaving mug to slosh his entire face. He dabbed it dry with a square of hemmed huckaback. "Keep the raisins for yourself. Those and the jerky will have to do you."

"Don't you ever get hungry?"

"Try 'n get some sleep. We'll be moving in an hour. I'll be right back."

She hated when he said that, not knowing if it would be in five minutes or an hour or maybe never.

Chapter Thirty-Two

Under the pearly light of early morning, they followed a well-trodden trail that pastores used to move sheep to the grassy meadows in the higher elevations. The sheep trail took them past several meadows, one with deer foraging and presently with sheep grazing on carpet-like sod.

The shepherd had a small sleeping tent set up near his campfire. He invited them for coffee and pan de campo and asaderos and campfire conversation. His camp bread and goat cheese were very much appreciated by Dominica, whose stomach knew only raisins and leathery jerky for over thirty and some hours.

No Apaches from the reservation or otherwise had come his way, the shepherd reported, although on occasion Domingo would pop up his head. Speaking Spanish, the shepherd said, "That *malino viejo*"—calling without malice the Apache blusterer *old evil one* or the Devil—"likes to harass the pastores but never, so far, has gone beyond the threatening gesticulations from a distance."

The gunman gave the pastore a half-eagle for his hospitality, which the shepherd appeared dumbfounded at seeing in his palm, as if he might not know what it was, or was dazzled by the yellow brilliance of the coin, and tried to return it, saying he could not accept so much for so little, and the gunman said it was not payment, but a gift. It was not polite to refuse a gift. One gift for another. In that case, the humble shepherd accepted graciously.

No matter what he said, Dominica thought, she saw the good in the gunman that her heart could not deny or resist loving.

For Dominica it was a relief to have met up with another human being who was not looking to scalp or shoot them. Her senses detected they were out of the wilderness. Her senses were reinforced by signs of civilization—a farmhouse and buildings here and there in the distance from the sheep trail, and then a real road. The well-traveled road was widely hoof-trodden and wagon wheel-rutted. She was further heartened by a mule-drawn wagon that passed, with a man and a woman on the bench seat in front and children with a goat and a dog in the back. They waved as they passed, and Dominica waved back. She would have never thought to be so glad to see people when not too long ago she had sought reclusion from them.

"Dominica," the gunman said, "see that white rock up there?"

"Where? Oh, Piedra Blanca."

"Good. You remember. Pay attention to me. That mountain is about three hours from here."

"Puma Mountain."

"I'm glad you have such a good memory. Below that white cliff is where the main house is. Casa Grande the vaqueros call it. There are villitas about the ranch. The field and farm workers live in them. There are goatherds who have shanties, jacales, in the desert. If you get lost, you can ask any of the peones the way to the Casa Grande. The white outcrop up there is what you keep in your sights," he said, as would be expected of a gunman, "and aim for."

She looked at him, her eyes widened. "What do you mean *you*? *Me?*"

"All you have to do is stay on this road. There are forks you don't want to take. Some go into side canyons you don't want to go into. Stay on this road, always going north. You know north, south, east, west, don't you?"

"Of course," she said indignantly. "That's west, that's east. That's north." She twisted herself in the uncomfortable, hard horse-soldier's saddle and pointed behind them. "South. It's easy up here in the open where you can see everything with no trees in the way." She looked at him with a worried frown. "But why are you talking like this?"

"If you stay on this road going north, the white cliff will always be in sight to your right. East."

Panic had already set in. Her heart was flopping around in her belly. Her voice took on a threatening quaver. "Where will you be? Why won't you be with me? Where are you going? I thought you had to go to the ranch. I thought you said—"

"This road comes to an end at a main canyon road that goes east and west. Going west it comes to a town called La Luz. When you come to the canyon road, there will be a sign with an arrow pointing west that reads 'La Luz.' Just remember to go the other way. East. Got that?"

"I don't want to get it. You said you were going to the ranch."

"Which way are you going to turn on the main canyon road?"

"East. But I don't want to—"

"Keep going east until you come to a little settlement. The Mexicans there speak very little English if any. They all know the Corvalan ranch. There's a store. On the front a sign: Tienda. You can buy something in there to eat. Ask *¿donde es Corvalan rancho*?"

"I know how to speak Spanish," she retorted, her apprehension exacerbated to exasperation.

"Anybody around will point you the way. For a silver coin, any muchacho will see you there."

"I don't have a silver coin."

"Let's stop here for awhile."

★ ★ ★ ★ ★

With her skirts bunched and stuffed between raised knees under the blanket poncho, Dominica sat on the ground, weary and worn. The black sombrero pushed off her head and hanging on her back, the wind blew long, oily strands of too-long-unwashed hair across her face and about her head like waving appendages. She watched him, fearfully knowing and waiting for what was coming. Not knowing what to do about it. How to stop him. Desperation building inside her.

She watched him load the chambers in the Mexican bandits' pistols and slip them inside the waistband of his breeches.

"How can you do that?"

"What?"

"Put those pistols in your calzas like that? You are not afraid they will shoot?"

A genuine laugh she could not recall hearing from him, except the one time when he was playing Topetada's butting game, broke the grim set of his features, like a crack in a rock splitting open. His teeth were small and scarcely showed but for the even edges when his lips moved tightly in speech, but in a full grin or smile they were displayed healthy and beguiling. He pulled one pistol out and held it for her to see, but she flinched away.

"It won't hurt you. I want to show you."

"I am always afraid a gun has a mind of its own."

"Look." He released the cylinder pin, which allowed the bullet chamber to rotate freely, and he slowly spun it and held it for her to see the empty hole. "You always leave one chamber empty and position it so the hammer rests on the empty chamber. If the trigger is pulled, the hammer strikes on a chamber that is empty, so no bullet fires. It's a good safety habit. I never knew any shooter who didn't practice it."

He replaced the pistol in his waistband with the other and

proceeded to take out the cylinder of the six-shooter from his holster tied on his thigh. His gun looked more deadly than the smaller pistols, maybe, she thought, because it seemed so much bigger and heavier. He inserted metal cartridges into the disengaged cylinder and replaced it in the gun. From somewhere that she did not see, as if a second cylinder magically appeared in his hand, he checked the loads of that one and put it in his jacket pocket. It seemed he was getting ready to fight a war as a one-man cavalry, and she knew he was.

"What kind of gun is that?"

"Remington. Old army model. I had it in the war. It's undergone some changes since."

"What war?"

"The one between the states."

"Between what states?"

"The states in the north and the states in the south. You probably were not even born yet when it started. At most a baby."

"When did it start?"

"Eighteen hundred sixty-one."

"How old were you?"

"Twenty. I was in a military academy at a place called West Point, New York."

She held a studying gaze on his face as if trying to fathom the depths of the man. She had told him she knew all she needed to know about him to love him, and that was true. But the more she learned about him, the more she wanted to know. She didn't want slices any more, much less mere crumbs; she wanted the whole loaf. She wanted to hold the whole loaf tightly against her and never let it go.

As Dominica, she had never had a sense of true belonging, always feeling a displacement in life. She so desperately wanted to be a part of his life, to have a place of belonging in his life as she could only imagine she might have had in her lost family life. Now in only less than three weeks, having developed a sense of belonging with someone, she felt him slipping away from her.

"I will never see you again, will I?" she softly murmured.

He did not answer. She watched him get up and go to the dun and slip the Winchester back into the scabbard and loop over the saddle horn the one Mexican's gun belt, to which he had transferred all the cartridges from the other belt left lying on the ground. He loosened the girth and breast straps and checked the horse for galls before readjusting the blanket and saddle and tightening the straps.

Desperation at last impelled her. She blocked his way. He looked down at her. She looked up into his face cold and hard as stone frozen in ice, yet holding a dangerous allure too powerful for her to overcome.

"Kiss me. At least kiss me goodbye."

At once he dropped his mouth to hers. His kiss was not a kiss, but a brutal assault. His arms around her not an embrace, but an iron vise crushing her. His overpowering masculine aggression gave her a glimpse of the violence inside him and threw her into a panicky struggle like a mouse caught in a lethal trap. He released her. His glacial stare was vacant of all human emotion.

Still she said, "You do things to make me believe you are something you are not. I can't stop my feelings for the man inside that machine that my heart knows is in there."

He walked away from her before he did something he would regret. Even he did not know if that was making tender love to her or beating her black, blue, and bloody. Either one, regret.

Without looking at her, he said, "I am no good for you, child."

"Don't call me child. I am not a child."

"To me you are." He turned to face her as they spoke over a

safe distance between them.

"I don't care. You will have to kill me to make me stop feeling what I do," she cried and whirled herself around, to put her back to him this time.

"We're wasting time," he said.

"Well, go! You don't have to wait on me. I know where to go. You told me. I'll leave when I feel like it. Go hurry! Get yourself killed!"

"Dominica, it's my fight."

She brought her angrily tearful face around to confront his. "It is not your fight. I should put on a gun belt and go with you. They killed Padre Zxavian. They destroyed good people's lives. They destroyed everything good I knew. All I knew." Her green eyes shone with a fury fed on her very powerlessness. "The one called El Lobo took away my life not once, but twice. Do you forget he murdered my family? Violated my mother?!"

"I didn't forget."

"When I wanted you to kill them for murdering Padre Zxavian, you told me you get paid for the work you do, your price is high, and, even if I had money to meet your price, you weren't for hire. I still don't have money to pay you, so why are you doing this?"

"El Lobo's got a personal grudge against me. Not just for making a mockery of him, besides giving him a very sore throat. I brought down three of his men. And wounded another. Whether any live or are dead, that's reason enough for him and what is left of his gang to want my blood. It's my fight. I don't want to bring my trouble to the Corvalan family. I want to stop them before they get that far. I know Ramón Corvalan and his son. They would come to my defense. I don't think the Lobo gang would stand a chance against the Corvalan vaqueros. But some of the Corvalan men could be seriously hurt, if not killed. I don't want any of the people on the Corvalan ranch involved.

It's my fight."

"What about the man behind the murder of your wife and unborn baby?"

Following a moment's hesitation, he said, "That's another reason I can't have any Corvalan people putting their lives out on a limb for me." He continued before she could interrupt, "I put the gold in the bay's saddlebags. It's yours."

Impatiently brushing away tears with the backs of her hands, she cried, "I don't want your gold! I want only you. I don't want you to go." Then she said, "I want to go with you. If you must die, I want to die with you."

He mounted the dun. "You know the way. You know what to do. Oh. I wanted to give you something."

"What?" she breathed out as if on the very last breath of hope.

"Let me have your hand."

Her eyes narrowed in puzzled suspicion, she lifted her hand. He slipped a turquoise and silver bracelet about her wrist.

"It was Nadie's. I want you to have it. And one last thing." He slipped a hand into one of the saddlebags and withdrew the suede envelope containing his writing paper and pencil. He unwound the leather string to open the flap and withdrew a folded-up paper and handed it to her. "A letter for Don Ramón. Give it only to him, Dominica. Don't lose it. Put it in your skirt pocket." She did. "This is most important to remember: do not trust Frutozo Armendariz. Don't tell him about the gold. Only Don Ramón. He will put it in his safe to keep it for you. Trust nothing to Frutozo Armendariz. Do you understand?"

"Trust only Don Ramón. Tell only him about the gold. Don't trust Frutozo Armendariz," she said with wooden resignation.

Tears streaming down her face, she watched him ride away. She cried out, "Mister! I will always love you!"

He did not look back.

She looked at the beautiful bracelet on her wrist, and tears splashed down on it.

Chapter Thirty-Three

"Easy, kid."

"Uncle, it hurts," the kid moaned, grimacing.

"I know. I know. Jes try'n relax. Here. Take some of this. And call me Al, remember?"

"Sor . . . unc . . . Al." The kid lifted his head from the saddle blanket used as a pillow and sipped from the mouth of the whiskey flask held to his lips. He coughed and sputtered, and a hairy hand clasped over his mouth.

"Jeez, kid. I ain't got but only so much left, and you spittin' it out all over."

"Sorr. . . ." The kid's head fell back into a stare at a bright orange spot on rock.

"Kid? Kid?"

"How's it look, Al?"

"Not good. I don't think he's got much life left in him."

Al took a sip of the laudanum-whiskey mixture before slipping the flask into his coat pocket. He pivoted on his boot soles, remaining hunkered beside the boy. His tawny, shaggy head was topped by a slouch hat shoved back, fully exposing a face not merely bearded but hairy over the cheeks almost to the eyes. The yellowish-brown hair fell from a low hairline to thick, broad, dark-sandy brows that concealed what little forehead there was. A stolid stare of pale-brown eyes with yellow flecks giving them a topaz glow and unusually long, protruding canines among crowded, crooked, pointed teeth certainly could easily be said to resemble the Mexican wolf that struck terror in many rural people's hearts. A former member of his following lay a skeleton in the desert somewhere between El Paso, Texas, and La Mesilla, New Mexico, for having had the audacity to retort in an altercation between them that he belonged in a carnival freak show. Anyone who rode with Al Parson never hinted at his unusually abundant hirsute condition, even amongst themselves.

"Well, what we gonna do? Jes set around here and let 'em get away? We wasted a day already."

The hunkered leader looked up at the shadowed figure of the other man in the firelight. "Lenard, you wanna jes leave the kid here like this?"

"Well, whatta we gonna do, Al? Call it quits? Go back?"

Al glanced at the boy, whose eyes were closed. He stood up and took several steps away in case the boy was conscious and could hear. He spoke huskily and low, touching his cloth-wrapped throat. "Lissen, he's my sister's kid. I dint want him to join us, but she couldn't handle him and feared he was gonna get in trouble with the law. I promised I'd take care a him. You know her old man took off, and she's tryin' to make it on her own."

"Awright, awright. It ain't like ya to give the sob story. So what ya wanna do? The others are gettin' antsy. Can't dawdle here forever."

"I can't leave him here like this, Lenard."

"How 'bout we leave Leaman with him? He's a chicken shit anyway when ya come down to it. He can nurse him 'til we get back. You, me, Boyles, and Logan should oughta be able to take care a one fast-gun and one little gal, providin' we don't come up against those damn bah-kay-rows if he gets that far."

The leader noticed the other massaging his wounded arm. "You okay with that? Your shootin' arm."

"Don't worry 'bout me," Poke said. "Just a crease. I can still use it. What we gonna do?"

The leader wordlessly looked at the kid. It appeared the laudanum had given him some quieting comfort. Maybe by dawn, he would be quietly dead.

"Reckon you're right. We can leave Leaman to stay with him. We'll start out first crack a dawn." He added vehemently, "Jest remember: we catch up to 'em, he's mine. I want him to know what it feels like to get his gullet smashed in afore I plug a hole between them snake eyes. Damn devil. He's gonna pay for this." The leader sorrowfully gazed at his mortally gut-shot nephew.

In the purplish-gray light of early morning, Poke banked the fire with some dead branches, causing sparks to fly.

"What the hell you tryin' to do, Lenard? Send out an invitation to ever' Patchie in these hills?"

"Thought you was sleepin'."

"What you doin' up?"

"Can't sleep."

"Me neither. Kid's still breathin'," Al Parson said, as if he had been hoping otherwise.

They brewed coffee in the pot.

"You know, Al, ain't no chance for him, you know that. If you can't do it, I will do it for you."

Al's wolfish face glowered, showing his fangs. "What can't I do?"

"Put him out of his misery."

"You never did like the kid, Lenard," Al accused Polk.

"He was such a smart-ass. I can see why your sister put him on you."

"Let's jes let Leaman stay behind with him."

"Leaman ain't gonna cotton to that."

"It was your idea."

"Aww, jeez . . . what's all the jabberin'? It ain't daylight yet.

What idea?"

"Leaman, wasn't you spost to be on watch?"

"Shit. Pete ain't woke me. Bet he fell asleep," Leaman said groggily, sitting up in his blankets, scratching various body parts, ruffling his hair, and wiping sleep from his face.

Lenard Poke made a slow sweep with a suspicious-eyed gaze around the inky periphery of the campfire light. His two comrades' eyes followed.

"Sounded like sumthun was stirrin' up the hosses awhile ago. What woke me," Poke said. "Figured Leaman'd gotten 'em calmed down."

"Not me. I'm here," Leaman said. "Pete dint wake me. Remember?"

"Then Boyles, damn it. If he calmed the hosses down, that means he dint fall asleep. How's come he dint come git ya to relieve him? I'm feelin' sumthun's mighty amiss."

"Wake up, Logan," Al Parson rasped.

Boyd Logan was kicked and came up out of his blankets grunting, "What the hell?"

"Ever since them broncos back there, I keep waitin' for more," Poke said.

Logan was up wide awake, gun drawn. "Patchies?" he hissed.

"I been edgy, too, since them gut-eaters."

"Leaman, don't take much to make ya edgy."

Terror seemed to make a surreptitious entrance into the camp and slowly crept up each man's spine. Each man had his pistol drawn and cocked. All four pairs of eyes roamed over the dark-purple shadows beyond the firelight, up the low walls of the bluffs, dimly skylined above them.

"Somebody go check on Pete."

"Who somebody?"

"Leaman, you go. Since you was spost to be on watch. Tread softly."

"Damn shit," Leaman muttered as he cautiously slunk out of camp toward the quiet horses.

Chapter Thirty-Four

Riding the back trail, he mulled over the past four years. Killing had not been a pleasure for him. His Spartan existence was without sensuous or sensual pleasures. Eating was merely a mandatory function he performed automatically, his tastes basic when conscious of tasting food at all. Even sex was not a pleasure, only another bodily function as perfunctorily performed as defecating, and which could be achieved with or without a woman to the same effect of physical release and relief. The occasional whore had only been an optional implement, like using a fork when handy to transfer meat from a plate to the mouth instead of using the fingers. Even tobacco smoking was merely a savorless habit.

He took the unlit stogie butt from his mouth, where it had been smokelessly fixed like a strange black facial protruberance, and put it back into an inside jacket pocket.

At the dun's naturally fast walk and intermittent jogging, and the horse's favorite loping gait whenever the terrain allowed, with frequent short rest stops, the dun traveled the ground they had covered coming in quicker time going back. The eastern serrated ridges were still edged with deep-gold sunlight when he came to N'ii's cairn. He paused to reflect upon it.

He let the dun graze and took himself a doze. He had come to need little sleep. A short nap was enough, and four hours was more than plenty. He did not like to be in the place of sleep. It was less restful than disquieting. Presently, it evoked the painful pleasure of her. The soft flesh of her mouth under the hardness of his, the feeling of her youthful womanliness in his arms, her touching closeness when she had slipped beside him while he slept. Dominica would never know the gratification she had gifted to his empty existence, even for such short while. Therefore, all the more keen, all the more sweet, all the more painful to give up.

As usual he came out of his sleep abruptly, wide awake, ready to tackle the day, or night, in front of him. As he rode away from the spring-water pool in the mesquite trees, he hoped that she would not hate him too much for abandoning her again. He hoped the saints that had been watching over her before he had come back into her life guided her safely along the trail to the Corvalan ranch. By now she should have been there for hours.

Perhaps she would have a new life with the Corvalan family if, despite all his connections, Don Ramón could not locate and reunite her with the people she had come from, as he had requested in his letter to the well-known nobleman. No doubt Don Ramón would be surprised to get his letter after so many years of no communication from him. It would be as if he had arisen from the grave for the Corvalans.

The waning gibbous September moon was still ninety percent full and bright. The round swells of darkly dappled tawny hills glowed luminously. Emerging from the oak-juniper woodland to the nearly pure grassland in the vast hollow, he halted the dun and skimmed the meadow with his gaze. The field shimmered silver-gray in the moonlight and rippled in the strong nocturnal breeze.

He smelled it before he saw it. He brought the binoculars to his eyes. A dark blotch not a juniper or piñon or oak tree in the lunar pale grass marked the spot where the carcass of Dominica's black pony lay. Even at that distance the shifting breeze carried a whiff of decomposing flesh. He skirted the source of the putrid stench by a wide margin. Movement caught his eye, but he could not make out what caused it. Maybe fox or ring-tail, some small, nocturnal carrion feasters. The dun kept one eye and ear turned their way and tossed his head and snorted as a vegetarian might in disgust as they crossed the meadow toward the oak-juniper hills on the other side.

There were no signs where the men hit by his rifle shots had left their saddles in the high grass early yesterday afternoon. He had only his own judgment to determine an approximate place in the meadow where the gang had quit the chase and turned back. But he did not believe they were in full and permanent retreat.

Possibly, the three lived, and, if alive, doubtlessly an encumbrance, which could explain why the gang had not resumed the pursuit so far. Enough time had passed for them to have buried their dead if all of the three gunned-down men had to be buried, and by now, well over thirty and some hours, the gang would have gotten back on the trail. In that case, he would have met up with them or seen some sign of them hours ago a good many miles back. Since he had not, he surmised there were wounded among them, and they had retreated to somewhere not far in the juniper brakes. Delayed but not defeated, he reasoned they would have a desire for revenge inflamed to resolute perseverance. There was no doubt in his mind that El Lobo wanted to kick in his throat before filling his hide with lead more than he wanted the gold.

In the bright moonlight, he picked up the tracks of the eight horses and horse droppings that got fresher along the way. The moon had reached its summit and begun its westerly descent when he came on a place where they had stopped and done a hasty burial job. The telltale odor led him to the common grave of two corpses evidently dug up by scavengers. The grave defilers had gotten into the bowel cavities and chewed through the limbs, carrying parts off. Badgers or wolves came to his mind, both having the jaw and tooth power to tear apart a carcass, in this case human corpses, limb from limb.

He ruled out wolf. As an army officer, he had learned from Indians and trappers that wolves were night hunters that liked to start out at dusk, preferred fresh meat of their own or somebody else's kills, and settled for old, decomposing meat only as the degree of hunger dictated. Among the Indians, Brother Wolf was known to pass up a carcass that had gotten too putrid. For a wolf to dig up a grave it had to be starving, and he presumed starvation among wolves was not all that rare either. Badgers were natural diggers for insects and rodents that burrowed, having the claws for it, and were not so fussy as to pass up overly ripe carrion, so he thought they were more likely the grave robbers.

Whichever scavengers did it, he had to thank them for the telling sign. The Lobo gang was down to six men for sure. Knowing their reduced strength gave him an edge. They could be down to five able-bodied men, since the third one down by his shot, while apparently not dead, could have been seriously wounded enough for the gang to be digging another grave. He knew he had merely grazed one man earlier when they had been pursuing arrow-shot Chago/N'ii, and his hit had made them fall back. His shot got a visible reaction but did not knock the injured man out of the saddle. That might or might not have been one of the men shot later. In any case, their number was down by two for sure, possibly three, and crippled by a fourth winged man. So informed, he was emboldened.

His mind focused on the leader of the gang, the one called El Lobo. Dominica's story of her family's massacre by white men contriving to make it look like the diabolical work of Indians was the kind newspaper bloodhounds ran their noses around the frontier sniffing out to make headlines that white society, especially Easterners, ate up. The local publicity alone was not what a man with dreams of being a cattle king would want, if the cantinero's hearsay, which was all he had to go on, were true. To be identified as one of the perpetrators of a savage massacre of white pilgrims would be bad publicity that could get a man not only arrested, tried, convicted, and hung, but tarred and feathered for the ignominious nature of the crime.

In his calculations, Dominica was a threat to El Lobo to be eliminated. Even if she had not recovered her memory, in the guilty mind, she had witnessed his crime, and so long as she was alive, the possibility existed that she could put an incriminating finger on him. Why El Lobo had not eliminated her when he had had the chance was something only El Lobo knew and could be sorely regretting. So long as El Lobo lived, his threat to Dominica existed.

He equated his strategy against the El Lobo gang with chopping off the head of a poisonous snake, although he might have to chop the whole damn body into pieces before he got to the head. Either way, the snake would be rendered harmless against Dominica. The risk of the venomous fangs sinking into him did not prevail as a possibility. He had become so inured to danger, had looked into the black face of death so many times, it was as if death could not touch him. Not that the Devil couldn't. His soul could be claimed by the Devil whenever the Devil decided, since the Devil already owned it. So long as he still had the Devil's work to be done, his reprieve from Hell continued. With that self-assurance he anticipated getting the snake out of the way and then proceeding to the matter of his personal vendetta. He was inexorably committed to that. With Dominica at the Corvalan ranch, he had had to rethink his strategies of how he was going to accomplish his goal. After the deed was done, he wanted to disappear as if he had never been. The Corvalans would never know he had come back. Most of all, he wanted Dominica to be unaware of his presence; it was best he never re-enter her life again.

The way the plan formulated in his head, he wouldn't have to go anywhere near the Corvalan ranch. He knew where Frutozo Armendariz spent his time in Santa Fe. Frutozo Armendariz did not associate with the influential powers of Don Corvalan's political-social class. Armendariz enjoyed gregarious prestige in the lower affluent ranks in Santa Fe, where he owned an inherited general store and patronized a high-class gambling house run by a woman who herself flaunted her reputation of being his paramour. It might take some patience, but, after four years of dogged perseverance he had the rest of his life to wait until one day Frutozo would show up in Santa Fe, and taking care of him in a dark alley in the city teeming with off-the-trail rowdies, riffraff, and criminal sorts would be no challenge.

But first things first.

Chapter Thirty-Five

The memories of her long-forgotten childhood in a countryside without mountains, fishing in a pond with two younger brothers, playing with a younger sister and a shaggy dog . . . her father behind a plow pulled by a dray horse . . . her mother kneading dough in a kitchen . . . an unpainted wood-frame house with chickens in the dooryard . . . herself walking on a dirt road to a school house . . . her grandmother, who had lived with them, waving her off to school . . . all her lost memories came back with vivid clarity in daydreams as she rode the cavalry bay at a slow walk along the road well-trodden by animal hooves and human feet and rutted by wagon wheels.

None of the memories, which once might have had cherished meaning, held any significance in her present life. The disjointed segments of her life before Dominica did not fill her with elation. The memories of her life as Aleah Nicholson had no relevance to the person she was today. There was no sense of reality to a long-ago past in which images were transparent, could not be touched, smelled, tasted. Memories having no substance.

The memories of her most recent life as Dominica had more of a realness to them. Memories that conjured up smells of food that stimulated the juices of craving. Memories of hugging Sombra and his velvety muzzle nuzzling her neck. Memories of the gunman's body against hers snuggled up beside him, the sound of his voice, the way he walked, moved, talked, smelled, of detailed features of his face and hair. Memories of the gunman, still real in her mind as the bracelet on her arm, dominated her daydreams as the cavalry horse carried her along the dusty road.

Periodically she gave in to an uncontrollable fit of muffled sobs. Then she would get control of herself and beseech the cloudless sky: "God, please bring him back. Please, God, don't let anything bad happen to him. Please, please, please bring him back to me."

She frequently looked back but saw no sign of him. As usual God was deaf, mute, and blind. Padre Zxavian often repeated in his church sermons, in various ways: "God's answers do not come right away, and, when they do, they come in ways you did not expect. He knows what's good for you better than you do."

Well, she would have to debate that.

A distracting excitement momentarily took her mind off her heart's woes and worries about the gunman's fate and her uncertain future. She had to rein the bay off the wide road into a space between tall, thorny ocotillo wands and sharply serrated, slender-leafed bear grass for a small herd of cattle being moved by a man and a boy on foot.

They urged the sluggish beasts with *garrochas* and ineffective whacks on the rumps with the fancily carved canes of mesquite wood. The cattle merely bellowed and did not move any faster. A few stopped dead in their tracks and bawled their objections to the treatment, which was not really harsh.

"Buenos tardes," the man said as he passed. *"¿Cómo està usted, señorita?"*

"Muy bien, gracias, señor," she lied. She did not feel very well at all. On top of emotional distress, her hungry stomach was starting to gnaw on itself, not to mention physical discomforts in unmentionable places from too many hours applied to a wooden, split-seat saddle.

"Ventea. ¿Eh?" he said conversationally, although his studying gaze appeared leery as well as peculiarly curious.

"Sí, hace viento," she said, agreeing it was windy. It had only in the past half hour or so started to blow hard, and she had had to jam the bead up the strap to her chin to tighten its hold on her hat to keep it from flying off her head.

She realized how peculiar she might look, with the gun belt crossing her chest, the loops empty of cartridges and the holster empty of a gun. For whatever reason she didn't know, other than she was unable to leave a perfectly good leather holster on the ground where the gunman had tossed it aside, she had slipped it on over her makeshift blanket poncho for quick and easy carrying. Who knew, someday she might get herself a pistola, and she would have a holster to carry it.

"Por favor, señor," she said, employing her most polite voice to assure him she was no bandit. *"¿Voy bien este camino a rancho de—uh . . . um . . . Corvalan?"*

"Sí, señorita," he replied, pointing east, reassuring her she was on the right road.

Once the cattle drovers had the little herd moved on, she waited until the dust cloud dispersed before getting back on the road. Soon after, the little settlement emerged from the mesquite that grew in abundant colonies among the piñon, which she had come to think of as a ubiquitous pine in these mountains, from the lower foothills to the high forests. If the little, smooth, creamy, good-tasting nuts weren't so hard to shake out of the cone and crack and peel out of the shells, she would stop to pick some, this being the season, but for a few tiny nuts it was too much work. She wasn't that hungry. Besides, the gunman had said there was a store in the settlement where she could buy something to eat.

The settlement was all of several huts constructed of mesquite logs and yucca thatching, *jacales de leña,* with porches, *portales,* in front where a few men were taking a siesta in the shade of the thatched roofs. The tienda had been constructed in the same manner, only larger, and there was a hammock strung from one supporting post of the portal to another, and a sleeping figure in it, not seeming bothered at all by the wind and the dust whirling around. His hat was clamped down under his arms crossed on his chest to keep it from blowing away.

The high and hot mid-afternoon sun clued Dominica to it being siesta time. She had the notion to join the two other slumped figures at the base of an enormous trunk of a cottonwood tree with a wide spread that formed an umbrella over the whole store.

She tied the bay's reins to the hitching rail in the wavering shade of the wind-shifting cottonwood branches. The tinkling and clanking of metal and clay bells, and the sibilance of hanging baskets, rattlesnake skins, and other dry, pendulant objects swaying created a cacophonous accompaniment to the droning din of the wind.

She went inside through an open doorway and squinted her eyes to adjust them to the inner darkness. Unventilated earthy odors and stale, greasy smells stifled her nose after so long in open, fresh, breezy air. She stood around for minutes in a buzzing silence. Flies and gnats whizzed and darted about and alighted on all surfaces in the dim store, which was cluttered with sundry items from handcrafted wood and leather and metal goods to foodstuffs like cheese and hanging chains of *chorizo* links.

She called out a few times, bringing no response. She went outside and looked at the figure sleeping in the wind-swayed hammock, holding the hat on his chest. He looked too peaceful to disturb. Flies and gnats crawled on vegetables and fruit that emanated an odor of sugary putrefaction from a display stand.

She went to the bay and, cautiously, watching to see that nobody was spying, dug out a few gold coins from the sack in the saddlebag. Even though the gunman had told her the gold was hers, she felt as guilty as a sneak thief. She studied the three coins in her palm, having no idea of the value or buying power of any. She had never had money. When Consuela had sent her to get a piece of brown sugar cone from one of her women friends in the village, it was to borrow, not to buy. The people had bartered and traded among themselves; no money had been exchanged. Consuela had alluded to Padre Zxavian's money from the wine that he sold cached away, but Dominica had never seen it and was sure Consuela had taken it with everything else she had taken. Carlos Valenzuela had had coins jingling in his pocket, in different metals, sizes, and denominations, Mexican and American, and he had liked to show them to her, as if his possession of them gave him a certain elevated importance, while to her they were only a novelty, not a practicality.

Knowing her numbers and that the higher the number the more in quantity, Dominica's common sense calculated the five-dollar gold coin to be the least valuable in her palm and the ten- and twenty-dollar gold pieces she put back, instinctively knowing they were too much. But she could not determine a number to be applied to the peach that stood out firm and not overly ripened among so many too ripe and going to rot.

Her gaze regarded the sleeping man, who stirred to chase away a fly that had landed on his nose. He swatted the air with the hat and saw her and at once swung sandaled feet to the ground, uttering effusive apologies in Spanish, then English on the correct presumption she was a gringa in spite of her Mexican getup.

"*¿Ve usted algo?* You see something you like to buy, señorita?"

"I would like a peach, señor. Only one. That one."

"They are so sweet and juicy, after the one, you will wish you had another, chinita. Mira, look, niña. This one es muy bueno. A bunch of grapes? Mira. Aqui, taste." He plucked one from a cluster in the basket and proffered it to her. Her hunger whetted by the sweet morsel, she chose a bunch to buy.

"*¿Cuànto debo?*" she asked at length.

"Hmmm," he said, calculating behind rolled up eyes under the flimsy brim of the hat made of material like yucca leaf strips or some grass Mexicans used to weave into sleeping mats, baskets, hats, and myriad things. "Un momento, por favor," he suddenly said and vanished inside the store. He came out with a net bag, the open mesh weave of a desert plant fibre twine, into which he put her purchases of two peaches, grapes, and a melon, and handed the shopping bag to her by the drawstring. He said the bag sold for twenty-five cents, but for her it was free. "Dos dollares y fifty cents, señorita."

She gave him the five-dollar coin. Grinning widely, he stuck a hand in a pocket and brought out a bunch of coins. Among copper, silver, and gold centavos, pesos, and reales, he picked out two silver dollars and smaller American coins counting them out in her palm.

Without thinking she raised the drawstring of the net bag to hook it around the saddle horn, but there was no saddle horn. She had to use one of the straps in the three holes in the high rounded pommel of the ridiculous saddle to secure her bag of purchases. She missed the saucer saddle horn on her saddle lost with Sombra. She missed the whole comfortable padded leather saddle. Mostly she tearfully missed Sombra, however used to the taller bay she had gotten. There was no horse she couldn't love. But not so saddles.

The cavalry saddle had a slot splitting the rawhide-covered wooden seat from hornless pommel to high cantel, which she had secretly rationalized as a place for a man's private parts to keep from being smashed, until the gunman had enlightened her, explaining it was for the horse's comfort, not for the rider's, and prevented chafing the horse's back and withers during the unalleviated long hours a horse soldier spent in the saddle. Maybe it prevented a horse's back from getting chafed, but not her backside.

By the time she got herself back up into the wretched saddle, there were men, women, and children gathered around, all expressing curiosity among themselves but politely standing back and not directly assailing her with their inquisitive interest. Where did she come from? Who was she? Where was she going? Why was she there? Why was she riding an army horse? Not only the saddle but the U.S. cavalry brand on its hip made that conspicuous. She could hear their questioning remarks among one another.

The *tendero* delegated a muchacho to show her the way to the Corvalan ranch. As the gunman had said, for a silver coin any boy would guide her. Now she had some silver coins.

He walked in front of her leading the way. He had a wide-brimmed straw hat and the loose, white, cotton camisa and baggy pantalones of the campesino and was barefoot. Twenty or so minutes into their hot, windy walk, she withdrew the peaches from the net bag and shared one with him. He was effusively grateful, and while eating the peach his walk got jaunty, and she had to squeeze the bay into a faster walk to keep up with him.

He led her off the main canyon road into another canyon with the same features of the landscape she had been passing for the past few hours—spiny, thorny, brittle vegetation in the bottoms of arroyos and narrow hollows and wide strips of level grassy land between rolling hills, dotted and dappled and solidly manteled with piñon trees increasingly towered over by juniper trees. All crowded together, the evergreens formed an even edge on the ridges, unlike the serrated outline of pointy pine trees in the upper elevations of the mountains.

The single different feature in the landscape that had become monotonous for so many hours was the Piedra Blanca. In closer view, its white limestone configuration was more definable to the eye. It stood out from the piñon and juniper that cloaked the summit of the hill like a crocheted shawl. The outcrop resembled a human neck projecting up from the shawl about the hill's rounded, wide shoulders.

Then came the Casa Grande in view, in a wide squat on a long bench of land lacking pines. Cottonwood, box elder, willow, and oak prevailed on the bench. The boy suddenly stopped and told her he would go no farther. The road they were on would take her to the house. She dug out a silver coin from her skirt pocket under the poncho and gave it to him. Again, the effusive expressions of gratitude, both words and gestures. Then he was skipping back home.

Approaching so close, her nerves began to get knotted. When digging the coin out to give to him, she had felt the paper in her pocket, reminding her of the letter. She supposed for moral support, she pulled the gunman's letter out of the pocket and unfolded the paper, carefully holding it in both hands. Nevertheless, almost at once a gust of wind snatched it away.

"No!" she screamed.

The boy came running back. He saw the paper fluttering like a white dove, swirling up and around, over the desert brush and cacti, in fleeing flight. He chased after it. Dominica wheeled the bay around, but by the time she got the horse into a haphazard, hopping, and leaping gallop, zigzagging around the clumps of vegetation stippling the rough up and down terrain, the gunman's letter had flown up like a kite in the sky and dipped down out of sight.

They—she on the bay and the boy on the ground in bare feet—stood at the edge of a deeply cut arroyo and forlornly stared out at the foothills dropping to the vast desolate-looking sprawl in the west, where once again lay in her vision the snow-like patch of white sand dunes.

"No . . . no . . ." she drily wept.

The boy looked up at her. *"Lo siento."* He apologetically shrugged. *"¿Es importante el papel, señorita?"*

She merely nodded. She had never felt so empty, as if all her insides had dropped out.

Chapter Thirty-Six

The oval gibbous moon was still bright and high in the dusky western sky. The spearhead forms of pine were beginning to take distinguishable shape on the dark slopes silhouetted against a livid sky in the east. Directly beneath him, thirty or forty feet down the vertical scarp of a bluff, the orange light of a campfire illuminated two men in the pool of dark shadow within a cove formed by the bluff and a copse of deciduous trees. The horses were beneath the treetops, which were vigorously shaken by the strong, shifting winds.

The whistling, whirring variable gusts obscured the men's voices. Every so often a voice was swept on an upward current that swirled about his ears, but he couldn't distinctly make out any words said. The entire breezy night had picked up to a hard blow. He had left his hat wrapped in the jerga, with the dun. He wasn't chancing the thing to blow off and sweep past his targets' eyes. It was not a good night for sighting the rifle when the bullet would meet so much variable resistance from shifting directions. He wanted all sure shots, not inaccurate hits and misses, and for that he would have to be a lot closer in the gale-force winds.

He made out lumps on the ground in the dark shadows to be three sleeping figures, presumably the one wounded, leaving one unaccounted for. His narrowed gaze scanned the rocks for sign of a lookout. He soundlessly backed away from the edge of the bluff and slunk into the shadows of the rocks above the wind-shifted treetops.

Dominica wove in and out of his thoughts against his will. In time she would forget him. She was young, with a whole new life ahead of her. The important thing was that he had made sure she would have the chance to obtain it. Don Ramón Corvalan was one of few men whose integrity had gained his trust implicitly and the only man he knew in whose charge to put her that would assure her all the advantages of realizing the best he could wish for her. Dominica had come to be the only redeeming factor of his doomed existence.

The guard simply slid down from his sleeping slump into a peaceful forever slumber. He set the corpse back up into the sleeping position, head fallen forward, concealing the slit across the throat, although the dark stains down the front of the jacket would be revealed for what they were in the imminent light of dawn.

Beneath the sounds of the wind he heard the horses' restlessness, whether it was the wind that unsettled them, his sensed presence, or some nocturnal animal. On silent moccasin soles he swiftly got to where they were tied to a rope strung out from one tree to another. His unthreatening presence quieted them to a curious interest as if waiting to see what he was up to. He sliced the line from the trees and led the whole string slowly several yards away. One by one he took off their bridles and the bits out of their mouths and slipped away before the eight horses knew they were free.

Gradually they moseyed farther away from the camp into the juniper and ponderosa, foraging for palatable plants and grass. Soon they had wandered into the night and kept wandering. Before long they would be a mile away, grazing in the light of pre-dawn.

He waited, and, as sure as he counted on it, another man

came slinking in the shifting shadows of the wind-jostled trees.

"Boyles? You there?" the man called out in a loud whisper. "Pete, where the hell are ya? It's me. Leaman." Low mutters. "Damn it. Makin' me tromp around like this. Where the hell—? What? Whadja do with the hosses?"

Before he could alert the others, he was slumped to the ground as silent as the other in the rocks.

He wiped the blood off the seven-inch blade onto the dead man's trousers and replaced the knife in the sheath at his waist. The Winchester recovered from where he had placed it, he stole to the base of the bluff and inched his way around it in the cover of brush toward the campfire.

The kid cried out in awful pain, and one of the three men with pistols drawn fired a shot into him.

"Goddamn you, Logan!" Al Parson growled.

"He was gonna die anyway. Everybody knew it. Now he's outta his pain and don't set my teeth on edge anymore with his yellin'."

At once Logan fell dead.

"Al, for godsake! Whatchya do that fer?" Lenard Polk squawked.

"Fer killin' my sister's kid."

"Now that that's done, let's get Boyles and Leaman and the hosses and hit the trail."

"Where are they?"

"Whaddya mean?"

"One a dem should a been here by now. What the hell the two a dem doin'? Havin' a tea party?"

"I don't like it, Al. Like I said afore, sumthun's not right."

Both men fell quiet and turned their heads in various directions, listening to the ominous voices of the wind, howling and whistling around the rocky heights of the bluff, rustling in the trees, whispering and whining in the bushy and spiny close surrounds of the camp.

"All right," Al said. "We can't jes stand here yakkin'. Let's split up."

"I'm thinkin' we should stick together. Cover each other's backs."

"Reckon yer right. You feelin' what I'm feelin'?"

"Sneaky Patchies again."

"Thems back there wasn't so sneaky. Let's go see about these ones if that's what it be spookin' us fer damn sake."

Before the two men could get the gumption to investigate, white explosions flared from the shadowy brush at the base of the bluff. Both men fell before either could react. Beneath the sounds of the wind, which extinguished the fluttering flames of the campfire and simultaneously blew glowing life back into dying embers, the thunder of the Winchester stopped, and a leaden quiet dropped.

The gunman checked to make sure neither would be surprising him as the Mexican bandido had.

"Logan . . . why . . . Logan . . . ?"

He spun around to realize the voice was coming from the wounded man in the blankets. He hunkered down beside him and saw he was a boy, as Dominica had claimed one to be. Guessing him to be no more than sixteen, lying helplessly in obvious agony, his sallow face had the innocent look of an eight year old.

"Unc . . . hurts . . . Logan . . . ," the kid blindly moaned a supplication of the man hunkered over him, examining his wounds.

There was dried old blood of a gut wound, the gunman assumed from his rifle. Fresh bleeding high on the left side of the chest indicated a recent shot, the gunman assumed the one he had heard.

Perhaps mere curiosity motivated him, or maybe a predestined reflex compelled him to lean low to the boy's face to hear what he was saying. Did it matter? What stalled him from the inevitable? What postponed what he had to do? The boy was as good as dead. He was going to have to make him that way. He felt the boy's hand come up and grasp his side under the short-waisted jacket as if needing to brace himself against his last painful breaths. Maybe needing the human touch to stem the lonely terror of entering the Stygian realm of death. He obviously was on his last breaths. Another minute—less, seconds—and the job would be done, without having to waste a bullet.

He saw a vengeful rage flare in the boy's glassy eyes. And at once a shocking pain in his back as, empowered by a last surge of strength, the seven-inch Spanish blade plunged through muscle, cracked through bone, and pierced viscera. The gunman recoiled as an impaled worm. The boy fell dead, his hand falling away from the handle of the Spanish blade. The gunman gasped over him, trying to reach back to pull the lethal weapon out of his spine. He gasped for air. Pain ripped through him like a lightning bolt.

He lay for a long while, forcing himself to take only sips of precious air, fighting the compulsion to gulp. Slowly he reached his hand back to feel for the knife. His grasp on the familiar silver handle was too weak to yank the blade out.

He forced himself to his knees. The pulsing of his life's blood pounded in his ears, behind his eyes. His vision blurred. He fought the debilitating pain to stay conscious.

His single thought was *the dun*.

The sun's crest broke over the high horizon, and, by the time he crawled, inch by inch, to within sight of the horse, sunlight splashed over every ridge and poured into every canyon. The dun curiously watched him for several minutes, then slowly ambled over and sniffed his hatless head, blew into his hair, nudged his face as if attempting to turn it up from the ground. The horse pricked his ears forward at the murmured instructions. Like a faithful dog, the horse licked the exposed side of his face.

He stirred and on sheer will pushed himself up from the ground. The horse patiently waited. Blood loss made the world spin. Pausing at intervals of great lengths, he dragged himself up by the stirrup. At long last, he staggered to his feet against the puzzled horse. With the intent concentration of a bumbling drunk, he managed to get one rein in hand. Gripping the horse's black mane with one hand and the saddle with the other, with agonizingly awkward difficulty, he managed to lumber up into the saddle. As if the horse knew the man's desperation, he stood stock still. He felt the familiar weight in the saddle, the man leaning forward to his right side. The horse felt shifting of the weight and heard the familiar voice mumble meaningless utterances. The horse waited and continued to wait for a cue that instructed him on what to do.

At long last the dun's head picked up at the sound of the man's voice: "Go . . . boy . . . take me . . . her."

The horse dropped his head and started a slow walk. Soon he felt the man slump forward on his neck. He heard incoherent murmuring. The horse, feeling only the dead weight of the man, paused and lifted his head and looked around at the landscape, waiting for some signal to guide him. He looked around at the man slumped on his neck. He stood indecisively. Waiting. No cue came.

The dun responded to his first nature and dipped his head to crop grass. The long reins dallied at their ends around the saddle horn tightened and tugged at the bit, pulling his head up. At the release of the bit, he started walking, slowly, uncertainly, hesitantly. He put his nose up to the wind that had decreased in velocity to a breeze in the advancing morning. He walked slowly, feeling the inert man on his back. He paused again and called out. His whinny drifted far into the mountain canyons. Echoes of a single, lonely call vanished into emptiness.

The horse resorted to his own feral senses. He made his way through the high ponderosa and higher conifer forests, pausing to graze on the high grasses. The long reins allowed his mouth to reach and browse on branches and to drink at streams and water holes familiar to him.

At last the horse, with the dead weight on his back, came to a halt over a small valley. The embracing hillsides of piney green were mottled with autumn's pale yellows, deep golds, and oranges. The smoky dun snorted through sooty nostrils in his sooty muzzle and pawed the ground with hooves of his lower sooty legs. He lifted his black-maned pale head and called from the very depths of his great smoky-beige chest, a tremulous scream that vibrated across the dawning sky.

Chapter Thirty-Seven

Frutozo Armendariz had never seen such a sight. Not on the ranch, much less in the relatively new and sparkling clean tile and marble vestibule of the Casa Grande. A shabby, black hat aslant on a jumbled mess of hair too dirty to tell of what shade of brown. A gun belt with an empty holster crossing the chest like a bandolera empty of cartridges over a shabby blanket worn like an oversized poncho. Saddlebags over a shoulder, small might they be, cavalry type, looking too weighty for the scruffy wench to easily bear. Skirts of the mestiza slut variety seen among the dregs of society littering the fetid, slop-strewn, back streets of Santa Fe. The ranch's peonas had more class. And what appeared to be men's boots also of the plebeians under the ragged, dirty ruffles of the compesina skirts. The better-quality whores of Santa Fe kept their ankles decorously hidden under tastefully fashionable silk skirts. She reeked of horse, dirt, wood smoke, and God knew what else. Her eyes got to him, though. He appreciated emeralds. Luminous emeralds in a grimy face.

"Eso es todo. Gracias," he said, dismissing the leather-clad vaquero who had escorted the wench to the *zaguàn,* main entry of the house, instead of going the back way. The vaqueros esteemed themselves above the peones, such arrogance, when they are peones themselves, all of them mestizos, Indian blood mixed with other blood (he hated to admit Spanish), gringo, even negro. The man plainly of higher breeding disdained the

man before him and all of his lot. Holding in front of him his *sombrero galoneado,* with the tall cone crown that arguably could hold ten gallons, the vaquero gave a slight caballero bow, clicking star-shaped *rodajas* at the ends of the spurs, causing a metallic clink, and musically backed himself out, jinglebobs jingling, bringing after him the elaborately carved, heavy, wood door to shut with its twin as if he had practiced painstakingly to execute the performance with such smooth precision.

Her green eyes were wide with childish wonder as they roamed over the round vigas of the high ceiling, higher than the low ceilings of the casas in the village she was used to, except in the church. Her green gaze took in the long and narrow vestibule, exquisitely carved high-backed benches, and massive wood tables topped by white marble . . . niches holding hand-hewn santos and gilt plaster statues of saints and the Lady of Guadalupe . . . mirrors in gilt baroque frames . . . Talavera-tiled archways leading into interior rooms.

The man was proud of what obviously awed her. The Casa Grande incessantly underwent modernization and enhancement with materials and new furnishings imported from Mexico and all the way from Europe by way of Mexico or the United States and the Santa Fe Trail, and soon the much-anticipated railway to Santa Fe would facilitate importing. The original packed mud floors of over twenty years ago were now paved with glazed terracotta tiles and the walls newly whitened with a purer gypsum brilliance than the original wheat-paste whitewash. Some rooms had gotten patterned cloth coverings pasted on the walls. The real pride was the Talavera from not Mexico but Spain; the more a house displayed on the inside and/or the outside, the greater the proprietor's wealth. The iron grillwork was a recent addition for cosmetic enhancement as well as security, fashioned after that of the Spanish elite in Mexico. It, of course, originated in Spain, as did the more elaborately hand-carved doors and cabinetry by the finest craftsmen he himself had found.

Her gaze came back to him when he asked more as a demand than a polite inquiry, *"¿Cómo se llama?"*

"Dominica."

"¿Pues qué quiere aquí?"

"Señor, por favor, ¿usted es el señor Ramón Corvalan?"

Not a tall man, nor excessively stout, but large in the chest, and dressed in a lounging coat of cinnamon-brown velveteen, with quilted lapels and cuffs, he used his chest as a heraldic shield of authority. Muttonchop whiskers, meticulously barbered, emphasized his look of authority.

"¿Qué quieres?"

"Por favor, señor. Señor Ramón Corvalan. *¿Se le puede ver?* I must see him."

"You are americana?"

"Sí. Yes."

"I am the *administrador.* Any business you have with Señor Corvalan can be done with me."

"It is Señor Corvalan I must see."

"You cannot see him. You must go. I don't know who you are, and I don't know what you want, but it is impossible for you to see the señor. Go now." He began pushing her toward the door. "That stupid maid should not have let you in."

"What have we here, Frutozo?"

Flinching at the name, she glanced at the breezy entrance of a young man full of flourishing vitality. He was of medium height and slender build, and there was a careless poise about him that instantly captivated. Black, satiny braid decorated the lapels of a well-tailored short, black jacket and the seams of slim, form-fitting trousers that flared slightly at the bottoms. Black boots of smooth leather had a polished shine, with tapered toes and a trim contour that gave his feet a dainty look. *Botinas.* A white shirt beneath the jacket had twin rows of ruffles down the front. Side-parted, raven-black hair and sideburns were meticulously clipped, and above a boyishly disdainful mouth a pencil-line mustache boasted self-assured manhood. The devil danced in glittering, coal-black eyes.

She had never seen a man so well-cut and extraordinarily handsome she would have to say *beautiful.* Formidably so. He hardly looked real to her and made her want to shrink inside herself.

"This . . . er, señorita," the administrator said with derisive emphasis, his large, square head of black, ram's-wool-like hair stiffening on a thick, stumpy neck, "asks for your father."

The dashing young seducer of female hearts glanced at the pompous administrator, and his patrician levity deigned to formal politeness.

"Señorita, allow me to introduce myself. Raul Cipriano Jovian Corvalan Santana y Larrieta de Montealegre." As if he could not stay serious for too long, flirtatiousness flashed in his roguish eyes as he added, "It goes on. But I can only remember so much."

At once he clicked the silver spurs as the vaquero had, bowed from the waist, and smoothly took Dominica's ragged-nailed, dirt-ingrained hand in his immaculate one and brought it up to his lips. *"A la disposición de usted, señorita."*

She quickly snatched her hand back as if he had bitten it, her eyes wide with dismay.

His smile was indulgent. "I am the first, last, and only son of Don Ramón, my lovely desert blossom. How can I be of service?"

The administrator let out a noise like somebody had punched a needle in his puffed chest letting air out. "*¡Basta!* Enough of your pretty games with the ladies. I will handle this matter,

Raul." He put out his shield of authority again.

Raul Cipriano Jovian Corvalan Santana y Larrieta de Montealegre-and-it-went-on did not take his dancing, black eyes from the bewildered emerald gaze as he spoke. "I think, Frutozo, I shall like to handle this matter myself." His glossy, raven head swiveled around to look at the administrator. "If you don't mind."

The administrator lowered his shield as if in begrudging deference. "Perhaps, Raul, we should both handle this matter."

"Then stay if you wish," Raul airily said and turned his attention back to Dominica as if dismissing the other man's presence from his mind, if he could not rid him from the room.

"Señorita, you look as though you have had an arduous journey."

"I came a long way, señor."

"May I ask if you have a name?"

"She said Dominica," Frutozo said.

Raul's attention did not waver; his glittering, ebony eyes steadily held her glistening, green gaze. He waited for her to answer.

"Dominica," she said.

"Only Dominica? No family name? Not even half as long as mine?" He had an engagingly teasing way.

"No. Yes."

He cocked his head, amused. "No? Yes?"

"Well, it's a long story, señor. And I have to see Señor Corvalan. I mean the other one. Your father."

"A matter of urgency, I detect in that sweet, distressed voice?"

She licked her painfully weathered dry lips and glanced around uncertainly. "I was told to talk only to him."

"*¡Vaya!* Now we are getting someplace. Who, may I ask, might that be? The person who told you to talk only to my father."

"A friend of Señor Corvalan."

"May I inquire of this friend's name, my sweet?"

"I, uh, *lo siento,* don't know, señor," she said, lowering her eyes, abashed.

"Hmmm, I see. You regretfully don't know."

"I only called him 'Mister.' "

"Uh-huh."

"You must believe me."

"I am trying to."

She blurted out, "He was married to an Indian woman. She was called Nadie. Her mean owner treated her like she was a nobody. Nadie was killed by"—she quickly recovered her involuntary glance at Frutozo and put it back imploringly on Raul's face, sternly set now and eyes narrowed in a closed expression, as if he had already shut the door on her, and no matter what she said, he would not hear. Still, she rambled fast, ". . . by some men that Mister spent four years searching for. He lived in a high valley once a part of this ranch, he told me. He showed me the valley. It has a waterfall running down a rock wall between lots of pine trees all crowded together. The cabin is still there. He said he knew the Corvalan family when he was an officer in the cavalry. Then he quit the army and went to Mexico, and he came back with his Indian wife and bought the valley from your father . . . no, I think he bought it when he was a horse soldier; that's what he said. He raised horses and sold them to the army, and he and his Indian wife lived in the valley until she was killed. He was away taking horses to the fort." She added, "She was with child. His wife."

Dead quiet fell on the room.

Raul stood before her for a long minute, staring at her with his hands held behind him, then gave Frutozo a side glance and remarked quietly to him, *"Pues no puede ser."*

"¡Sí!" Frutozo exclaimed. *"¡Cuàndo! ¡Imposible! ¡No lo crea!"*

"Digo verdad," she said, on the verge of frustrated tears. "It's the truth."

Frutozo was about to say something, but Raul proceeded ahead of him in a cordial voice. "I don't think you will be seeing my father, my dear. If this is some kind of practical joke that somebody is playing, it is a cruel one. My father is on his dying bed. That is the reason you would not be able to see him under any circumstances; certainly not this one." His voice had turned progressively more unyielding as the ebony of his eyes had to shiny, hard coals. "I shall see you out and that one of my vaqueros will see you off the ranch. Did you come on foot?"

"Horse."

Having navigated her to the door with a firm hand and opened the door, he looked out into the spacious, adobe-walled courtyard, where the bay stood, head hanging, looking glum, obediently ground tied.

"A cavalry horse?" He noted the saddlebags over her shoulder. "Army saddlebags?"

"It's a long story, señor. Not so easy to tell in five words. Mister—he—he was coming with me. He sent me alone because he turned back to stop El Lobo and his gang from coming here. Mister said he didn't want to bring trouble to you and your family. He had to stop the gang. They came after us all the way."

" 'Mister.' "

"Yes, señor. He was . . . a gunfighter but—"

Raul's face flushed red with anger. "¡Basta! Enough! The only man I can think of who fits your description is Quinn Harden, and Quinn Harden was no gunfighter, and he is dead. He has been dead for over four years. I was there at his burial."

"No!" she screamed. And screamed and screamed.

Chapter Thirty-Eight

Raul allowed her to see his father the morning after the afternoon she had fainted on him when he had been trying to kick her out and off the ranch, as if she were a conniving gypsy who had wheedled her way into the house, scheming to steal the Corvalan treasures, when she had more gold in her possession than she knew what to do with.

It had been his sister, Leida, who came on the scene to save her and had the servants tend to her in their quarters. They gave her a bath, or tried to—she gave herself her own bath—but submitted herself to a head scrubbing and examination for lice. She had never had maids work on her as if she were a two year old, toweling, combing, and brushing her hair dry and dressing her in their clothes that best fit her, not unlike the cotton skirts and blouses she was used to wearing. She had to be grateful for the clothes, pressed smooth with a hot flat iron, feeling crisp and clean on her clean body, since her own had been lost along the trail but for what she had been wearing when she got there.

She bore many unsightly blemishes and scars of her journey, but most would eventually disappear. Her nails would grow again to be evenly maintained, and the scratches and cuts would heal with little or no scars, but for the one on her forehead. However, that was mostly in the hairline and not so noticeable. All in all, she felt relatively civilized again.

They fed her in the servants' dining room adjacent to the kitchen, a meal fit for royalty—a cold soup she had never had of tomatoes, onions, garlic, olive oil, and spices, called *gazpacho,* and a chicken-rabbit *paella* with beans and vegetables and rice, not new to her palate but of a different, stronger, not distasteful spice flavor than Consuela's paella, which could have had goat, mutton, and chicken mixed in, followed by a dessert of fried dough rolls most familiar to her, *sopaipillas,* drizzled with honey, all served on porcelain dishes, not earthenware or copper or tin or gourds or wood, and eaten with silver forks and spoons, though she had rather eat with her fingers and drink right out of the bowl. She didn't like the metallic taste that the silver gave to the food, which her fingers did not impart.

Her night of supposed rest was restless, her dreams bizzarre, of she and the gunman chasing after the El Lobo gang and Apaches across hills of white sand, she shooting a pistol at them, and Padre Zxavian watching her from the belfry, shooting a rifle at Consuela and the people in the village for no reason she could fathom upon awakening. Throughout the night, between muslin bedsheets on a mattress of straw and horsehair on a narrow bunk bed, she jerked awake, feeling for the saddlebags and pulling them close to her to protect them from Frutozo Armendariz, who in her nightmares covetously aimed to steal them.

After a common breakfast of *churros* and *champurrado* in the servants' dining room, Raul had taken her, clutching the saddlebags—more to stem her tremors than to secure them from Frutozo, whom she had not seen since she had fainted the day before—into the sick man's richly appointed bedroom.

The ceiling was as in the other rooms of the house, *latillas* or straight, thick twigs diagonally set between round viga poles running parallel to one another the width of the narrow room. All the rooms were narrow. The larger rooms were still narrow but longer. The wooden floors of the adjoining sleeping and sitting rooms of Don Ramón's bedroom were covered in what she later came to know were Belgian carpets. In a corner of each room of the bedroom suite was a tumid, white-plastered *fogón,* a smaller replica of the huge, bell-shaped fireplaces in the larger principal rooms.

Upon entering, Dominica almost turned about and fled, driven by compunction for disturbing a dying man in the privacy of his bedroom.

However, he was ready to receive her, propped up against many plump pillows in a huge bed with high, timber-thick corner posts, having been prepared beforehand for her visit. His full head of white hair had been groomed, as had his white mustache, and he appeared immaculate in a white nightshirt with lace trim about the neckline against the white bedding. It made her feel glad she herself was clean, and her hair brushed and neatly woven in its customary braid. Upon her approach, ushered by Raul to his bedside, the *patrón*'s pale face seemed to acquire an enlivening pink color.

Dominica had to think it was plain to see where his son had gotten his handsome looks, although a gilt-framed oil painting in one of the other rooms, depicting *los don Ramón y doña Victoria,* had already verified that Raul had inherited the best features of both his parents.

"Señorita Dominica, eso es mi papá, el señor don Ramón Corvalan. Papá, esa es la señorita Dominica Aleah Nicholson." Raul made the formal introduction. Her name in her other life only so recently recovered in her memory sounded alien to Dominica's ears.

"Tanto gusto en conocerle, señor Corvalan," she said, making a conscious effort to remember the good Spanish learned from Padre Zxavian, who had often corrected her bad Spanish picked up from Consuela, who, like a horse, could not be re-trained easily to unlearn bad habits, the padre had tolerantly said.

"El gusto es mío, señorita Dominica Aleah," Don Ramón said in a voice manifesting his weak state. He motioned for her to come nearer to his bedside, upon which he came out of his lethargy with a surprising spurt of energy, sat up more erect against the pillows, and promptly demanded in a stronger voice that gave her an inkling of the authoritative head of the family he was: *"Déjame ver esa carta. Mi'jo, mis anteojos."*

"No, Papá," Raul said. "I said she said she had a letter for you from the man who sent her here, but she lost the letter on the way."

"Señor," she said nervously, "I think he wrote about the gold." She was hugging the heavy saddlebags so hard, her arms trembled.

"What gold?" He looked at his son.

Raul shrugged. "She passed out some coins to the servants. They told Leida and asked if they could keep them."

"For these clothes they gave me," she self-defensively said, more to the father in the bed than to the son, who had already chastised her for giving out money to the servants, although he had let the servants keep it. He had derisively muttered to her that she certainly knew how to win friends. "It's the gunman's gold. He told me it was mine. But I feel it's his and am keeping it for him until he comes here."

"A pistolero is coming here?" Again the elder man inquired of the younger with a look.

Again the son shrugged. "She says. But he hasn't arrived yet. I await his arrival with interest."

"When should we expect this gunman to arrive, *mi querida*?" the patrón asked.

"I don't know, Señor Corvalan. I fear he might be dead."

The two men exchanged looks.

Quickly she explained, repeating what she had told the son yesterday about the El Lobo gang following them and wanting to kill them and the gunman going back to stop them from coming to the ranch and causing trouble.

The father appeared more receptive to her story than the son had yesterday. "Is this gunman wanted by the law?"

"He is not a bad gunman, señor. People hire him to kill only bad men."

"Yo veo," the father said and looked at the son. Bringing his gaze back to her, he said, "What is it so important you had to see me?"

She became speechlessly numb. She honestly did not know or forgot.

She heard the impatient sigh of the man who had been standing beside her as still as a statue. He said, "I believe we have bothered my father long enough for nothing."

She felt his hand slip firmly under her arm, and she quickly said, "The letter. He said to give you the letter and nobody else."

"But you don't have a letter to give to me."

"The wind took it. I am sorry." She stood her ground against the forceful tug on her arm. "He said trust nobody but Don Ramón with the gold. You will put it in the safe."

"Where is this gold?"

"Here, señor." She indicated the heavy saddlebags clumsily clutched in her arms, the rebozo about her shoulders and arms slipping loose and exposing her one arm to the elbow.

The father's black gaze beneath thick, white brows seemed to rivet on something other than the saddlebags. He said, *"Raul, mi'jo, mis anteojos, por favor."*

Raul quickly snapped out of his stance, dropping his hold from her arm, and retrieved the eyeglasses standing in a velvet-clad case from a bedside table. The patrón fitted the wire earpieces about his ears and the glass lenses over his nose and eyes. He beckoned Dominica to come near. He tilted his face back to better see through the spectacles.

"Where did you get that bracelet, querida?"

She looked down at the turquoise stones set in four rows of silver that made a wide band about her arm halfway above the wrist where it fit snugly. It was too loose about the wrist where she feared it could slip off. She murmured, "Mister gave it to me."

"Mister?"

"What I call him." She looked up. "As I call you *señor,* señor," she said.

"Entiendo," he said. "May I see it, the bracelet, *por favor, mi querida*?"

Raul moved in close to look at the bracelet on her arm, as if he had not noticed it or had deemed it a gypsy trinket not meriting notice. He looked at his father. *"¿No cree que es suyo?"*

The father glanced at the son. *"No sé. Hay una semejanza fuerte."*

He patiently waited for Dominica to remove the wide cuff bracelet from her arm in her contortions of juggling the weighty saddlebags gripped between her elbows.

"Permit me to hold those for you," Raul at last said impatiently.

She let the saddlebags drop with a heavy thud to where they straddled her boots, which looked almost new, polished up by one of the servants, who had done it without her knowing until the girl had handed the men's boots to her all clean and shiny. Then the girl had stood there as if expecting something. Dominica was a fast learner and was not going to be reprimanded again by Raul. The servant girl had taught her the gist of his reprimand: servants got spoiled as quickly as little children and pets—give them a treat, and they expect it all the time, like Sombra and Padre Zxavian's horses, constantly nipping at her for the treats with which she had spoiled them. The *criada* had flounced away—one less of the friends she had made with the gold. The bracelet slipped down and off easily She handed it to the patrón.

He shoved the blankets away from himself and tried to swing his bare legs around to boost himself to sit on the edge of the bed, with little or no regard to the young female presence. Maybe during his bedridden sick days he had gotten inured to females' seeing him in his bedroom state. However, in spite of her somewhat immoral behavior with the gunman, Dominca still possessed her sense of proprieties that did not presently go unscathed. She turned her head away decorously, hiding her embarrassment.

The father resisted the son's attempted assistance, as the four or five stacked soft mattresses sank down as low as they were high. He had to push and shove and grunt to get enough momentum to get the best of the bedding and not fall back, with his bare legs and feet up in the air. He finally succeeded without anybody's help. For a man who was dying yesterday, perhaps even only some minutes ago, Dominica had to think that he had stubborn will, if not healthy strength.

He called for his robe, and his son hopped to retrieve the dark blue, velvet garment and held it for his father to stand and slip his arms into it. The obviously proud and independent patrón closed it and tied the belt and, having slipped his bare feet into slippers, shuffled to the daylight of one of two sizable windows looking out past a porch under an arcade into an inner courtyard. Never having lost his grip on the bracelet in his hand through all the gyrations of getting out of the bed and into his robe, he inspected the bracelet closely in the daylight, with his bespectacled eyes.

Raul moved in to bend and look at it in his father's examining hands. Don Ramón said, *"Es Zuñi. No Navajo."*

"¿Cómo lo sabe?" Raul asked.

"Navajo is heavy with the silver. *Grueso.* Thick. If Navajo, the stones would be different shapes and sizes and even different shades of turquoise. Zuni have always been masters at the stones. To them it is the stones that matter more than the silver. Even before silver when they learned the forge from *los españoles* and used only copper, tin, and iron, they were particular not only to match colors and shapes and sizes but to put the stones in symmetrical designs. Not so random as the Navajo."

"I did not know you had such interest in Indian jewelry and knew so much about it."

"Quinn told me. He learned from the pueblos. He got a little into trading it when he was in the freight business, he told me. That's how he got the silver knife of his, with the jade stones. He got to know a silversmith in Mexico who traded him for Navajo pieces. *Mira. Ver aquí.* See here."

"*Yo veo.* I see." Raul's glossy, black head came down close to the white hair, both looking closely at the four rows of silver bars on the inside, soldered together by narrower vertical bars. Raul squinted very close. "But what I am looking at?"

"Looks like an inscription. It is hard for me to see. Can you see it?"

"Could it not be any smaller? I see. *N.*"

"What else?"

"Marks. And under the marks, *Q.*"

"That's it. It is known among Indians that wolves mate for life. In Zuni when two wolves are drawn together, it symbolizes a pair mated for life. That's those marks. A pair of wolves. Such symbol is put on gifts to a man and wife newly married. Quinn had it inscribed for Nadie. That's Nadie's bracelet. No doubt."

Dominica listened quietly, absorbing what she had not known. Mated for life, his life even after his wife was gone. Hadn't he tried to tell her that?

Bringing himself up erect, Raul said, "I would have thought

he buried it with her."

"Don't you remember? He said they took her bracelet, and he was going to get it back. He said he was going to find each and every one of them and make them pay, and he would have her bracelet back."

"Instead he got himself killed," Raul said. At once he turned to Dominica and demanded accusingly as if she were the killer, "Where did you get this?"

"I told you. Mister gave it to me. It was his Indian wife's. He said he wanted me to have it."

Raul's face flushed as if his blood was so hot it would blow off the top of his head. He disdainfully snorted. "It is likely that Mister Gunfighter of yours was the man who so hideously murdered our friend's wife, Nadie, and took her bracelet. He probably is the killer of Quinn, too."

"No! He loved her. She was his wife. I saw him kneeling and weeping at her grave. You must believe me."

The father seemed to have more heart than the son and put his hand up and out toward the enraged man, whose vehemence shocked Dominica. "Raul, *eso basta. Por favor.* You cannot accuse the girl of something that is no fault of hers." Extending the bracelet toward Dominica, he said, "Here is your bracelet back, querida. Now, the gold. I am assuming—*¿en esas pesadas alforjas?*" To her nod, he said, "Raul, why don't you take them for her? She looks tired from holding them." And to her he assured, "We will keep it safe for you."

She let the saddlebags back down on the floor and opened them. "It's in sacks."

Raul lifted the heavy sacks of coins as if they were feather pillows and placed them on the floor against a long credenza of elaborately carved wood below a large oil painting framed in gold baroque. Dominica supposed the man and woman depicted in the painting, as in other portraits in other rooms, were of more Corvalan family. She had never seen such oil paintings, the closest thing having been the retablos of the Virgin and the saints in and about the church. The realistic oil portraits of people and not saints, some transmogrified by the santeros to grotesque figures, were a new fascination to her. Raul took the painting down to reveal a metal door in the wall. He used a key to open the lock.

"Do you not think we should count the specie to have a record? Frutozo—"

"No!" she blurted out. "Not him." She frowned. "What's specie?"

Raul's patrician face registered dismay at her outburst, followed by a look of aristocratic disdain for her ignorance. "Coins, my dear. Counted and recorded in Frutozo's ledger book so we can have an official account of your money put in our trust."

His attitude had undergone quite a change toward her from the courtly conduct he displayed initially upon their meeting the day before. If there was any one person who could be two different people, in her mind that was Raul Corvalan. How did she really know it was Frutozo Armendariz the gunman had found out was the mastermind behind the devastation of his life, and not Raul Corvalan? It could be the gunman had warned her about Frutozo only because he had unscrupulous avarice in him, not the capacity for plotting murder. Her suspicions shifted from the administrator to the patrón's son.

"Nobody has to count the coins," she said. "Mister said his guess was close to twenty thousand dollars."

The senior Corvalan said, "Perhaps you and I can count it together, querida. To be more precise, I am tired of being in bed. We can sit here at this table. I have nothing better to do. I am sure Raul does."

At that, with the pointed look of the father's eyes, the son made a miffed exit.

Chapter Thirty-Nine

Over the weeks that passed, never did the sense of waiting diminish. To the contrary, it only intensified. In Dominica's mind, she knew he was not coming; in her heart, she continued to hope, pray, and wait. The not-knowing was emotional torture to bear. Not knowing what had happened to him. Deep within herself she intuitively believed what she did not want to emotionally accept. If he were alive, surely he would have arrived at the ranch by now.

She could not believe he would have relinquished his implacable dedication to avenging the death of his wife and unborn child when so near to the end of his vengeance trail. There was only one thing that could have forced him to abandon what she came to believe was the inexorable and only purpose of his existence—death. And if he were dead, it wasn't that he had died four years ago. She could not believe that. How could she after having lived with him twenty-four hours a day every day for almost three weeks? The gunman, the man she had come to love, surely had not been a killer of himself and come back a ghost!

For Raul's Quinn Harden and her gunman to have shared identical circumstances in their lives was too coincidental for them to have been two different people. Yet, by all logic they could not have been one and the same man since Raul's Quinn Harden had been dead for over four years, and her gunman certainly had been alive only weeks ago. This enigma baffled them all, frustrated Dominica, and provoked Raul's pragmatic rationality.

The waiting and wondering and wishing never stopped and was torture when she was alone. Fortunately, she was virtually never alone outside her private chambers in the Casa Grande, which consisted of twenty-six rooms. Her bedroom was comprised of two rooms—one to sleep in and one to sit, write, read, or simply be alone if she wanted. However, other than the fifteen- to thirty-minute siesta customarily following the heaviest meal, at midday, and the unconscious nocturnal hours, she rarely was in the solitude of her bedroom during the active parts of the day and evening. There was always some activity going on to distract her mind from dwelling on the gunman.

Raul's younger sister, Sorena, was approximately Dominica's age in years, but she was older in terms of experiences of travel, formal schooling, and worldly wisdom. She opened her two wide armoires to Dominica to pick and choose any dresses she might like to try on and wear, and some she said Dominica could keep. The vivacious girl began opening trunks and pulling out fabrics that Benita, the head servant and also an excellent seamstress, could sew into some everyday dresses that would give Dominica a start on her own wardrobe, which called for a future shopping trip.

Sorena, who wore her hair, black and glossy as the rest of the Corvalans' abundant tresses, brushed smoothly back, parted in the middle, with the thick, heavy length of it piled on top in coils and locks, persuaded Dominica to let her do her hair, which Sorena envied for the red cast that she said accented her enviable green eyes. The result, which Sorena thought had transformed Dominica into a princess, Dominica had thought uncomfortable and as unnatural as wearing a strange, top-heavy hat.

Sorena exhorted exasperatedly, "You are as hopeless as Leida

Hermonosa Corvalan, Dominica Aleah Nicholson. Except she is a *pajuela,* a boy inside a girl's body, and would be happy in pantalones. How do you expect my brother to escort you to a baíle with your hair like a campesina?"

"I have no intentions of going anywhere with your brother," Dominica retorted. "What makes you think he would even want to escort this campesina to a dance?"

Sorena had her brother's thick-lashed dark eyes, right down to the devil dancing in them. She flounced herself about in swishy skirts and chimed flippantly, "You'll see."

It was by way of Raul's sister Leida's suggestion that he give Dominica a tour of the ranch that they fell into frequent horseback rides together, as the entire ranch could not be toured in one or even two days. His attitude toward her again underwent a change from stuffily aloof back to gallantly charming, so long as the gunman was not mentioned.

He appointed a palomino gelding as her mount for the indefinite duration of her stay, and she accompanied him on his rounds about the ranch. That way he could give her a tour while he performed his directorial duties over the vaqueros and field workers, to whom she was introduced when an introduction was called for as "la señorita Dominica Aleah."

"In the early times the term *estancia* was used and passed down from my great-great-great-great grandmother. I have to stop and count on my fingers. Easier in Spanish. *Mi quinta abuela.* Juana Talamantez de Corvalan."

She laughed, charmed by his jaunty humor in contrast to his aristocratic austerity. He was a man with two opposing sides she was getting to know.

"La doña Juana," he continued, "came from a silver mining family in Zacatecas and—Am I boring you with all this about my family?"

"No. It is interesting to hear about your family," she replied sincerely. "I wish I had a family I could tell you about."

He became silent for a thoughtful moment. "I am sorry, Dominica, about the tragedy of your family. Hopefully the letters of inquiry will bring back something on a missing Nicholson party. But that was over seven years ago, and such things take much time to find the right person in the right place who might dig up information that might be recorded somewhere." He sounded so sincere, she almost believed he believed her. Up until that moment she had thought that he believed her assertion of a massacred family to be a ruse.

"I have no way to thank your father for having Frutoso write the letters to those he thinks might help. But back to what you were saying. About your fifth grandmother."

"She married Terciero Lazaro Corvalan, direct descendant of an *encomendero.*"

"Forgive my ignorance," she said, with a hint of sarcasm in recollection of his derisive attitude toward her not knowing what "specie" was, "but I never heard that word before."

"*Encomendero?* That was back when the Crown granted distinguished conquistadores great pieces of land called encomiendas along with the Indian inhabitants to work on them. My fifth grandfather left la doña Juana a wealthy young widow with two sons. It is not clear how she came from Zacatecas to Albuquerque, but there she settled with her sons in the early part of the 1700s. She never remarried and acquired much property over her lifetime, passed down to her sons and their families. My father through his father and so forth going back and, therefore I, coming forward, are directly descended from my fifth abuela's son, Cipriano, whose name I carry second from my front name."

The Corvalan family enterprise, comprised of not only the Puma Mountain ranch but also ranches in Albuquerque and

Santa Fe and other real estate holdings, as well as other business investments and undertakings, was all too complicated for Dominica to comprehend beyond her condensed conception that the Corvalan family was very rich.

The palatial opulence of the Casa Grande alone had made such a visual impression. The bed that she slept in was a wonder—four corner posts of hand-sculpted, heavy wood, standing three feet up from the pine wood floor, two mattresses of cotton tick filled with a flock of fleece, which a servant fluffed up every day, and smooth, cotton bedsheets between which she slept. Fine-textured, thin, wool blankets were folded on a leather chest with brass hardware at the end of the bed, and there were more blankets in the chest, should she need any in the night. Never would she have imagined such luxury. Compared to the woven-grass mats most of the village people had slept on on hard dirt floors, her fleecy sheepskin on a one-foot raised support of wood planks had been a luxury.

The wealth of the Corvalan family was substantiated further by the vast expanse of the rangeland, spreading over desert foothills and juniper-piñon woodlands and up into ponderosa timberland.

"The ponderosa and other pine used to build the house is from up there," Raul told her, "as well as much of the furniture, too. When I was a boy, everything we had was made right on the ranch, that is, what was not brought from the Albuquerque ranch where my father grew up. My tio Iban, my father's older brother, took over the Albuquerque ranch when my grandparents retired and moved to live in the city. My mother came from a wealthy family in Seville, but she did all the sewing, cooking, washing, and more when she came with my father to start this ranch. I was four years old. The servants *helped* her; they did not *wait* on her. My sister is spoiled. Not Leida. She might not like to do women's work, but she is not afraid to do men's work. Sorena has an aversion to all work. Sorena has only two passions in life: acquiring new dresses and wearing them. Sorena better marry a man with the money to employ a seamstress dedicated to sewing only dresses for her.

"You do more justice to Sorena's riding outfit than she," he said, observing her on the palomino as if he had not commented on how well the short-waisted jacket and split skirt of a smooth, rich, black cloth—*melendre,* Sorena had called it—fit her the first day she had appeared in his younger sister's riding habit.

Unlike Leida and other females in the Corvalon family, who had mature figures, Sorena was not so overall fleshy and was closer to Dominica's more girlishly slim build. The plump relatives called Sorena *puro pellejo,* emaciated, and teased how was she ever going to attract a man? The black sombrero with flat crown and rigid round brim was similar to Raul's and Leida's hats. Many of the vaqueros wore such style hats, which they called *poblanos.* Both his sisters rode astride like Dominica, who had never ridden a horse any other way and even had often ridden Sombra bareback. Sorena had shown her sidesaddles in the tack room of the stables, for the use of visiting female family and guests.

"I think I should not like to be the horse under that," Dominica had remarked about the unnatural and awkward looking contraptions. "I think the horse must feel too heavy on one side and off balance. It must hurt the horse's back."

"My brother and father think the same way. So do the vaqueros. They believe it is much safer to ride the way men do and think there is nothing *indecente,* unbecoming, for a girl to ride the way they do. Tia Honoratas tells us the sidesaddle protects ladies' delicate lady parts. She said it is the only way for proper ladies to ride. We are not proper ladies here on the Corvalan ranch," Sorena had said in her delightfully flippant way. "I don't like riding anyway, so it matters not to me."

That Dominica had learned was true. Sorena would rather ride in the family carriage, with somebody else doing the driving. That was why Sorena had been glad to donate her whole riding outfit to Dominica. "It is only collecting dust and taking up room in my *armario,*" she had said.

Presently, she and Raul were leisurely walking their horses past the fruit orchards where farm laborers were bringing in the last of the late harvest of peaches, pears, plums, and grapes. Pumpkins, squashes of other varieties, wheat, corn, and other crops also were being harvested on farm fields within view in the flat part of the valley at the foot of Puma Mountain, where the springs in the mountain provided irrigation water.

"Raul?" Dominica said.

"Sí, mi hermosa flor de desierto," he responded, to let her know she had his ear.

"I knew Frutozo was married to your oldest sister, Encarnación, but I—I apologize to say—but I thought she was not living. I never see her. I was surprised to learn she is in the house. Sorena said she stays in her own private chambers?" She looked at him for confirmation.

"Yes. Encarnación has sequestered herself from the world. Only her personal maid is allowed to enter her rooms. Frutozo has shown no ill effects due to his wife's denial of his boudoir privileges. He has his *amante* in La Luz when he cannot make the five-day trip to his other one in Santa Fe. It is no secret."

"Well, I can understand why Encarnación locks him out," she said a bit indignantly.

Raul's anthracite eyes glittered with their devilish humor above a teasing grin. "I am to assume you would have no tolerance for such conduct from a man of your own? You would expect absolute fidelity to you and you alone?"

Blushing, she averted her gaze to the scenery before indirectly glancing at him. She was thinking of the gunman's fidelity to Nadie, how she envied his dead Indian wife. "But she never comes out? Ever?"

"It is her choice," he said. "She can come out whenever she wants. She is her own prisoner or, shall I say, *carcelera.* She holds the key."

"May I ask how long she has closed herself off like that?"

"Four years. Since Quinn Harden's death."

She eluded the piercing look of his stare. Was he baiting her? For what? She evasively said, "Sorena misses living in Santa Fe . . . when she was in school there. She is afraid she will become a spinster like Leida living on this ranch."

"She told you that?" He turned his head to hold a steady gaze on her as they walked the horses side by side. "You and Sorena have come to have *la relación de confianza mutua.*"

"She has no one else to talk to. Not confidentially."

"She has Leida."

"Leida is so much older. More like a mother. I think Sorena likes that we are the same age."

"Ya veo," he murmured his understanding of that.

"I think she's afraid of you."

"What is she afraid of? I have never done anything to make her fear me."

"You keep yourself distant, a stranger."

A silent minute went by before he said, "Perhaps that is true. Our mother died giving birth to Sorena."

"She told me."

"My mother had two miscarriages after me. She had come close to death both times. The last time the baby made it, and she didn't. I was eleven, Leida fifteen, and Encarnación seventeen. She, being the oldest, became mother to Sorena until Sorena was sent to the sisters of Loretto school, the Academy of Our Lady of Light. I did not share the girls' lives. They had their interests, and I had mine."

He paused and lit a slender roll of dark tobacco, permeating the air with a sweet, smoky aroma that quickly dissipated in the breeze.

"I was twelve," he resumed telling her, "when I went to Seville to live with my mother's parents and go to school there, as my father had. Only he went to the university, and I did not. That's where he met my mother. I was impatient to come home. When I came back at fifteen, I spent all my time with my father, helping him as I learned the operation of the ranch. I got to know Leida because she already was ahead of me in that. She was my father's right hand until I came back. Not that I pushed her out of the way to take her place at my father's side; we have come to be good compañeros. We work well together. She can ride a horse and handle the cattle as well as if not better than the vaqueros. When it came to Sorena, I believe our father neglected her as well as I did. Her very physical presence undoubtedly is a constant reminder of his loss of my mother. *¿Entiende?*"

"Sí." Following several minutes of silence between them as they walked the horses slowly, she took the opportunity to ask about Frutozo Armendariz.

"His father was a friend of my father, a sheep rancher and merchant who owned stores in Doña Ana, La Mesilla, and Santa Fe. Frutozo was his bookkeeper and buyer of merchandise. His father was getting up in his years and wanted to see Frutozo married before he died. Frutozo was already in his forties. His father arranged with my father for Frutozo and Encarnación to marry. She was not receptive to the idea, but she would be thirty in two years, and the one man she wanted didn't want her." His incisive black stare appeared to penetrate her gaze to the depths of her being as he said, "Quinn Harden."

Chapter Forty

"How far is it, the high timber?"

"About an hour, the shortest but roughest way. There are different, longer ways not so rough, such as the way the loggers used. But no logging has been done on the ranch for some years. I don't like the closed feeling up there in the trees. Even in the lower piñon and juniper hills the trees can get too high and thick and closed up. I would like to clear some of that so more grass can grow." He gestured with an arm over the sweeping views of sky and lower desert hills covered with tawny grasses on which he had told her the cattle thrived. "I like the openness of this."

"Where I came from, the village on the mesa, I could see forever it seemed all around. There were no trees. It looked all flat. Crossing that flatland coming here I saw nothing but grass as far as I could see. This Carlos I knew told me there were men who would love that grassland for cattle. Why did you not pick land like that?"

"For one thing," he said, grinning, "I had no say in the matter. I was an infant in my mother's arms when my father heard about this land. The original owners—I should say the heirs of the original owners—were friends of my grandparents. In 1855, the descendants sold the land to my family. Originally the Crown granted three individuals over twenty thousand hectares to farm and run livestock, and in the ratification process of the grant by the American Surveyor General Office, it was reduced to thirty-two hundred hectares. It was not made final by Congress until only ten years ago, over twelve years after we had been living on it and had already purchased more adjacent land directly from the government."

"What are hectares?" she asked.

"The Spanish measurement of land. In American measurement, the original Spanish grant was fifty thousand acres. The American government cut it down to about eight thousand. What we added on to that brought it up to twenty-five thousand acres, more or less."

"I would not know one acre."

"I will show you. You stay here. I will ride there to about one acre away. You have to try to picture a square of the size of my distance away to understand how little an acre is."

She watched him jog his black stallion across the field of tawny grasses, skirting the bristly segmented cholla arms reaching out so one of its fingers could attach itself to skin or hide. Those cholla fingers were a painful ordeal to pick off for the hairy barbs gripping the skin like tiny hooks. She knew, having tangled with the cactus more than once in her life, considering the red flowers were good to eat, and the buds from which the dried up flowers dropped were good to boil and eat or add to soups and stews. She watched him and could not but think what a striking figure he made on that spirited black. He himself dressed in black, the hat and short-waisted jacket and slim trousers, with the excellent form of a gallant caballero. When he came back, which took all of about five seconds, she said, "I still don't know how to tell what an acre is. I only know this all seems like a lot of land."

He laughed and said in a proud but not bragging voice, "The longest way from one point to another is about eight miles. I made it in an hour once. There are some long flat stretches you can gallop until it gets up into the trees. To ride the perimeter of the whole ranch, about twenty-nine, thirty miles, would take two or three days, because once you go around the whole thing it comes to more like forty or fifty miles. One can get lost and wander around in circles in one square mile for a week and die of thirst. You must promise me if you go riding by yourself, you don't wander out of sight of the house and stay out of places you might not be able to get yourself out of. There are many rugged, rocky places and deep arroyos."

She almost told him about her experience with a flooded arroyo but decided against it. He would think she was making it up, since he didn't believe anything she said, it seemed to her.

"Also, there might be Apaches from other mountains roaming around, who might not be as friendly as Paco."

"Who is Paco?"

"An old Apache my father made a friendly peace pact with, when my parents first settled here. Paco was then about the age I am now. He and his band have been welcome to continue to use their old rancheria in the canyon near the springs on Puma Mountain. Feeling they are privileged ones, it is in their best interest to protect their benefactors from depredations by their relatives or tribal members. Apaches see nothing wrong with eliminating any of their own if it's for their own good. An Apache will kill a blood brother if it is to his own benefit. You might say having a peace pact with Paco has been like having insurance against Indian depredation."

Almost forgetting herself, but quickly remembering not to mention the gunman, she said, "When we were coming here, we met up with some horse soldiers. They told us some white ranchers sneaked on the reservation and murdered one or some Indian families. The sergeant told us to watch out for Apaches on the loose looking to get revenge for the murders. Did you hear that?"

"Yes. We were visited by a troop before my father's stroke, or what the doctor believed was a stroke. But, with the way he has rebounded, I am put to wonder. Our *trabajadora milagrosa,*" he said, his black eyes twinkling at her in an insouciant way, more teasing than serious.

"You have been a blessing," he said soberly. "Since your arrival, mi papá has grown stronger to almost complete recovery of his former good health. Dominica, my lovely desert blossom, you have brought a miracle to our house."

Her raised defenses against the suave man made her regard his glib flattery as insincere. She did not see herself as a "miracle worker." She had only encouraged the sick patrón to leave his sick room and walk with her in the courtyard gardens and take an interest again in things other than waiting to die. She had only spent time with him in ways his family was too busy to do, with their own responsibilities or interests. Besides, he liked her a lot better, the somewhat rakish patrón had told her. She could see where the rake in Raul had come from. The patrón had quite openly remarked to a visiting guest at a recent small dinner party, "There is no elixir of life as that of a beautiful young lady to rejuvenate an old man." She had to sheepishly glance around to see if his son might be in hearing range lest he start looking at her as a gold-digging gypsy not just after the family treasures but after his old man.

They came to a large pond, bordered by cottonwood, mesquite, hackberry, and other trees. *"Estero,"* he said, "a natural tank kept full by underground springs where the free-ranging livestock drink."

Pigs and poultry for ranch use were raised by *peones* who lived in adobe huts clustered together in *villitas* about the ranch. They halted their horses, and Raul conversed with two women doing laundry, one scrubbing on a wooden washboard in a wooden tub beside a kettle steaming over a small fire, and the other sloshing the scrubbed article in the water and slapping it against the side of the tub, then wringing it out and depositing it in another small wooden tub of rinse water. He and the women conversed with an easy familiarity as if he were a passing neighbor, which softened Dominica's adamant resistance to his charm.

As they continued to ride past the little chapel that served the villitas, Raul rationalized his employment system of the peones, who sustained their impoverished way of life by producing for him the sources of his wealth.

"They have all the essential necessities provided for them. Sturdy places to sleep out of the weather on land they would not otherwise be privileged to live on without worry about being chased off, fabrics of better quality than most campesinos have to make clothes—they get fleece to make blankets and woolen garments—and all the food they need to feed themselves and their families. Should any get sick or injured, we provide medical attention and a doctor when needed. Of course, they have their own *curandera,* and sometimes we have had to rely on her ourselves."

He pointed to a woman busy in a garden beside a small adobe. "That is her. Maria. Tending to the herbs she grows. She is the mother of a vaquero. Her husband was a vaquero who unfortunately was gored by a bull. She will always have a place here. They have no need for money. I do not object if any want to leave the ranch for a money-paying job. But very few want to leave the security they have here. Some have and came back. I have never refused to take any back. Another son of the woman I pointed out, the curandera, Sabino, left and came back to tell me he learned the trade of saddle making and was afraid to ask, but I guessed what he wanted. I asked how much he needed and already had the safe open in the oficina. I did not expect to get paid back, but he did pay the loan back with interest. So far, he is doing very well in his own saddle shop in La Mesilla. He made this one for me," Raul said, indicating the handsome silver-trimmed black saddle.

"And I paid him well, as well as gringos expect to get paid. I have had some leave to work in the mines, and they get paid one dollar and fifty cents a day when the white workers get twice that. One came back, wanting his old job for no pay and a better life. The other I have heard died in an accident in the mines. If the peones did not work on our ranch or some other, they would have nothing. At most misery. Leida wants to start a school for the children. That is her project with my support."

The horseback riding tours with Raul were an education for Dominica in more than the operation of the ranch and the Corvalan family history. They were a distraction from the unrelenting emotional despair she suffered alone in her bed trying to fall asleep every night.

Chapter Forty-One

They sat their horses at the edge of a high cliff overlooking several canyons far below and the Tularosa Basin far beyond. Today he wore a coordinated outfit of taupe leather—*chaqueta,* boots that came up to the knees of snug-fitting *calzas,* and even a *poblano*-style hat of leather the same color as the short-waisted jacket and breeches. There was an imposing elegance about him that he imparted to the clothes, not the other way around, Dominica could not deny. Even in a peon's baggy garments, she imagined that, Raul Corvalan would still possess an innate debonair quality, which reduced the gun in the holster about his slim waist to an understated presence.

He told her the revolver got no more use than for target practice, which sometimes might be a rattlesnake that threatened. He had more occasion to use the rifle in the scabbard for killing suffering livestock that were dying of thirst, disease, or injury, such as the time he came upon a mother elk in the labors of birth, with her vulva eaten away by a wolf while she struggled to give birth.

"Sometimes man must play the part of a merciful God when God is looking the other way," he said.

Not wanting to dwell on that image he had formed in her imagination, she looked out at the white patch on the dun-colored desert far below their high overlook. He told her the desert winds constantly shifted those white gypsum dunes, the sand blown from a great dried up lake that filled up in the rainy seasons to become what was called a playa. She almost remarked that the gunman had told her that very thing when, in the high forest part of the mountains, they had come to an open view of the same white sand dunes. But she held her tongue.

Raul prevaricated around the subject of the gunman. The very word rankled him. He adamantly believed his Quinn Harden was not her gunman, whom he continued to be inclined to believe had been the killer of Quinn Harden and his Indian wife. He had no patience to hear anything that could not be rationally explained.

"On the other side of that mountain range," Raul started to say, pointing, then looked at her. "You are bored."

"What?"

"I am boring you. You are somewhere else. Come. I will show you something. We are not so far."

"Not so far from what? Where?"

His teasing laughter intrigued her, and she followed him in the way a horse might be lured by a handful of grain.

The one-hour ride was through tall juniper scenting the cold late-autumn air with fresh green, up through ponderosa pine, spruce, fir. The aspens and oaks and maples rained down on them leaves of browning golds and dark siennas. The horses' hooves crunched through crisp fallen leaves and then soundlessly padded on cushiony beds of brown pine needles. Birdsong warbled, trilled, chirped, cheeped, twittered, and tweeted high overhead throughout the forest dazzling with sunbursts through the trees.

"You are not cold?" Raul asked.

"If I get cold, I have a rebozo," she said. The woolen shawl was tied behind her saddle, as she had been warned this time of the year the weather could change from chilly to freezing in minutes at the higher elevations of the mountains, where even snow could fall when at the lower elevations it was warm.

The mountain forest trail gave her a sense of déjà vu. And then they were gazing down at the small, secluded valley, held in a pocket of the ridge against a backdrop of ridges rolling over one another in a hazy distance.

"That was Quinn Harden's valley," Raul said.

"I know," she said.

He looked at her as if she were stubbornly set on deliberately bedeviling him. She squeezed the palomino into a jog farther ahead to where the land rose, closing off the view of the valley.

"Here! We made camp here. Look! The packsaddle is still there. There's where the Apaches came down from the trees and killed the roan packhorse." She dismounted and walked up the gentle grassy slope. "Look! Here! The roan horse! What's left of it. Now do you believe me?"

He stayed where he was in view of the valley. She mounted the palamino and jogged back to him. The knotted muscles in his clenched jaws worked.

"I never said I did not believe you," he said tightly. "I simply don't believe the man you were with was Quinn Harden. Of course, your Mister Gunfighter knew this place to bring you here. He was a party to committing the crime that was done here."

She bit her bottom lip to keep from turning a pleasant day into an unpleasant exchange. He averted his peeved gaze from her.

"It has come to be called Squawman's Valley. I have no doubt the name was started by the Indians who knew Quinn and his wife. Stories spread among the campesinos. There are many men who could be guilty of this tragedy. There are bad sentiments about a white man who lives with a red woman as if she is his wife."

"She was his wife. They got married in Mexico."

Pretending he didn't hear, he went on to say, "To make matters worse, expecting when he brings her into town that people should show her the same respect that they would a civilized Christian woman. There are *criollos* and *peninsulares,* pure Spanish bloods born in New Spain or the mother country, who often have the same sentiments, even though I hate to say the Crown at one time encouraged the mixing of the blood in Nuevo México."

His pure-blooded self-importance never ceased to abrade her own sense of human dignity. He must regard her as one lowly Anglo creature. "And you?" she said. "You are criollo, are you not?"

"Yes. I was born in Nuevo México to pure Spanish parents. I am not like Frutozo."

"Frutozo? He is not pure Spanish?"

"Yes, he is. I mean I don't have his prejudices."

Her head lifted with a slight jerk as if she were jabbed with a pin. "Frutozo had a prejudice against Quinn Harden for being married to an Indian?"

"For more than that, green-eyes. But, yes, that, too."

Her brow furrowed from curiosity, but she didn't have a chance to ask what the *more* was. Raul's black stallion, Negro, got fidgety from standing in one spot, which got her gelding squirrelly. She backed her mount and brought him forward again, which got him still and alert as if waiting for the next cue. Raul reined the stallion in a circle and, upon bringing him to an obedient stand, lighted a slender, dark cigar. He exhaled smoke and words.

"Down there is where he is buried, next to his Indian wife and their unborn child. Do you want to go down there and see?"

"I was down there," she said. "I know what's down there."

"I don't doubt your Mister Gunfighter brought you here. I

have heard murderers can be compelled to revisit the scene of their crime."

Not responding to him, Dominica stared, trying to remember if there might have been another mound next to the mound settled nearly flat under the grassy, weedy overgrowth. Why did she even try to remember as if she doubted herself? If there had been two overgrown mounds, she hadn't noticed. And if there was another grave, who was in that one if not Quinn Harden? If the gunman was not Quinn Harden, then who was he? She had not dreamed seeing him kneeling at the grave and weeping. Why would a murderer do that, unless he had murdered his own wife carrying his child? *Stop it!* Never had she had such suspicion of the gunman. If she allowed him, Raul Corvalan would have her disbelieving her own reality. Doubting her sanity. She would be back to being *la loca santa.* Only not holy. La loca. Just crazy.

Her throat tightened. Turning watery eyes away from him, she stared at nothing. Memories not even three months old were fading into an irrevocable distance of time. Her heart ached as though it would never, ever stop. Then anger overpowered despair.

She snapped a glaring look at Raul and in an evenly controlled voice said, "I have come to think many things about you. But one thing I did not think was that you were cruel. Why did you bring me here? Does it amuse you to taunt me?"

Raul's face, so perfectly featured it could have been modeled by an artist's sculpting knives, lost its color to the pallor of the artist's modeling clay. He was plainly speechless.

"I wish to go back."

"Mi querida—"

"Don't call me that. Take me back. Or I will find my own way."

"Dominica—"

"I am going to have Don Ramón or Frutozo Armendariz help me to make the arrangements for me to go to the States. I am not going to wait for any living relatives I might or might not have to be located. I will be an old woman by the time that happens, and I don't want to grow old on this ranch waiting for things that will never happen. It does not matter. No matter where I go, I must start a new life. I will do that with or without anybody's help. Your Quinn Harden, my Mister, whoever he was . . . I don't know any more. The more time that goes by, the more it seems a dream, seems he was a dream . . . Dream or ghost or whatever, whoever he was, the gunman, Quinn Harden, seemed to have been put in my life twice. The second time maybe a ghost, but both times for the same purpose. To save me from disaster and give me a chance for a new life. Whoever he was, I am thinking he was my guardian angel."

Raul so swiftly swept her from her saddle into his embrace in his saddle that Dominica did not realize what was happening and could only hang onto her hat with one hand while the other hand flailed the air. Next thing she knew her mouth was being smothered by his, but the sensual contact only lasted a few seconds.

His black stallion excitedly half reared, and Raul and Dominica both went tumbling to hard gravel. They lay on the ground, hatless, catching their knocked-out breaths, and, when each determined the other was alive, they both started laughing.

Dominica had not laughed so hard in all her recollected life. The treetops whirled around her head as she guffawed hysterically. Then her laughter was stilled under Raul's mouth and body on top of hers. Her immediate resistance yielded to the pleasure of him that swooped her into a dizzying realm of sensual awakenings never experienced, coupled with emotional desires unrequitedly suffered and suddenly satisfied. Though not by the man she loved, still bemusedly satisfied.

He pulled his face up from hers. She felt swallowed in the glittering, ebony depths of his profoundly adoring eyes. "Those shiny, emerald jewels are the devastation of me," he said huskily. "They haunt me in my dreams. My lovely desert blossom, do you think I would let you go now that your guardian angel has brought you into my life, out of where I don't know and I don't care? All I know is fate brought you into my life for me to cherish and to protect and be dedicated to forever."

"Oh, Raul," she wept drily, "don't say things you don't mean."

"Mi amor, I do mean them."

"I don't know what to think. I am confused."

"Believe me."

"Feeling I don't believe you, can you understand how I feel you not believing me?"

His reaction was equivalent to candlelight going out. Cold darkness where a warm glow had been. "I can't believe what can't be true!"

"Do you believe in God?"

"Of course."

"How do you know God is true?"

"Do you doubt?"

"Sometimes."

"Your faith is not deep. I have deep faith."

"And blind. Yet you cannot accept what I can prove."

"Prove how?"

She began to stutter and stammer, finding herself on shaky ground. "The carcass of the horse right over there and the packsaddle you refuse to go look at. Why? Is it simply the stubbornness of a jackass?"

"I told you I did not say I did not believe you. I simply cannot believe this gunman of yours is Quinn Harden, whom I saw dead and buried over four years ago. I don't have to listen to this. To be called a jackass!" He backed himself up away from her onto a knee.

"I am sorry to hurt your delicate *machismo* feelings." She pushed herself up and reached for her lost hat, tugged it down carelessly on her disheveled head, and got herself not too gracefully on her feet without the help of his extended hand.

He got to his feet and recovered his own hat. "You cannot prove your Mister Gunfighter was Quinn Harden, Dominica. Quinn Harden is down there under the earth. I saw him put there with my own eyes. I am convinced your Mister Gunfighter was one of the murderers, the one who took Nadie's bracelet and knew enough about Quinn anybody could learn in any town around here from the rumors about him to feed you a line of bull . . . manure, which in your naivete you swallowed, and he had you thinking it was honey. You obviously were too taken by him to see him for the killer he was. Trying to make my father and me believe he was a 'good killer . . . only killed bad men.' " He concluded his scathing tirade with an uttered sound of disgust.

"Oh! You! Oh! You—you—you—jackass!" She was too beside herself to think of any more articulate retort.

He looked at the sky and, with calm composure, said, "It is clouding up and will be dark soon. Let us start back before we could be caught in a snowstorm."

The scream averted their attention. It seemed to echo across the darkening sky. She looked up and around as if she might see a steed somewhere in midair or on a ridge or down in the valley. Raul urged her up on the palomino.

"It is nothing," Raul said. "Only a wild caballo. Perhaps being attacked by a predator. Something we can do nothing about. We cannot change God's laws of nature."

As they rode away, she glanced back. It was as if a very tender piece were being pulled from her heart.

★ ★ ★ ★ ★

"We'll go Quinn's way. I should say it is the Indian way. I suggest you don't attempt it by yourself," he said, putting ideas into her head that she had not had. "You could easily get lost and hurt, and nobody would ever find you. There are bears and pumas up here," he said as if to scare her, which of course he did. Now she kept looking into the trees.

As they descended through the timber, she perceived why the gunman had taken her the long way to the canyon road for her to find her own way to the ranch without him. She undoubtedly would have never found her way to the ranch this way, though shorter it might have been. She would have gotten lost in the forest with no distinct trail to follow.

"Quinn had many Indian friends. He let them hunt the valley the same as we did, as they have hunted this land centuries before us. That is another reason you should not come up here alone. Never know when there might be Indians in these woods. And they might not be friendly."

"He told me he quit fighting Indians because he came to see their side of it."

She knew she was dangerously pressing his jackass stubbornness—and everyone knew how hard a jackass could kick—but she needed Raul to face the contention between them for them to come to some kind of resolution. The mutual passion of their earlier kiss and embrace was not a sound basis for a romantic relationship unless he had more regard for her than a courtesan. How could she put belief in a man who did not put belief in her out of sheer stubborn denial? Just because he witnessed the burial of a dead man he could not believe came back to life as her gunman. Well, she had to admit that was a long stretch for the imagination, and so always she had retreated in surrendered silence. Until today.

"I met one of his friends," she said and glanced at him observingly. "Chago."

Her mention of the name did cause a startled reaction in Raul that he could not completely conceal. But then in his pragmatic way, he said, "Yes. Chago. He was one of the most civilized Apaches I have met. He was known by many, not only by Quinn, although they were very close friends. Chago often went hunting with Quinn. I had gone with them myself a few times."

"He changed his name to N'ii, which means, The One Who Was. We met him and his band on the trail. He had a woman warrior in his little band, and she killed him. It was one of her arrows in his back. Quinn," she used the name deliberately to push Raul against the wall, so to speak, "broke the shaft but could not pull the arrow out. Chago, or N'ii, identified it as hers before he died. We buried him somewhere in these woods. I did not know we were so close to the ranch. Quinn took us to a sheep trail that led to the canyon road, where he left me to go back to stop the El Lobo gang and told me to keep on the canyon road to your ranch."

It was plain to see Raul was disturbed by the news about Chago. Surprisingly he continued to let her speak, controlling his impetuous temper, which normally absolutely refused to hear what to him was impossible. He did not speak until they reached solid, level ground and Piedra Blanca was in plain view not far ahead, brilliant white in the glow of the lowering sun in the far west.

Raul reined Negro to a halt, which brought her to pull rein on Oro.

"I believe, Dominica," he said slowly, evenly, apparently trying for self-restraint, "you believe that somehow, by some miracle, I suppose, my Quinn Harden and your gunman with no name but Mister were one and the same."

"Does your deep faith not believe in miracles?"

He ignored her gibe with admirable forbearance considering the short wick to his hot temper. "I concede there are coincidences that make one wonder. What is important is that you are here, no matter how you got here. I feel it was fate that I cannot deny. And knowing Quinn as I had known Quinn"—the emotion that crept into his voice revealed the affection he had had for his friend—"if I believed in ghosts, I wouldn't doubt his ghost might have played a part in bringing us together. *If* I believed in ghosts, mi querida. And don't tell me not to call you that, because you are my dearest to my heart."

"Raul, did you ever see her? Quinn's Indian wife?"

"Yes, of course. I had been to their cabin many times. He only brought her to the house once, though, when he first came back. We had them to dinner, but Nadia was not comfortable, I could feel. I never could pronounce her name *nadie*. That is not a name, not in Spanish. Who would want to name a child 'nobody'? Nadia is not a bona fide name either. Maybe it is in some other culture. I asked him once why he didn't give her a different name. He told me she was his wife, not a dog. That put me in my place."

Dominica glanced at him, surprised to hear him make such an admission. There was some humility in that nobleman's arrogance after all.

"He told me he thought she kept it out of proud defiance. She did carry herself with dignity. She did not cover the scarred side of her face because she was ashamed, but to spare people the sight of it. When I told her I would not be offended to see it, she showed it to me and after that did not try to keep it concealed from me. She was a woman I had to bow to. I could never call her *nadie*. She was Nadia always to me. Not a nobody."

His remarks gave Dominica an insight into the man she had not had, which gave her *genuine* respect for him. Raul Corvalan possessed high esteem of himself, but he was not as haughty as she had thought.

Chapter Forty-Two

A sunbeam from a high rectangular window slashed across the wooden crucifix above a stand of devotional candles at which Dominica lit several. She had many to pray for, all of whom she wished the divine powers to bless, as well as herself for forgiveness for her own sins, especially wishing death to men, no matter how bad they were.

She could not stop wondering about the Lobo gang and the outcome of the gunman going back on their trail to stop them in their tracks to keep them from coming to the Corvalan ranch. Since the weeks had begun to turn into months, and there was still no sign of any of the gang, she could only assume the gunman had stopped them in their tracks. But what of him?

The *capilla* in the house was for the family to pray any time of day or night, a small chapel room with two short rows of benches. But, of course, as usual, whether she prayed at her bed or more formally in the family chapel, the saints never answered her, nor did God, and so another day went by with no word of or from the gunman. She had forgotten her first impression of him in her observation from the belfry, the devil out of the desert foothills, and, recalling that, the notion crossed her mind: *maybe he was.* Could her guardian angel have been a fallen one? How many times had he told her that it was too late for him, that his soul was already in hell?

She left the chapel by a heavy, carved wooden door similar to the one in the sitting room of her bedroom, which let out into a large family courtyard. She walked along the terracotta walk of the portal covered by the roof of the arcade that went around the entire rectangle of the inner sides of the house, which encompassed the courtyard. Passing windows and doors, she slipped the black mantilla, crocheted of a string to resemble delicate lace, from her chestnut hair worn in its customary campesina braided fashion.

She used the entrance into the large main sala where there was a piano at which Encaración used to play. It had been her virtuoso mother's, shipped from Seville by her parents when she had married Don Ramón. Encaración had taught Sorena to make the music on the instrument that had amazed Dominica when first hearing her play, never having seen or heard anything like it. Sorena had promised to teach Dominica if she would not go away and would stay with them always.

She proceeded through the large living room to the placita between it and the dining room. The placita was a small, intimate, tile-paved patio, open air as the plaza, enclosed by adobe walls with niches holding *bultos* and *retablos* carved out of pine and cottonwood by the *santeros* among the peones on the ranch. She approached the elderly Corvalan, dressed in a fine suit of black broadcloth, white shirt under a patterned vest, and red silk ascot puffed up dandyish, waiting for her at the marble-topped wrought-iron table, with wrought-iron chairs.

Don Ramón had come to expect her for breakfast with him in the placita every morning. Breakfast was not a heavy meal, only coffee or the common cornmeal drink flavored with chocolate, champurrado. They also had the customary churro, a fried dough, and lately, because the squash was in season, pumpkin-filled empanadas. After breakfast, if he was feeling up to it, Señor Corvalan liked to stroll with her in the outside gardens and show and tell her about the plants he had cultivated, some native and many exotic from Mexico and other places.

The patrón, astonishing the doctor with his remarkable recuperation, was not totally recovered. He exhausted easily, was often found sleeping in the library with a book in his lap, and retired to his room after the midday meal for a much longer siesta than anyone else who observed the tradition. There were some who did not, as Dominica, who used the nap time in her private sitting room to write in the diary she had started. She had never cared to nap in the afternoon; it only left her groggy for the rest of the day.

She had always hated interruption of what she might be engrossed in and even forwent the midday meal, which conversely enervated instead of energized her, and it took the rest of the afternoon to get charged up again to resume her engrossment, which lately was sewing herself dresses out of the fabrics from Sorena's trunks. Sorena had said Benita's feelings would be hurt, thinking Dominica didn't have faith in her ability. If that were true, Dominica had precluded the potential slight beforehand by consulting Benita's expertise on certain tailoring details Dominica did not know, such as darts. The obliging head servant had been flattered to instruct the *invitada americana de honor.* Guest of honor was how she had come to be made to feel, not the undesirable intruder, as at the onset of her arrival.

"Buenas diàs, señor," she said. *"¿Comó està usted?"*

"Muy bien, gracias. ¿Y usted?"

"Bien, gracias."

A girl servant appeared with their breakfast and quickly departed without intrusion. The patrón told her that she looked beautiful this morning, and she said so did he, at which he burst into laughter, saying, "You are the best medicine for this old man."

"Señor, you are not so old."

"I did not think so myself, mi'ja, until the problem with this heart."

Their conversations covered many subjects. He was interested in hearing about her, but the patrón became most stimulated when talking about himself, reliving his experiences in the telling with the attentive listener that she was, relating without boasting about his triumphs, and readily admitting his failures. He had told her about his ship travel to Seville, Spain, where he had gotten his education and meeting his wife, which he reminisced about nostalgically with moist eyes, tugging at her heart with the realization that life must irrevocably pass as it did. This morning she broached the subject of Quinn Harden.

"Mi'ja, what is there you want to know? It seems you told us what we know about him."

"But you don't believe the man I knew is the same one you knew."

"It is true. If the remains of the man we buried were Quinn Harden, then it is impossible that the man you told us about was him. However, the longer I think about it, the more I wonder if the remains the Indians found were for sure those of Quinn."

"Indians found him? You or Raul never mentioned that, only that you were at his burial."

"Our Indians. I call them 'our' Indians because they are a peaceful group who had a rancheria in the canyon long before we settled here. We let them continue to camp and hunt on our ranchland."

"Paco?"

His eyes, shiny coals that he had passed on to his son, queried her. Then it dawned on him. "Ah, sí. Raul. He must have told you."

"He mentioned your peace pact with Paco and his band."

"What is a cow or a sheep now and then," he said, shrugging, "to keep some families from starving? They preferred to hunt in the old way for meat they were used to, but when hunting was poor and bellies had to be fed, beef or mutton tasted good even to the primitive palate. They never took more than what they could use. It was a small price to pay for peace with a people, I must say, who had my sympathy. The American government kept breaking the treaties that the Indians were loyal to keep, so what can one expect? Quinn and I shared the same sentiments. We often had discussions on that before he quit the army. When he got his discharge, he stayed with us for a month before going into the freighting business. He had been our overnight guest before that often. He escorted Encarnación to a few bailes. I remember she was so proud to be in the company of a cavalry officer in his uniform." Grinning, a familiar devil dancing in his ebony eyes, he winked. "The ladies do like the uniforms, eh, mi'ja?"

He paused to take a sip of champurrado and resumed.

"In those years Quinn had taken part in our hunting parties and shooting matches. There was no beating him. Pistol or rifle. For him hunting was not sport as for some of our guests from the cities. Nor did he ever just wound an animal. He was a dead shot, a sharpshooter. His kills were always clean and instant. What meat he did not use for himself, he gave to the Indians. Nadie tanned the hides and used them to make their clothes and furnishings for the cabin. Raul admired him immensely. With three sisters, Raul looked up to Quinn as an older brother, I believe. I myself regarded him as I would a son. That was eleven, maybe thirteen years ago. How old is Raul now?" He paused to think.

"Twenty-eight. No. Twenty-nine. He recently had a birthday. It is terrible I forget the ages of my children. I think I forget because when I remember I am that much older. He was sixteen, seventeen back then. Yes, because he was fifteen when he came back from Seville the year we met Quinn, who was an officer with the federal army that came back and took over the New Mexican volunteers after that war over there in the States. They say it was about freeing the Africans from slavery, but it was more about the cotton, I think, although, I suppose, one went in hand with the other. We did not get involved. However, when the Texans came and for a while it seemed the Union was going to lose the territory, we were ready to take up arms with the volunteers. But the Texans never reached us, so we didn't see any battle in these parts. Paco and his tribe kept us informed on what was happening at Fort Stanton. The Indians took part with the Mexicans and Anglos plundering the fort after the Union soldiers abandoned it to the Texans. The Texans didn't stay long. They tried to set it on fire when they retreated, but we had some storms come through, and the rain put out the fire."

Although that was all interesting to her, Dominica steered Don Ramón from his digression back to Quinn Harden.

"Quinn bought into some freighting outfit. He scouted and was guard for the drivers. He was in that for two or three years. Then he came back with Nadie, an Indian woman who grew up more Spanish in Mexico but retained her native language and ways. She was dressed like a Mexican when we first met her, but after she lived with Quinn in their cabin for a while, she started dressing in skins as he did. Raul no longer being a boy formed a closer friendship with Quinn as men. But it was still a brotherly affection between them. They went hunting and fishing the two of them, sometimes with an Indian friend. I forget his name. I haven't seen him for years."

"Chago," she said and explained how she knew.

The patrón listened with grave interest and regret. Then he put on his hat, and they went for their walk in the garden on the outside grounds of the compound.

"Then it was your Indians who found Quinn's body," she said.

They sat on a timber plank supported by rocks, one of several such benches about the garden of wild and cultivated foliage and boulder rock placed by nature. Holding his hat in his hands between spread knees, he nodded his white-haired head.

"They came to tell us, Paco and some of his followers, women and children among them. They were taking the remains up to his place to bury them next to Nadie. To them Quinn's valley became sacred ground. They honored him and his Indian wife as if they were one of the tribe."

"Could it be the remains they found were of somebody else?"

"Raul and I looked at what they had bundled in a blanket on the travois. The flesh was dessicated on mere bones, the hair could have been his, but, truthfully, the corpse was grotesque and unrecognizable. It looked bypassed by any predators, or not found, and decomposed naturally and dried up by the wind and sun. What we had to go on were the clothes and the knife. It is true, many men wear Indian moccasins such as Quinn wore. And buckskin clothes. They, too, were hard to identify from being in the desert for who knows how many weeks, sand blown over them. Considering that Mescaleros don't like touching the dead, Paco probably would have left it where he found it. But he recognized the knife, the silver handle with the green stones that changed color, sticking out of the corpse's back. Paco said it looked like somebody stabbed him with his own knife."

"Then it was only the knife that was positively identified as Quinn Harden's?"

The patrón shrugged. "Paco said there were no weapons but

the knife. It is reasonable to believe the killer took Quinn's weapons." He added, "And horse, too."

"A zebra dun? Pale with black points?"

The elderly gentleman appeared awed. "Why, yes."

If it were Raul, he would have said that proved the gunman had killed Quinn Harden and stolen his horse, she thought.

"But left the knife in him," Dominica remarked as if skeptical.

"Well, could be Paco kept the revolver and rifle for himself. Who knows? I would think he'd have kept the knife, too. The knife was a handsome Spanish blade that any Indian would certainly find hard to resist, unless it had the blood of the dead on it, which could be why Paco didn't take it. The Mescaleros have their religious superstitions about the dead. After the burial, Paco and his tribe went through their ritual to cleanse themselves and banish any evil spirits that they believe linger about the dead and can contaminate them. I suppose they could have purified the knife as well, but maybe not. I don't know how Indians think. I know the knife was buried with the remains as it was found."

"The knife you described sounds like the one the gunman had. But how can I be sure they were the same knife? Raul would certainly argue it as an impossibility."

They fell into their own silent thoughts.

"Listen to it," Don Ramón said.

"To what, señor?"

"That *matraca grande.*"

She listened and heard only the low buzzing monotone of a nearby cactus wren. She laughed. "The bird? I have been hearing it often."

"We call it the big noise of the desert. Lately I have been hearing it more often than usual myself." He turned to her. "*Perdóname,* what were you saying, mi'ja?"

"I don't remember exactly. The man I knew told me you and Raul were outraged by the murder of his wife and unborn child, and you offered to do what you could to help him bring the killers to justice. Raul wanted to go with him to look for them. But Quinn told me he had to do it alone."

By Don Ramón's look, she realized how naturally the name came out of her. She didn't let him butt in as his son would have to object to her presumptuous use of Quinn Harden's name, as if there were any remote possibility the dead man and the living man could have been the same, which she had begun to see was not so impossible.

"Could it be Quinn found one of the men he went after and left him with the knife in his back? And that's who was found in the desert, not Quinn?"

Don Ramón came out of a long minute of silent thought with the remark, "I don't believe Quinn would put a knife in a man's back. Even if he did, I don't believe he would leave that knife. It was not a common knife worth little." Then an afterthought: "Perhaps he would. Considering that it was used in such a terrible way to kill his wife. And the unborn child. It was a terrible way for him to find it on the door of his cabin impaled with the knife. I don't know how I would have reacted if any such thing happened to me. I would have gone mad. It could be he had found one of the men responsible and used the knife with vengeful passion, not caring where he stabbed the man who ruined his life and then did not want it anymore; did not want to touch the knife or see it any more. Yes, I can understand that."

"And," she added, "that's when he became the gunman. Going after the others with his gun and rifle. You said he was good with guns."

He looked at her with new enlightenment smoothing out his handsome elderly features. "I think, mi'ja, you have solved the enigma—how your 'Mister' could be our Quinn Harden."

"Then the grave next to his Indian wife and child could be that of one of their killers."

The patrón crossed himself and uttered, "*¡Dios no lo quiera!*" He looked at her, grief-stricken. "In that case, where is Quinn Harden? Why did he not come here as he told you?"

"Señor, I fear the answer to that is he was killed when he went to fight the Lobo gang by himself." Following another thoughtful silence, she said, "One thing, though. The Quinn I knew had his Spanish knife."

They exchanged looks of persisting perplexity.

Chapter Forty-Three

One day while riding Oro, the palomino, she followed Puma Canyon, climbing to its heights in the juniper woodland. It was a relatively chilly winter day in the first week of December, and the brisk edge to the air was tempered by the rays of the sun. She continued up into the ponderosa and halted the horse and sat there and looked at the still and quiet forest. She listened. Looked around. Sensed something, not knowing what. A feral animal?

There were large predators in the canyons, especially in the higher elevations—bear, cougar, and wolves—as Raul had warned her. However, when traveling through the mountains with Quinn—whose name was now firmly entrenched in her belief that he had been the gunman—they had never seen any. He had told her it was rare that a bear, cougar, or wolves would attack a human being as prey. A bear with cubs might to protect her young. Wolves shied away from creatures not on their prey list, such as humans, unless they sensed a threat from the strange being. A mountain lion was more likely to slink away from human presence undetected than show itself in aggressive confrontation.

However, horse flesh was among a mountain lion's favorite meals, but usually the mountain lion picked on a horse that was weakened by injury, old age, or disease and not one carrying a rider. Quinn had told her that a cat had stalked him once but then retreated, probably deciding the potential meal was not worth the potential risk of the suspicious, strange thing on the horse's back. That did not mean one wouldn't attack a horse with a rider if desperately hungry. According to the Indians, he had said, once a cat did get a taste of human flesh it became a man-eater.

Quinn had taught her not to be afraid but cautious. Not to leave anything to chance. And to pay attention to her horse's signals. The palomino acted as if he did not sense any danger and showed interest in only the palatable vegetation within reach.

A cactus wren's buzzing warning cry from the lechuguilla and ocotillo below the piñon and juniper reached her ears as she urged the horse to continue up the slope. The grade grew steeper as they climbed to where the trees became more dense. She thought she saw through the trees a figure on a horse. Her heart quickened to the point she got dazed for several seconds. She had to take deep breaths to get her senses back. She stared into the trees for a long time, watching, looking, waiting for the rider to appear again. It appeared so much like the gunman on the dun. Or had it merely been a play of sunlight in the shadows? Her imagination? Her wishful thinking?

The ponderosa forest was very still, no breeze, even the bird calls were very high or distant, single cries of a few rather than incessant chirping and chattering of many. The palomino got antsy, wanting to do something other than stand there. Then she saw it again. A flash of a horseback rider through the trees higher up. Her heart raced. The hairs on her skin and head stood erect. Still she kicked her heels into the sides of the palomino and squeezed him into a jog up the slope. She cried out, "Quinn! Quinn Harden!"

Her calls were a lonesome sound that got swallowed up in the trees. She halted the horse, whose ears were perked alert.

By her sudden cry? Or had he seen the rider, too? His interest seemed more of curiosity than fear.

She was drawn to the forest again and again. Every day she went horseback riding, and up into the forest. The apparition appeared but always only as a flash through the trees. And always when she was in retreat, the scream of a horse echoed from high up as if calling her back.

One day she was compelled to go all the way to the valley. She got there and stared down, feeling something like disappointment as if she had expected, or hoped, to see him actively moving about down there, taking up residency of his and Nadie's cabin again. It stood appearing totally abandoned. As she was leaving, the scream of a horse stopped her cold. She looked around but saw nothing in the almost ghostly stillness that followed. Even the palomino stood stock-still, curiously alert, with ears flicking this way and that. He snorted loudly and wanted to go, pulling on the reins.

Coming to the broken rocky terrain where the juniper and piñon trees gave way to sotol, ocotillo, and lechuguilla among bunch grasses, as so often it did, a *chur-chur-chur-chur* greeted her. The cactus wren flitted from the lacy-sleeved, thorned branches of mesquite to the lance-leafed yucca to the paddle leaves bristly with darning-needle thorns of the prickly pear as if escorting her along the way until the Casa Grande came into view.

Early dusk had fallen. She hurried Oro home. She didn't have to urge him; he had missed supper and wanted to get to his stall and manger of hay and grain.

Ahead of her lay the adobe compound. The adobe walls encompassed two plazas, one formed the main living quarters and private courtyards, and the other included the workshops and stable. As she approached the tall, double, heavy timber entrance gates, which were normally closed before sundown for the night, she saw that they were open.

Raul was in front, outside the gates, waiting. He was bareheaded, looked disheveled in shirtsleeves. Practically even with him in height, and wider in the shoulders and hips, Leida was with him, her hat squarely set on her hair, which was confined in its customary *moño,* bun. They watched her ride in, standing like bookends, both with arms akimbo.

Dominica was going to ride directly into the plaza to the stables and put Oro in his stall and groom him, but Raul reached for the rein at the bit and stopped the horse in the open before the gate.

His expression of fury was frightening. Without a word, Leida stalked away, whacking the side of her riding skirt with a quirt as if in her mind she was striking Dominica.

"*¡Bajar desde allí!*" he ordered.

"Oro—he—I have to—"

"*¡Bajar!* Get down!"

She did, muttering, "I am . . . I am . . . hold your horses."

"*¿Mande?*" He paused and gave her a demanding look, while holding Oro's reins, which he had grabbed from her as a father might seize a prized possession from a misbehaving child, with the intention of the child never having the privilege of the possession again.

"Nothing," she murmured, keeping her eyes cast down from the blazing ferocity in his.

"*¿Cómo?* Speak so I can hear you," he commanded.

"Nada," she repeated loudly. But there was no defiance in her contrite gaze as it at last met his dark eyes with no devil flirtatiously cavorting about in them.

"Do you know how worried you had me?" he demanded.

"Raul, I'm sorry. I forgot time. I—"

"You forgot time. You forgot that I would be here wondering where in the hell you might be. Possibly at the bottom of an arroyo knocked out unconscious or something."

I already did that, she thought, and more wisely kept her silence to let him run out of his hot Spanish steam. Hopefully.

"Did you find it?"

"What?"

"What you have been looking for. If you had asked me, I would have taken you there. Perhaps you did not want me there when you met your lover. Well, did you meet him? Was he there waiting for you?"

She was too flabbergasted to speak. She tried not to fidget nervously.

"You still wait for him, don't you? You dream he will come back to his valley. That's what you wait and hope for. I cannot believe it. You and Encarnación. What has he got? Could it be, Dominica, when he turned back on the trail and sent you on by yourself to come here, he never intended to come? It was his way of leaving you?"

Her brain had stopped processing at the mention of Encarnación. That was the second, maybe third time he had aroused her puzzled curiosity with cryptic allusions to his sister and Quinn Harden. His sister, who had locked herself up away from the world at his presumed death. Her brain belatedly processed the rest of what he had said, and she nearly blurted out that nothing would have stopped him from coming but death, thinking not of herself as the reason but of Frutozo Armendariz.

"Do you love him so much?"

At once she realized with astonishment Raul's passionate jealousy. She had always sensed his protective guard over her around any of the men on the ranch, including his own father, who, yes, possessed the flirtatious chivalry he had passed on to his son but treated her as one of his daughters, calling her *mi'ja*, my daughter, and making her feel affectionately regarded as no more than that. However, Raul's jealousy of any man paying her any attention she had deemed typical behavior of a male animal guarding its marked territory. It had never been so fervent as he presently manifested regarding Quinn Harden. Apparently, he at last accepted the possibility that the man buried next to Quinn Harden's wife was not Quinn Harden, and that her gunman had been Quinn Harden after all.

She beseeched his gaze with her glassy own. "I won't lie to you. A piece of my heart will always belong to him."

"Only a piece?" His volatile disposition was reflected in an amused gleam in his black eyes.

"The rest belongs to you. You know that."

"How do I know?"

"You are the smartest man I know who knows all things."

It appeared to be a strain for him to restrain himself from laughing. She could literally see the muscular tension of his stance slacken as he exhaled a relieved and relenting breath. "Mi amor, you must never scare me like that again. I was about to round up some vaqueros and go searching for you, fearing what I might find. Promise you will never do that again."

"I promise," she said. She took off the hat and let it fall to the ground as she went to him.

Enclosing her in his embrace, he pressed his face into her hair. "If anything happened to you, I could not live. I want you to know, Dominica, I will wait for as long as it takes for you to stop waiting for a man in your dreams and to start seeing a living man who is willing and ready to give his heart, his home, and his name to you, *mi hermosa flor del desierto.*"

Chapter Forty-Four

It was a time on the Corvalan ranch and on all the ranchos and in the Mexican communities in Nuevo México for preparing for Las Posadas, the days before Christmas when the children, carrying lighted candles, went from casa to casa, each house decorated with pine boughs and paper lanterns, commemorating Joseph and Mary's search for lodging. At each house the children sang about Joseph and Mary's plight, and they were denied entry. Each new evening the children continued along the way lighted by little fires, *luminarias,* to guide them to the next house. Always the same answer: no lodging. However, at each house the children were given a party of treats and games, such as the piñata. On the day before Christmas, a Posada house was found where the children placed a baby doll representing Jesus in a manger, and the final Posada festivities ended with a midnight mass whether or not there was a priest to preside over it. At the Corvalan ranch, a padre from Albuquerque, a personal friend of the Corvalans, attended the ranch festivities as a guest and performed the midnight Christmas Eve mass in an outside altar setting for everyone.

There were traditional plays performed that had been brought by the ancestors from Spain, *Coloquios de los Pastores,* about shepherds going to Bethlehem, and *Los Tres Reyes Magos,* The Three Wise Kings. Starting on Christmas Day, the celebration of the birth of Christ began with the rodeo for the vaqueros. A steer, pigs, goats, and a sheep were roasted on the *barbacoas,* riggings of metal spits on which the skewered carcasses could be turned to roast over well-attended, smoking mesquite fires in pits and basted with rags tied to the ends of sticks and dipped into spicy sauces. There were fandangos with guitar and accordion music and plenty of casks of wine nearly every evening of the two weeks the fiesta lasted until the final night, when at midnight pistols and rifles were shot into the air, sending off the old and starting the new year. That was the end of the fiesta, although more festivities continued until about the second week of the new year, as Mexicans have a way of dragging celebrations out.

Dominica was drawn by Sorena and Leida into the excitement and busyness of the preparations, surrounded by the excited children. Then the days of the fiesta left her little time for anything else, and at the end of each evening after the full day's revelry, she fell into a deep, exhausted, dreamless slumber. At least when she woke up in the morning, it seemed she had had no dreams.

And then all the hectic holiday madness was over, and things settled back down to normal.

She kept her promise to Raul. When she went riding Oro alone, she never stayed out more than an hour, and she never again tried to find her way to Quinn's valley. Her longer, leisurely horseback rides were with Raul or with a group. When the horseback riding relatives came for a visit, they rode into the hills for the traditional family picnic, *merienda,* with panniers packed with food and wine.

As much as she once was so much *la extraña silenciosa,* the strange, silent one, she came to enjoy the ranch sociability, for they turned even work into play, a fiesta for every Saint's Day, and there were more saints than there were days in the year. Any occasion or event that could be was turned into a holiday—

birthdays, anniversaries, sheep shearing, cattle branding, informal dinners and dances for the neighbors (who brought contributions of food), visiting distant family dinners, and formal dinners and dances for the elite social and business acquaintances and associates. Life on the Corvalan ranch was not dull.

Still, her most enjoyable moments were in exploring and foraging on foot in the desert within the vicinity of the main grounds, riding Oro over the vast acreage within range of the house and villitas, and even just being in the same room with Raul, he absorbed in whatever he was doing—reading, paperwork—and she in a book or sewing, separate yet together, giving her a sense of companionable solitude.

On their wedding night a year following her arrival on the ranch, when they were alone while the celebration went on and would go on for days, and after the consummation of their conjugal union when they held each other in blissful contentment, she said, "Quinn told me that one day I would thank him for the day he refused me when I offered myself to him. He said he had the love of his life, and someday I would meet the love of my life. At that time, I resented his wisdom. The day has come as he said it would. I do thank him today for that day he pushed me away. As he said I would someday meet the love of my life, I have, my much-loved husband. I do love you with all my heart, Raul. You must never doubt that."

"But for the little piece."

She giggled. "No. I said my whole heart is yours. But, yes, that little piece you will have to share."

He chuckled. "I don't mind sharing a little piece of your heart with a man I, too, will always love as a brother and who brought you into my life. How could I begrudge him sharing a little piece?"

"But there is still what cannot be explained."

"The Spanish knife?"

"Yes. How can it have been buried with the man we think he killed with it and he have it when he took me from the deserted village to bring me here?"

Raul, who had to have a rational explanation for everything mundane, said, "I have come to believe that Quinn obtained another like it, very likely from the same silversmith where he got the original in Mexico. You said he told you he was in Mexico, in a prison or dungeon of some general? He got mixed up with some revolucionarios?"

"Yes. That was how he got the gold."

"Then it is plausible. He got another knife similar in Mexico from the same platero. The one you saw was similar, perhaps very much the same made by the same man, but not the same knife I knew him to have and that was buried with the man he killed with it. I accept that explanation because there is no other," Raul said in his way of confident finality not to be protested or argued with.

"I cannot help but be disturbed to think one of the murderers of his wife and unborn child is lying next to them."

"It is a disturbing thought, I agree. What would you have me do? After all this time have the grave dug up and have the remains put elsewhere? My consolation is my faith. All that is in the earth are earthly remains. The souls have long departed and do not lie next to each other."

"That is one reason why I love you. You make me see things in ways I cannot see for myself, and you make me feel better," she softly said and ran a fingertip over the hirsute terrain of his chest. He grabbed her hand in his and rolled on top of her.

"I am glad I won't have to have anybody dig up the grave," he said, his lips moving against hers. "I don't think Benito or any of his men would be up to the job. Especially for the superstition."

"What superstition?" she asked, although more aware of his body on hers than what they were talking about.

"Started by Paco and his Indians, I would not doubt, considering how Mescaleros view the dead attracting evil spirits. They would prefer not to touch a dead body, but when they have to, they have to go through a purification ritual to rid themselves of any of the dead's evil spirits that might linger around them."

"Your father told me that."

"Once they did the burial and did their purification dance and whatever else they do, Paco and his people left the valley not to return. To them it was cursed and sacred. Taboo. Such superstition spreads among superstitious people. From the Indians to the campesinos and any people who like to believe in such things. Even among the white people in these canyons, who would not even know how to get there, the legend of Squawman's Valley is told. Anyone who goes in the valley, does not come out."

"I was down there. I came out."

"And so was I. But we don't believe in such superstitious things, do we?"

"Let's not talk anymore," she said.

He was ahead of her, burying his face into places that made her squirm and then at once be still in total concentration of the sensual sensations of his lips and tongue teasing her sensitive flesh.

That was the start of her new life as la señora doña Dominica Aleah Nicholson de Corvalan.

One night during their intimate talk in bed, Raul asked, "Dominica, do you still long for his return? It is possible he is alive somewhere."

"If he is and he did return, I would embrace him tightly and be glad he is alive. But, mi amor, you are the love of my life. And I think he would be glad I found mine in you as he had found his in Nadie."

"I had to ask," he murmured into her neck.

"I don't think he is alive though, Raul. If he was, I do believe Frutozo would not be alive."

"¡Híjole!" His head came up abruptly. *"¿Por que?"*

"I have suspicions of him from remarks Quinn made. He never came out and said Frutozo was the man, but I believe he was."

"*¡Diga!* Don't give me little pieces."

"He told me he got his revenge on all the men who murdered his wife but one. He said there was one man he didn't learn about until the last man he killed, who spilled it all out hoping to save himself. The very last man hired the six to destroy Quinn's home and to kill his Indian wife. The man who planned it. I think he was Frutozo."

"¡Pucha!" Raul exclaimed astonishment and was sitting up on the side of the bed in an instant.

"Quinn told me not to trust Frutozo Armendariz. He repeated himself to make me think, 'that's the man' he was coming to the ranch to kill. The last man on his list. I believe the only thing that would have stopped Quinn from fulfilling his need to avenge his wife's murder is death. He must have been killed by the Lobo gang when he went back to stop them from coming here."

Raul sat unmoving, very quiet. He rubbed his forehead with his fingers in a gesture of trying to mentally digest and make sense of what she had said.

"I don't want to wrongly accuse an innocent man, Raul, but—"

"Pues, yo soy capaz de creer esto."

"You can believe it?" she said, surprised.

"You once asked me if Frutozo had prejudice against Quinn for marrying an Indian. I said he had prejudice against Quinn for more than that."

"Now that you remind me, I do remember."

"Quinn has always been a thorn in Frutozo's chest. I mean chest, where his heart is. It is true, his hate for Indians and men who consort with what in his mind are heathen women gave him a motive for wanting Quinn dead. But I don't think that was enough reason for him to have gone to such an extreme as having a woman with child, even an Indian woman, killed and in such barbaric manner. I do believe a man with a hate passionate enough could devise such a heinous crime against a man who made him feel like an *orejón* without him being one."

"*¿Orejón?* Made him feel like big ears?" She giggled.

"Mi amor, forgive my cow-pen Mex talk. I pick it up from the vaqueros."

"What does it mean if not very, very large ears?"

"*Cornudo.* What a man is called when his wife cheats on him with another man."

"Encarnación cheated on Frutozo?"

"I said he was made to feel as if he were a man who was cheated on by his wife, not that he was. Not in reality. Only in his mind."

Dominica raised herself to sit beside him on the edge of the bed in the shadowy dimness of the moonlit room.

"I believe Quinn Harden swept Encarnación's heart away the first time he came to the ranch, leading his troop of soldiers. She all but threw herself at him like a *churria* the times he was here."

She laughed. "Loose bowels?"

"Loose woman," he said with no humor in his voice.

"More cow-pen Mex talk? Oh, Raul. You will have to give me

lessons. I want to learn that vaquero talk."

"You are too much of a lady." He gave her his devilish grin, with glints of moonlight in his black eyes. "Now Leida . . . she can give me lessons."

"Then I will ask her. Don't stray."

"Never. I am yours wholly and completely forever."

"Raul," she purred, putting the side of her face against his arm embraced in hers. "Finish telling me before we both forget."

"All right, quickly. Because now I can think of only one thing."

"Quickly."

"I have to take a minute to get my mind back where I was with you up against me like that."

"Quinn. Encarnación. Frutozo," she prompted.

"Did I not tell you this? I feel I told you when you asked me about her sequestering herself in her rooms."

"You did mention she closed herself off from the world when Quinn died. Or you thought it was because of him."

"Yes. He was here a month, mostly hunting with me and Papá and spending most of his time with the horses, helping to train some, but she still managed to slink around him like a cat in heat. He left to get into the freighting business."

"Papá told me; so did Quinn. About the freighting business."

"She married Frutozo, I believe, to spite her feelings of rejection by Quinn. My father and Frutozo's father arranged a marriage between them."

"That you told me."

"She did not leave any doubt in anybody's mind that she was crazy for Quinn. He certainly had to know it."

"Quinn? Or Frutozo?"

"Both. Early in our friendship with him, when he was still in the cavalry, she got him to escort her to a baile or two."

"Your father said."

"Some other social functions, too. He was too much of a

gentleman to refuse her the escort, but he never showed an interest in her as she would like. When he left for his freighting business, she married Frutozo. Frutozo was well aware of her feelings for Quinn. I can imagine his feelings of impotent jealousy when Quinn came back with his Indian wife, and Encarnación locked Frutozo out of her rooms."

"I thought she did that when Quinn died. Or you thought it was Quinn the Indians found on the desert."

"She only locked him out at night until then. Then she sequestered herself after we thought it was Quinn we buried."

"She went into mourning."

"I believe that would drive a man to jealous revenge on the man responsible for his wife shutting him out of their bedroom."

"But why in such a terrible way?"

"I can imagine Frutozo wanted Quinn to suffer as he himself suffered."

"You make it sound as if you are convinced he is guilty. Frutozo would never admit to such a thing, even if he was guilty."

He pulled her down on the bed with him. "Enough talk, mujer. Leave Frutozo to me. I will find out."

Chapter Forty-Five

Dominica eased herself out of bed so as not to awaken Raul. She barely could lift herself up because of her swollen belly. This last month had been a misery. She could scarcely get any sleep, unable to find a way to lie comfortably. Besides, it was so hot. She went to the open window to breathe in some fresh air. Not a breeze. Not a bird chirped, not a horse neighed, not a coyote barked—the quietude in the twilight before dawn.

She stood at the window, trying to feel some relief from the airless room. She felt the kick under her arm across the cumbersome bulge. She watched the sky brighten over the flat roofs of the compound and heard the cactus wren's churring announcement of the birth of a new day. And far off in the distance the scream of a horse that echoed across the pearly sky.

"Trouble sleeping again?" Raul said close behind her, slipping his hands beneath her arms to rest with hers on the tumid mound of their child.

"It's so hot. I can't wait for this baby to come out."

His sweet-talking commiseration was not soothing, only annoying. He didn't have to suffer her discomfort. She said, "Raul, if it is a boy, I was thinking . . ."

"To name him Quinn."

She turned to him, put her arms up about his shoulders and gazed at his handsome face in the lustrous early light. "You always see into my mind."

"That is why you must be careful what you think." His black

eyes twinkled devilishly. "I had the same thought. And we will pronounce it the way he did."

"What other is there?"

"The Spanish way."

"How is that?"

"Keen."

"Oh. I never heard any of you say it like that."

"That's because we said it the way he did. But there are those of my relatives who would give it the Spanish pronunciation, I warn you. As there are those of our English-speaking friends who say my name their way and don't give the *R* the Spanish roll." He demonstrated the roll with great exaggeration. He could trill them out forever as fluidly as bubbling water.

She laughed. "You make me forget my miseries. If it's a girl, maybe Quinita?"

"I like it. I like it we are in agreement of honoring our beloved friend by naming our first child after him, boy or girl."

The years passed. Dominica made Raul a proud and happy father of four sons and two daughters. Sorena married a friar-educated youngest son of a sheep rancher, who became a foreman on the Corvalan ranch, and they had five children. Don Ramón lived to a ripe old age and was a doting *abuelo* to his grandchildren, who called him *grampa.* Leida started her school. One of the rooms in the kitchen section off the rear plaza was made into a school room. The carpenter had to make more tables and benches for her growing number of students that came from other nearby ranches. Dominica took half the class when it got to over twenty and expanded to another room.

Frutozo Armendariz never did confess to Raul any guilt of involvement in the murder of Quinn's pregnant Indian wife, much less admit to being the mastermind of the plot, but soon after Raul's interrogation, he began drinking excessively. His alcoholic incompetence led to Raul dismissing him from his duties as administrator, but because he was still Encarnación's husband, he was reluctant to take away his title. One day Frutozo went to Santa Fe and never returned to the ranch. The last Dominica heard was that he had sold the store inherited from his father for money, which was eventually spent, and that he was living a life no better than that of the Indian he so hated, no better off than those who sat against adobe walls in a drunken stupor in Santa Fe. Justice had found Frutozo and was less kind than Quinn would have been. Quinn would have been swift.

By Raul's and the family attorney's management, Encarnación obtained a divorce from Frutozo. She no longer confined herself to her rooms. Her hair was completely white and, though only forty years old then, she looked nearly as old as her sixty-seven-year-old father, who was happy to have her back at the dining table with the whole growing family.

Encarnación and Dominica eventually shared confidences about once having loved the same man, which bonded them not just as sisters-in-law but as sisters. They each confidentially thrilled at hearing each other's reminiscences. It seemed Quinn Harden had been two different men: the one Encarnación had known and loved, a lady-charming cavalry officer, and the one Dominica had known and loved, an emotionally inaccessible gunman. But they both concurred with the conception of a third man he had been, the one only his Indian wife, Nadie, had known and been loved by, as they once wished they had been. This secretly shared romantic despair was the thread that fastened them as intimate friends.

A wistful smile came to Dominica's face whenever she thought of Quinn and how he had known her better than she had known herself. Knowing that he would have never been able to change the unchangeable . . . *your idea of me doesn't change the truth of what I've become.* Knowing he would never have been able to give her the happiness that she had found with Raul. Knowing he could not change the course of destiny. And, again, she had to wonder if he hadn't changed it by having given his life for hers, for that was what in the very depths of her being she believed.

Dominica looked up at the stars winking out in a periwinkle sky, the clouds barely tinged with pink. It was a time in the early morning when all living things seemed asleep. The stillness in the twilight of predawn. She cocked her gray-streaked, night-braided head to listen to the quiet, not even a breeze. Her eyes passed once more over the dawning sky. She slipped back into bed besides her husband of forty years.

He turned over and put his arm around her and sleepily murmured into her cotton gown, "That dream again, mi amor?"

"*Shh,*" she said and stroked his thick, white hair. "Sleep, mi amor. It's early yet." She closed her eyes, and she heard again what had awakened her—the *chur-chur-chur* of a cactus wren. She became very still, holding her breath, and waited and listened expectantly, as if the wren's cry heralded a coming presence, which she felt to the soul of her being as the unearthly scream of a horse echoed across the dawning sky.

ABOUT THE AUTHOR

Donna M. Vesely was born in Chicago, Illinois and grew up to live her girlhood fantasy of living on a ranch out West. A horsewoman, her retired third-level dressage Chicago police horse, who came with the name Amigo as if prophetic of their future in the Hispanic Southwest, became a cow pony on a small cattle spread where they settled in Hill Country Texas before relocating to southern New Mexico near the El Paso, Texas border.

Her teachers through grade school and college predicted she'd be a novelist. Well, it was a long, twisting trail of many occupations from motherhood to entrepreneur and various jobs in the engineering and accounting fields, not to forget award-winning, professional visual artist—a Jill of all trades, master of none—to this first published novel. However, writing has steadfastly remained her first passion. She won third place in SouthWest Writers' Western Historical novel contest and made the short list in the Literary Awards Program of the Santa Fe Writing Project among other literary acknowledgements.

The employees of Five Star Publishing hope you have enjoyed this book.

Our Five Star novels explore little-known chapters from America's history, stories told from unique perspectives that will entertain a broad range of readers.

Other Five Star books are available at your local library, bookstore, all major book distributors, and directly from Five Star/Gale.

Connect with Five Star Publishing

Visit us on Facebook:
https://www.facebook.com/FiveStarCengage

Email:
FiveStar@cengage.com

For information about titles and placing orders:
(800) 223-1244
gale.orders@cengage.com

To share your comments, write to us:
Five Star Publishing
Attn: Publisher
10 Water St., Suite 310
Waterville, ME 04901